A DAIRYLAND RV PARK NOVEL

Desire in Dairyland

A Small-Town Contemporary Mystery Romance

Michelle Caffrey

Black Rose Writing | Texas

First printing

This is a work of fiction. Names, characters, businesses, places, events, and incidents are either the products of the author's imagination or used in a fictitious manner. Any resemblance to actual persons, living or dead, or actual events is purely coincidental.

ISBN: 978-1-68513-314-6
PUBLISHED BY BLACK ROSE WRITING
www.blackrosewriting.com

Printed in the United States of America
Suggested Retail Price (SRP) $22.95

Desire in Dairyland is printed in Baskerville

*As a planet-friendly publisher, Black Rose Writing does its best to eliminate unnecessary waste to reduce paper usage and energy costs, while never compromising the reading experience. As a result, the final word count vs. page count may not meet common expectations.

To Margo

Praise for Desire in Dairyland

"This delightful, entertaining small-town mystery with a robust set of varied characters kept me guessing all the way to the end. The elder citizens, a pet guinea pig, and a noisy goose warm the heart and keep smiles on a reader's face." **–Christine DeSmet, author of *Fudge Shop Mystery Series* and *Mischief in Moonstone Series***

"A fun, engaging story, with a lot of layers and plot twists, and a variety of characters, each one with a distinct personality including Gandalf, the attack goose." **–Kerri Lukasavitz Award-Winning Author of the *Oak Lane Stable Novel Series***

"*Desire in Dairyland* is a novel that appeals to anyone who has ever yearned for a community that means 'home,' and neighbors who mean 'family.' It's a page turner filled with charm and chuckles, drama and trauma." **–Beverly A. Jackson, author of *Loose Fish***

"A fun, fast-paced, five-star read!" **–Patti Liszkay author of *Tropical Depression* (*Equal and Opposite Attractions Trilogy*)**

Desire
in
Dairyland

CHAPTER 1

Ruth Markson perched atop the front stoop of her apartment building in Madison, Wisconsin, encircled by moving boxes. At her feet, her guinea pig sniffed at the confines of its cage in the dappled June sunlight.

"Ready for our next adventure, Oreo?"

Her black-and-white pet twitched its nose.

I'm not sure either.

On schedule, the Budget moving van squealed to a halt in the loading zone. A tall auburn-haired man exited the truck and strolled toward her wearing a lopsided grin. They'd attended different colleges but had been in touch on and off for years. When she needed help, she turned to her childhood friend.

"Hey, Tyler."

He pulled her into a hug. "Hey yourself."

As she leaned on his shoulder, she inhaled his clean scent and fought the urge to stay in his embrace.

"You carried all this?" He pointed at the piles surrounding her.

She hadn't wanted Tyler to find evidence of her ex-lover in the apartment. She flexed her biceps. "Strong woman."

He chuckled. "Oh, don't I know?"

After they'd loaded the truck and driven away, she stared in the rearview mirror at her six-flat building. Modest as her first apartment was, it represented everything she was proud of, including her independence and her scholastic excellence. Now she had a risky plan, one that had to work if she was ever going to fulfill her dreams.

Tyler glanced her way. "Are you okay?"

"Yeah. I'm fine." *Liar.* She stroked Oreo's fur through the cage to calm her anxiety.

In minutes, the Capital's cityscape gave way to villages lining Highway 14. The horizon stretched for miles. John Deere tractors combed the fields like huge alien insects, spreading fertilizer on corn and soybeans. The odor of manure permeated the air.

She raised the window to limit the stench. "You have to love Wisconsin." Her words dripped with sarcasm.

"Come on, Ruthie. Nothing beats being a Sconnie," he said with a grin.

The nickname students used for native Wisconsinites at UW-Madison made her cringe.

"I guess it's better than being called a Cheesehead." A herd of tawny Guernseys lowed, hock-deep in the muck. "I miss civilization already."

Tyler shrugged. "I couldn't wait to get home when I graduated last year."

"From Stanford? That's hard to believe."

"I love Eureka. Small towns are like having a big, weird family."

"Weird all right. On your part. You might live anywhere in the world with your virtual job."

"Just because you know a place well doesn't mean there's anything wrong with it. Besides, living with my folks means I can save enough to buy a place." He glanced at her. "At least you'll have your own four walls."

"True." *Surrounded by nosey foster grannies.*

The cow teat cleaning truck ahead of them came to a screeching halt, the rear panel looming closer. A cartoon Holstein with a shocking pink milk bag leered over its shoulder and bragged, *We're udderly superior!*

"Watch out!" *Just my luck. Death by dairy.*

Tyler slammed on the brakes and stuck his arm in front of her. Their moving van careened to a stop. She wondered at the fate of her stuff as something clunked in the truck's rear. Inside the cage at her feet, Oreo let out a series of high-pitched *wheeks.*

The service truck turned into an enormous dairy farm.

Tyler's well-toned arm continued to guard her as they inched down the country road. "You were saying?"

"Oh, where were we?" Her pounding heart slowed, and she released her death grip on the safety handle.

"I asked you why you're not taking a break after graduation before going straight into a job."

Ruth hesitated for a moment. "Can you keep a secret?"

He chuckled. "Oh, boy. This must be good."

Relief flooded her, even though she'd known the answer. He was there for her. "I've taken the MCAT, and I'm admitted to med school. The school's granted me a deferral for one year to get my finances in order." She regarded his raised eyebrows as she pulled her long, golden hair into a ponytail. "See, I even surprised *you.*"

"Outstanding. I love that you always go for it." His warm grin encouraged her to continue.

"Even with my scholarships, I need to pay off some of my crapload of student loans. I can't take on more debt."

"Your secret is safe with me. Although you should tell your mom."

"She's done enough with a rent-free trailer." No way would Ruth ask for money, since her mother had recovered her campground business from near bankruptcy.

An hour and a half later, he steered the truck into the entrance of her family's homestead, where a sign welcomed them to *Dairyland Acres RV Park and Campground*.

Motor homes, travel trailers, and smaller vans filled the sites along the smooth asphalt road. The aroma of campfire smoke evoked strong nostalgia and sentiments about *home*.

"It's busier than I remember," Ruth noted. "Looks like all sixty sites are full."

"Your mom worked hard to turn her business around."

"I know." Not for the first time, she marveled at her mother's tenacity and determination to hold on to the family legacy.

A flashy Allegro motor home sported a *Bling on the Block* sign. Betty Fontaine waved, her hand raised with a slight twist to the wrist, the sequins on her baseball cap glistening in the sun. Ruth waved, wondering if the woman still performed a striptease tap dance at the local Senior Talent Show.

A flash of white sprang from the bushes.

"What the—" Tyler pumped the brakes, and the van lurched to a stop.

Ruthie shook her head. *Welcome frigging home, Sconnie.*

In the center of the road, a towering goose spread its wings, hissed, and wagged its tongue like a rock star in concert.

Ruth slapped the dash. "Can you go around him?"

Tyler checked the clearance. "No way, not in this truck. Flattening your mother's pet would *not* go over well." He honked the horn, and the goose honked back.

When widowed and alone for three years, her mom swore that Gandalf the Guard Goose had been a terrific protector. Ruth doubted he was worth the trouble.

Tyler drummed the steering wheel. "My mom calls him the Spawn of Satan."

Their mothers defined the adage "best friends forever."

"I know. An apt description." She noted the gander's contortions. "He's going to twerk."

"Yep. He sure is shaking his tail feathers."

She lowered the window. "Get out of the road, Gandalf. *Now!*"

When the goose stretched its serpentine neck toward her, she flinched and wound up the handle.

The brazen gander stood its ground. Tyler studied his side mirror. "The cavalry has arrived."

A police car pulled in behind their truck. A tall man in uniform approached them. Luke Engel doffed his cap, revealing a salt-and-pepper buzz cut, and leaned in over the driver's side window. His warm brown eyes crinkled at their corners.

"Welcome home, Ruthie."

"Thanks, Luke."

He nodded at Tyler. "Mary Jo and I appreciate your help with the move."

"No problem, Chief." Tyler grinned. "Happy to do it."

No problem except a near miss with the cow truck. Tyler may have been handsome and a computer genius, but as a driver, he lacked concentration. Most of the drive home, she sat on the edge of her seat, gripping the safety strap or bracing herself on the dashboard.

"Ruth, your mom's waiting for you by the rental trailers." Luke glanced at the goose, now less riled, but still blocking the way. "Hang on. I'll take care of this." He strode to the gander, stroked its head, and the goose waddled into the bushes.

"No wonder he's known as The Goose Whisperer," Tyler said.

Luke shouted into the radio on his shoulder and jogged to his car. He drove off with his police lights flashing.

Tyler frowned. "Did you catch that? Something's going on at your new job at Golden Years."

"They needed the police?"

"I guess. The hospital called my dad to the ER before I left because another one of his patients has overdosed."

"Heroin or pain relievers?"

"Could be either drug. Dad says there's an epidemic."

She took in the information about Dr. Greg, Tyler's father. He was the foremost general practitioner in Eureka and had recommended her for the nursing job at the retirement facility in town.

Tyler put the van in gear and tapped the brakes as two kids rode by on bikes, streamers flying from their handlebars. He drove past the new building that had replaced her grandparents' A-frame '70s structure, demolished by a tornado. A wave of nostalgia swept over Ruth. The barnlike office sported geraniums planted in old milk pails on a porch filled with rocking chairs. A bright multi-colored barn quilt decorated the building, hand painted by Ruth's mom, and a huge burr oak dominated the front lawn.

She pointed to the tire swing hanging from one of the tree's limbs where Tyler used to push her higher and higher until she screamed in terror. Grinning at the memory, she jabbed him lightly on his side. "Rotten tease."

He chuckled, and his dimples showed. "You *never* retaliated."

"*Only* with the faux sundae." The surprise on her friend's face had been priceless when he dug into the disguised mashed potatoes and then spat them out.

"You acted like I'd poisoned you."

He gave her an eye roll and nodded toward two trailers across from the office. "There's your mom now."

He stopped the unwieldy van with a lurch, and they climbed out.

Mom looks the best she has in years. That chic hairstyle and outfit really suit her.

"You made it!" She threw her arms around her daughter, who returned the hug. Ruth inhaled her mom's familiar scent of Dove.

Mary Jo pointed toward a dark green Saturn sedan. "Let's check out your new ride."

Tyler inspected the drab gray interior. "Front-wheel drive. Good in the snow."

At the rear bumper, Ruth spotted the familiar sticker *I go where I'm towed.* That settled it. She'd christen the green vehicle "Toad."

"Seems... uh... safe." Tyler's mouth twitched.

Ruthie fought the urge to smack him for laughing at the sedate vehicle. "How much do I owe you, Mom?"

"She's your graduation present."

"Oh, no. I'll pay you in installments."

"Absolutely not." Mary Jo crossed her arms, her raised eyebrows signaling any argument was in vain.

Having lost the battle, Ruth said, "Thank you."

Mary Jo dangled the keys. "Do you want to test drive her now?"

"I'll take my car to work tomorrow. Too much to do now." Ruth gave Tyler a don't-say-a-word glare, and he shrugged.

"Tomorrow? Golden Years wants you to start that soon?" A flash of a frown crossed Mary Jo's face, and then she brightened. "You need to choose your new digs."

Both rental trailers were beige with side decks. One had a freshly painted picnic table. Scruffy hosta plants surrounded the other. Ruth wanted to toss a coin.

"You choose." Her mom pointed at the closest trailer with nicer outdoor fixtures. "This is where Luke and I lived when we were building the house."

Ruth squelched the image of her mother and stepfather in bed.

Mary Jo pointed to the other trailer outlined in bedraggled plants. "And this is where Mr. Schultz lived until he passed away."

Her mother saved his life when the near-deaf man hadn't heard the tornado sirens. Ruth was afraid to ask. "Where *exactly* did he die?"

"The meals-on-wheels gal found the poor soul in his recliner. He must've gone during his nap."

Ruth decided. "I'll take his trailer."

Mary Jo frowned. "Are you sure? The other one is better furnished."

Tyler raised a brow and remained silent.

"Well, it's your choice." Her mother glanced at her watch. "I'd help unload, but I have an appointment at my gallery."

Tyler nodded. "We can handle her stuff, Mary Jo. It's only Ruthie's ginormous collection of heavy books, and a wardrobe that might clothe all of Eureka."

"And Oreo," Ruth said.

"What? Cookies?"

"Your new grandpet." Ruth smirked. "A long-haired guinea pig."

Her mother grimaced. "I'm not much into rodents."

"No. Only vicious geese." Ruth imitated the gander, wagging her tongue and hissing.

Mary Jo barked a laugh at her daughter's impersonation. "Gandalf's only posturing. He won't hurt you."

"I'll take *your* word for it, Mom."

"Touché. These are for your breakfast." She took a basket of brown eggs from the Jeep.

"Thanks." The first and last time Ruth had attempted a cooked meal, the results had not been worth the effort. PowerBars worked fine. She took the proffered gift, anyway.

"Will you join us for dinner?"

"We picked up a pizza from Next Door Pub, Mom." She shrugged. "Traditional moving fare."

Mary Jo grinned. "Then can you both come tomorrow night? I insist."

"Sure. Love to," Tyler responded before Ruth opened her mouth.

"Have a great first day, honey." Mary Jo hopped into her Jeep.

Funny. Her mom had taken the dinner rebuff much better than expected.

Ruth and Tyler spent the next hour lugging boxes into the cramped trailer. They wiped sweat off their brows in the rising heat. Fortunately, only a few things had shifted in Tyler's near misses, and nothing appeared broken.

With the last of her possessions unloaded, she reviewed the 1970s décor. Mr. Schultz had been a fixture in her early life. The last time she'd seen him, he escorted her mom down the aisle at the wedding.

"Home Sweet Trailer, at least for the next year. Then I move on with life. Would you like a drink?"

"Something cold would be great." Tyler's Comic Con T-shirt clung to his broad chest in dark spots of perspiration. "Is the air on full?"

Her cheeks were warm. "I'll check." She adjusted the thermostat and the old trailer groaned. "Brewski?" When he nodded, she handed him a Spotted Cow ale from a cooler. "I appreciate your help." She took a deep swig of the yeasty Wisconsin brew. Boxes marked *textbooks* and *novels* cluttered the dinette. Oreo snuffled inside her cage on the kitchen counter.

Tyler glanced around the vintage trailer. "Why this instead of the one where your mom and your stepdad lived?"

"I prefer to think of Luke as my mother's husband." She pulled her hair out of the ponytail. "I don't dislike Luke, he's—"

"Not your dad. I get it. But you should know, most people think the world of the Chief." He reached over and touched her arm. "I remember you had a tough freshman year."

"I still miss him." Her throat tightened at the memory. Her dad's diagnosis of pancreatic cancer four years before had proven fatal in a matter of months. The speed of the disease at his young age had rocked her entire perspective on life. The futility had been so overwhelming she'd considered dropping out of school. Tyler had persuaded Ruth to stay. Now she was glad she had listened.

She opened the pizza box, releasing the scent of wet cardboard. "Ready?"

"You bet." He tore into the Geneva Meat Monster, studded with pepperoni, sausage, ham, and bacon.

He wolfed down a fourth piece as she worked on her first. "I don't know how you do it."

He wiped his lips with a paper napkin. "What?"

"Eat like that and not gain an ounce."

"Mom says I have a hollow leg." Tight jeans hugged his long limbs. He took another wedge.

"Not anatomically possible. More like a good metabolism."

"I've been working out at the Y. I guess it helps."

Tyler's strong biceps and broad chest attested to his workouts. Her stomach tightened at how handsome her childhood friend had become. She had trouble not staring into his emerald eyes.

They munched in silence until the box was empty. She fidgeted with the tab on her empty beer can. "You needn't come to dinner tomorrow if you have other plans."

"Your mom's a skilled cook."

"Suit yourself." Ruth experienced a surge of relief, knowing she'd have an ally at a potentially awkward dinner.

She rose to feed Oreo fresh lettuce.

Tyler put his finger near the cage, and the guinea pig ignored him. "Cute." He aimed his phone at her pet and began videoing. "I'll post this."

"Hard to believe what techies find interesting." Most of Ty's computer pastimes eluded her, especially his *Better Geek than Never* blog.

"Oh, you'd be surprised."

"And you'll keep med school between us?"

He locked his gaze with hers. "I'm honored you trust me."

She sighed. "At least someone in this town can keep a secret. Golden Years might not have hired me if they suspected I was only short term."

"Never fear." He looped his arm around her. "You can count on me."

A jolt of electricity she hadn't expected shot through her. He wasn't the boy she'd known all her life. Tyler was a great catch for a lucky someone. *Too bad I'm leaving in a year for school.* And her ex-lover had left her with a deep mistrust of commitment. There was no way anything serious would happen between them.

CHAPTER 2

A piercing noise akin to a cross between a yodel and a scream startled Ruth awake.

"What the?" She brushed the sleep from her eyes. A glance at her phone told her she'd overslept. Another shriek shattered the morning calm. A raucous rooster. *The eggs.* Her mother was keeping chickens, besides a goose. What was it with poultry as pets? With the windows closed all night, the stuffy trailer smelled of Mr. Schultz.

She spoke into her phone, "How to get rid of old people's musty odor," and read the response.

"What do you think, Oreo? Kitty litter or fabric freshener?" Her pet's nose twitched. "You're right. I'll pick up both."

Ruth fed Oreo a carrot and filled her water bottle. The rooster's call resumed, and the source of the annoying blast seemed to be located nearby. She eyed the speckled eggs on the counter her mother had given her.

"Geez, why can't Mom *buy* food like a normal person?"

The guinea pig answered her by gnawing on the carrot.

By the time Ruth found a PowerBar for breakfast, she was running late.

She groaned at the sight of blue-black circles beneath her eyes in the mirror and went heavy on the concealer. The whites—the sclerotic coat, she reminded herself—were red from lack of sleep, so she skipped her contacts and put on her dark, horn-rimmed glasses. After braiding her hair into a single plait, she chose navy blue scrubs to match her Crocs, deciding the matronly style might fit her new job.

Ruth sprinted down the deck stairs, missed the last one, and twisted her ankle. She gasped as something white flashed in the trees near the trailer. She peered through the brush. Afraid of an impending goose attack, she stayed on high alert, scanning the area for Gandalf.

Climbing into the Toad, the sedan was so low to the ground she misjudged the distance, lost her balance, and landed on the bench seat with a *thunk,* her ankle throbbing.

Her nose twitched. A pine air freshener, reeking of condensed cleaning fluid, dangled from the rearview mirror. After tossing the pine tree onto the floor, she caught a reflection from the back seat.

Oh boy.

Stretched across the rear of the car was a clothes bar. Only old people headed to Florida for the winter drove with their clothes hanging in the rear of their cars. It confirmed her suspicion. The Toad was a Snowbird-mobile. Her mom probably had taken the car in trade for campground rent, and her mother's generosity touched her.

As she drove the sedan through the park, she had to stop for power walkers swinging hand weights. Betty Fontaine, a.k.a. Bling on the Block, led the Walkie-Talkies, a gaggle of grannies who ruled the park. The shapely sixty-something woman, in tight yoga pants and a sports bra, called them to a halt.

Betty Bling yanked out her earbuds and leaned in the car window. "Hello, Ruth. Welcome home." Her collection of diamonds sparkled in the sunlight, including a giant rock on her left hand. "You want to join us?"

"I'm into running these days." Not wanting to appear rude, she said, "Speaking of which, I'm running late this morning. My first day at work."

"Come to my water aerobics sometime. Easier on the joints." Betty urged the group, "Let's get a move on, ladies!"

The sunny June morning matched Ruth's optimism on the first day of her nursing career. As she drove through her family's campground, she viewed familiar RVs, campers, and smaller vans lining the smooth asphalt road.

I never thought I'd live in Dairyland Acres again.

Once on the highway, she gunned her Saturn's engine, and the sedan struggled up to the speed limit. Instead of the bustling streets of Madison crowned by the State Capitol's glistening dome, the flat Southeastern Wisconsin landscape stretched around her in a limitless expanse. Grain silos studded the horizon instead of high-rise dorms. Starlings sat like sentinels on power lines and blue chicory weeds bloomed in the ditches.

She drove past the *Eureka, Population 7,209* sign and silently added one more to the total. Temporarily, she reminded herself. Once she lived rent-free in her mother's campground for a year, Ruth hoped to follow her dream. In the meantime, she had to keep her plan a secret at the nursing home or risk her job.

She eased the sedan up a curved driveway and stopped beneath the sign *Golden Years, a Retirement and Assisted Living Community.* She glanced at the clock—she'd barely made it in time. To the left of the building, an ambulance pulled away with lights flashing. *What's going on?*

The automatic entrance door opened with a *whoosh,* and Ruth entered the light-filled reception area. Coffee tables flanked by orange Naugahyde couches, and dusty Ficus trees decorated the atrium. A signboard read *Bingo tonight in the recreation room at 7:00.* She prayed she'd never have to officiate since the games at Dairyland Acres could be brutal. Growing up in the campground, she'd witnessed her grandmother refereeing arguments between campers that almost came to blows.

At the front desk, Lillian McNulty grinned. "Welcome to Golden Years, Ruthie, where happy hour is a nap." Her short, purple-streaked hair stood on end like angry cockatoo feathers.

"You live here?" It surprised Ruth to see one of her mother's long-term campground residents behind the desk.

"Hel-heck no. I'm not old enough. I work here part time for spending money."

Ruth nodded. Lillian was well into her eighties and had an addiction to buying things at Goodwill. Where she kept all her finds was a source of speculation since she lived in a fifth wheel RV.

"What's with the ambulance?"

"Don't know. There's been a lot of those lately." Lillian pointed to the clock on the wall. "You'd better hustle. Your new boss is a bi—" She hesitated. "A stickler for punctuality."

Ruth hurried down the corridor, wondering if the pious woman was attempting to stop swearing and telling off-color jokes. That would be too bad.

She knocked on the closed door of her supervisor's office.

"Hello, Nurse Markson. Have a seat." Head Nurse Steele waved at a side chair. Ruth judged the woman to be nearing her retirement. "You come highly recommended by Doctor Kelly." She peered at Ruth over wireframes, her florid face framed in tight graying curls.

Ruth flushed. She hadn't requested the favor, but her mother's friend had helped her get the job. "I'll try to live up to his reference."

"We have high expectations for you, since second in your nursing class at UW *is* impressive." The Head Nurse tapped on her desk. "However, you'll have a six-week probation period like everyone else. Today, you were nearly late. We expect you to arrive on time, or earlier."

"Sorry." Ruth hated to start on the defensive. "I'm usually punctual."

The stress of the move from Madison gave her insomnia. When she slept, nightmares plagued her, only to awaken to find she'd overslept. No excuse. *As Dad used to say, "If you have to explain, it's too late."*

"Rules are rules, you know." She thrust a pile of papers across the desk at Ruth. "Please fill these in by tomorrow. You can check in with Nurse Deborah Peterson. She'll be training you."

"Where might I find her?"

"She'll probably be in Mr. Bettini's room, number 13." Her thin lips lifted into a smile, but her tone remained cool. "Welcome to Golden Years. I'm sure you'll do well here."

Perhaps Doctor Kelly had suggested Ruth for the job over Nurse Steele's inclinations. Ruth vowed to prove they'd made the right decision to hire her.

She found the gleaming corridor for rooms numbered 1-20, redolent of wax and bleach. Most of the doors were ajar, displaying residents sleeping or staring at blaring televisions. Crocheted afghans draped side chairs, stuffed animals perched on dressers, and framed photographs covered the walls.

Ruth spotted the nameplate *Tony Bettini* and knocked on the door.

"*Entrare.* Come in."

A man in a tracksuit reclined in a La-Z-Boy. He wore his silver hair in a pompadour, and around his neck, a religious medal dangled from a gold chain.

"I'm Tony. And you are—?"

"Good morning. I'm Nurse Ruth Markson."

He ogled her. "You're tall for my taste, but not bad."

Will I be so rude when I'm much older?

"I'm looking for Nurse Peterson."

"We go by first names here. You mean Debi." He rolled his eyes. "Hubba-hubba. You should get fashion advice from her."

She bit back the retort that her job description didn't include being a fashionista.

"Now, To-ny." A nurse entered the doorway, pursing her lips. "You know I'm a professional." Ruth judged her to be in her late thirties. She wore a short, white uniform above UGG boots. *Boots?* Strict as Nurse Steele was about punctuality, she apparently wasn't fussy about a dress code for the staff.

"*Dolcezza*, sweet nurse." He straightened and broke into a grin, baring his even shiny dentures. He stared at her shapely legs above the boots.

Ruth read the woman's nametag and introduced herself.

"Welcome to Golden Years." Debi's tone was cool despite the phrase.

"Thanks." Ruth's shoulders tensed. "I understand you're my trainer."

"I am." Debi glanced at her wristwatch. "Shall we get to work?"

Ruth nodded. "Have a nice day, Mr. Bettini."

He winked. "Call me Tony."

She knew fans of the Rat Pack, none of whom were so over the top.

"Call me Nurse Markson." She left, following her trainer to a claustrophobic break room.

Debi smirked. "Well, *Nurse Markson*, here's your list of patients and duties."

Ruth scanned the documents. Most of the work comprised providing medications to the residents and checking their vital signs, nothing she hadn't done at her part-time nursing home job in Madison.

"The procedure is to 'assess patients' mental health and provide emotional support.' What protocol do you use?"

"Here's what we use. If a patient is going bonkers, let Nurse Steele know."

"Oh. Does it happen often?" Ruth studied her coworker's flawless complexion. Few women could get away without makeup, but Debi was one in a thousand.

"Not much. We keep them medicated and calm most of the time."

Ruth wanted to ask if it was for the good of the patients or the staff. She examined the lists of medications each patient received. "These are a lot of meds."

"We follow orders." Debi tossed her honey-hued hair over her shoulder. "If you want to pass your probationary period, you'd be wise to do the same."

Ruth spent the morning meeting her patients and learning how to use the antiquated computer system. As she shadowed Debi, she noted her trainer had no time for small talk, accomplishing her tasks with ease. Ruth was a fast learner, but she had to pay attention to keep up with the more experienced nurse.

When Debi finally allowed them a break for lunch, Ruth limped to the dining hall, relieved she'd passed a test with her trainer. Her head ached and her shoulders were tight as bungee cords. She scarfed down a tuna salad sandwich, eyeing the clock.

A man in khakis and a golf shirt approached, aided by a cane. "Hi, Ruth. Remember me from the wedding?"

"Of course, Mr. Engel." Her widowed mother had married his son, Luke, a few months before. Standing, Ruth stuck out her hand for a shake.

"It's Howard, dear." Ignoring her hand, he drew her into a hug. "Mind if I join you?"

"Please." Technically, she guessed, he was her step-grandfather. She'd only met him once, but he'd seemed like a nice man. She'd been busy studying in Madison, and she rarely came home. A wave of guilt combined with regret swept over her. *And there were other reasons I stayed away.*

"How are you finding your first day?"

Ruth resisted a banal reply since his face reminded her of her deceased Grandpa Fred when he wanted to help her. "Challenging."

Howard snorted. "The Head Nurse is a stickler for the rules."

"And Nurse Peterson is my trainer."

"My condolences."

She took a sip of water. "She's distant, but she knows her stuff."

"She's part of the Bettini group." He sipped on his coffee from a Styrofoam cup. "Most of the men here adore her."

"Not you?"

"Nope." He regarded her with caramel brown eyes. "The prettier the gal, the colder Debi gets."

She flushed at the implied compliment and fiddled with her horn-rimmed glasses.

"I need this job." Her stomach tightened. If he only knew how much the income contributed to her plan, she was certain he'd understand.

Howard patted her arm. "I'm sure you'll be fine here." Throughout their conversation, people stopped by, shaking hands and exchanging pleasantries. He made a point of introducing Ruth as a member of his family.

Loud laughter erupted from a table of residents, and Ruth spotted Tony Bettini in the center. "You were saying there are groups? Cliques?"

Howard shifted in his chair and scanned the dining room. "There are two factions here at the Home. Tony heads one."

"And who leads the other?"

"I do."

She raised a brow. "Am I supposed to kiss your ring or something?"

"No, and don't you dare genuflect." He pointed at her plate. "You wouldn't have fed that tuna to your cat before we got the administration here to up the ante."

"I own a guinea pig with black and white fur named Oreo."

"Unique pets run in the family. Your mom's gander is—"

"Vicious." How her mother tolerated Gandalf the Guard goose was beyond her. Every entrance or exit from the RV park was fraught with peril. "I hear your son is a Goose Whisperer."

Howard chuckled. "Luke grew up on a farm, same as me. We know our way around animals." His face grew serious. "Anyway, I've been president of the Residents' Council for the past four years. I've had enough time in the barrel. I want to warn you, there's something funny going on here. A few nights ago, a friend passed away, not the first one." Howard focused on a spot behind Ruth.

"Hi, How-ard." Debi stretched out the two syllables of his name.

He gave Debi the barest nod of recognition. "We'll talk later, Ruthie. Good luck today."

That afternoon, Ruth's only task was entering patients' vital signs into the outdated computer system. None of the prompts were in the order she expected, and the wait time between screens was insufferable. She wondered what Tyler would think of the software. He would most likely write an app to replace it. She checked the wall clock in each room, yearning for the day to end.

As Ruth entered the last room of the day, she read the nametag on the wall: *Ethel Jankowski.*

Ruth introduced herself and set about taking notes. After they finished the interview, Ethel asked, "Would you mind looking in my closet? I'm missing a dress. My aide couldn't find it this morning. It's one of my favorites."

Ruth rummaged through the closet and didn't find the described apparel, a navy blue shift with white embroidered flowers across the yoke. "I'm sorry. It's probably not back from the laundry."

"All right." Ethel's face sagged. She ran her hands along a granny square afghan. "Now *this* I'd hate to lose, a gift from a late friend."

Ruth sympathized with the woman. Residents valued their personal items, which often represented the last vestige of their independence. As she left the closet, one of her Crocs caught on the other and her ankle twisted. Stumbling, she landed on the shiny linoleum floor, spilling her paperwork.

"Oh, my! Are you injured, dear?" The patient's eyebrows rose over thick glasses. "I'll call for help,"

"No!" Ruth sat up and rubbed her ankle. "I'm fine."

"I took a fall myself last week." Ethel raised her arm, enveloped in a bright blue cast, covered in scrawled autographs. "Old bones don't take spills well."

Ruth struggled to her feet and bent to scoop up the scattered papers. Mid bend, a voice behind her sang out.

"Oh, my goodness." A middle-aged woman rushed into the room and began helping pick up the documents. Her plump face broke into a grin. "Some welcome to Golden Years, huh? By the way, I'm Miriam."

"I'm—"

"Ruth Markson." The plus-sized woman winked. "We don't get many new people around here. We're all *so* excited to have you join us."

Miriam wore a shirt that read *Recreational Therapy Wanna Play?*

Ruth noted the shirt. "You're in recreation?"

"I'm the Head of the department. Best job *ever*. I get paid to party." Miriam glanced at the wall clock and gave Ruth a hug. "See you tomorrow. We'll talk more."

"She's a cheerful sort, isn't she?" Ruth said after Miriam left.

"Relentlessly so." Ethel sniffed. "Makes you wonder how she can be so damn happy all the time."

"Time to get to work," Debi announced from the doorway.

Before Ruth responded, a commotion erupted in the hall.

Debi rushed out, followed by a limping Ruth. A group of aides gathered in an open doorway. One man called out, "I dialed 9-1-1."

They charged into a room where a man lay prone in bed.

"Where's the closest AED?" Ruth asked.

Debi tested for a pulse and shook her head. The patient's face was pale and lifeless. "I'm afraid Mr. Coldwell passed away hours ago. I'll contact the doctor to make this official."

Ruth picked up his chart. "Arthritis. No history of cardiac trouble." She frowned as she scanned the list of medications, treating everything from anxiety to pain. *Do Not Resuscitate* clearly marked.

Debi snatched the clipboard. "Doctor Kelly will want this." She trotted out the door.

Howard's attempted warning niggled at Ruth, even though older people often died unexpectedly. A surge of sympathy flowed through her. He was someone's son, perhaps a father or a grandfather. She pulled a sheet over the deceased man's face with a silent prayer.

CHAPTER 3

The middle-aged clerk at Rexall Pharmacy greeted Ruth. "Good evening. Is this all?"

"Yes." She dug through her wallet for change.

The woman glanced at the bumper sticker as she slid it into a paper bag. "New car?"

"Not exactly." Ruth counted out pennies.

"You're Mary Jo's daughter, right?" The older woman scrutinized her over an Altoids display. "Welcome home."

"Thanks." Ruth bade her goodbye, wondering if people in a ten-mile radius knew she had returned. She trudged out of the pharmacy and drove home.

She couldn't stop thinking about the patient they lost today.

Arriving at her trailer, she opened the side door and yanked out the clothes rod. She was just about to put a new bumper sticker over the existing one when Tyler's Triumph sports car showed up.

He strode over and drew her to him. "I heard about your patient."

She relaxed in the familiar comfort of his arms. News certainly got around fast. Finally, she pulled away, pointing at her scrubs. "I have to get out of these."

Tyler settled down on a step. When she returned a few minutes later, she'd changed into her running shorts and UW T-shirt, carrying two cold beers.

She popped the tab. "I need this."

"What happened?"

"It's never easy to lose someone, but the patient appeared to be in good health." She frowned. "Howard, Luke's dad, warned me something's not right at Golden Years. How did you know about the patient?"

"They called Dad to sign the death certificate." Tyler touched her arm. "Is there anything I can do to help?"

"Their computer system is slow and outdated. But I don't know how you could improve it."

"You never know. Send me specifics."

Nodding, she checked her phone for the time. "Finish your beer. We should go."

They strolled along the twisting road, past the sites where the permanent residents lived.

"What's up?" Tyler pointed to the kerfuffle near the small Coachman motor home.

"I don't know. Something with Rupert and Aunty Cordelia."

An eighty-something couple gesticulated at the small greenhouse next to their camper. Luke, still in his police captain's uniform, stood with arms crossed.

"It's medicinal. These are from heirloom seeds." Rupert's lined face was purple with indignation beneath his floppy-brimmed hat.

Luke frowned. "You can't grow it. It's not legal in Wisconsin."

Cordelia waved her large sunhat. "It is in other states."

"Not in a greenhouse on someone else's private property." Luke shook his head. "A police chief's, no less."

Ruth and Tyler exchanged questioning looks. As they approached, Cordelia turned her head in their direction.

"You're here!" Cordelia enveloped Ruth in a patchouli-infused hug. "Welcome home." Her late grandmother's best friend could still pass for an AARP model, with her lean figure and chiseled features.

"Congrats, Nurse Markson." Rupert blocked his greenhouse. "I hear you already started your job."

"Yeah." A wave of frustration rushed through her.

Cordelia frowned. "You should take some time off. You've been at school for years."

"Can't afford to with my student loans to pay off, Aunt Cordy." Ruth peered around Rupert's wiry build. Spiky green plants populated his small greenhouse. "Is that what I think it is?"

Rupert's voice went up an octave. "It's medicinal, I tell you."

Luke ran a hand over his buzz-cut and sighed. He addressed Ruth and Tyler. "Are we having dinner tonight?"

Ruth said, "Yes, we're on our way."

"Oh. Good. See you up there." Luke turned toward the older couple.

Ruth and Ty strolled up the road toward the house on the ridge, past camper sites festooned with hanging lights shaped like hot peppers and beer cans. Dappled sunlight flickered through the early summer maple leaves. They followed the lane bordering a meadow to a pond that glistened at the bottom of the hollow.

"The swimming hole looks popular." Ruth pointed toward the beach where kids squealed as they skimmed down the water slide like playful otters.

"Your mom's stroke of genius, using the pond instead of the broken pool."

"True."

Two women strode along, their Sheltie barking at kids jumping rope. The scent of lighter fluid filled the air as campers fired up charcoal grills.

"I love a good grilled burger, don't you?" Ruth's mouth watered.

"Yeah. I'll make one for you someday."

"You cook?"

"Sure. Can't you?" He raised his brows.

"Um." Ruth's diet comprised takeout food and enough Ramen noodles to feed the entire population of Eureka during a major disaster.

As they strolled by a fifth wheel trailer, Lillian emerged, shouting Ruth's name. "I won't ask you how your first day at work went."

Ruth's stomach knotted. Addressing Tyler, Lillian added, "I haven't seen you in a while. You could double for Prince Harry."

Ruth glanced at his strong profile. Lillian wasn't far off in her judgment.

A little girl in a pink tutu and tiara at Lillian's trailer held a whimpering Chihuahua in a matching outfit.

"Grandma! Check out Taco!" She dangled the dog over the edge of the deck.

"Son of a bi-biscuit," Lillian muttered under her breath. "No, Princess! Don't drop him!" She sprinted off.

Tyler raised his eyebrows. "She moves pretty well for her age."

"I'm surprised Lillian didn't cuss. I hope she hasn't stopped her racy jokes." They continued up the hill. "She was my one-woman Sex-Ed class. Now we work together."

They approached her mom, and Luke's farmhouse perched on the ridge above the campground.

"They hadn't finished it by the wedding." The farmhouse had been a set of plans and blueprints when Ruth attended.

"Nice wrap-around porch. I like the blend of traditional and contemporary."

"I prefer a city loft, but it's nice," she allowed. "Since when have you become Mr. HGTV?"

"I've been looking at buildings a lot lately."

"Want a place of your own, huh?"

"Yeah. I'm working with the Historic Committee."

A green and gold banner flapped in the breeze on a flagpole. Beneath it, a bed of yellow marigolds framed a plywood football helmet emblazoned with a capital G.

Ruth knocked on the screened door. "I take it Luke's a Packers fan."

"Big time. So is your mom."

"You're joking."

Tyler pointed to a partial foundation. "This is supposed to be his Packer Shed." Cement bags, stacks of lumber, and cement blocks littered the otherwise pristine wooded area.

"Ah. What Mom refers to as his never-ending project."

"Come in, guys." Mary Jo opened the door. "How was your first day, honey?"

Miraculously, her mom hadn't heard. Rather than rehash the painful events, Ruth answered, "Fine. Just the usual acclimating to a new place and all."

As they entered the front door, Ruth said to Tyler, "She used to hate football. Wouldn't watch it with my dad for anything."

He shrugged and wandered toward a laptop on the coffee table.

Over the mantle was a painting of a chubby toddler in a red and white bikini perched on the shore of a pond. Her fat-folded legs splayed out and her hair hung in damp ringlets. Nearby was an overturned sand bucket. Next to her, a pale, skinny ginger-haired boy held a shovel, which she reached for with a determined look on her face.

"Do you like it?" Her mom glowed with pride.

"Geez. I hope no one recognizes me." Ruth squinted at the picture.

"What? You look cute."

"I look fat. And crabby." She recalled punching Tyler after her mom took the photo. Ruth flushed with embarrassment at having hurt her mom's feelings. "It's beautifully painted."

Mary Jo stirred a wok as the appetizing aroma of peanut oil filled the air.

"I'll move it to the gallery." She carried a pot of fragrant Basmati rice. "Cordelia knits wall hangings and her fiber art's selling well."

"That's cool."

Mary Jo frowned. "Why are you limping, Ruthie?"

"Oh. I missed a step this morning and twisted my ankle."

"Ouch. That must've made your first day on the job difficult." Mary Jo fiddled with a placemat. "So, was it hard saying goodbye to your friends in Madison?"

Ruth studied her mother's face, wondering if she was being deliberately nonchalant.

"No. We all graduated and then took off. I'm sure we'll keep in touch."

Mary Jo fussed with a folded napkin. Then she met her daughter's gaze. "And your former roommate? Anything new?"

For two months, Theo had promised to start divorce proceedings. But when Ruth demanded paperwork, her ex-professor justified his procrastinating that he'd been too busy with finals to talk to a lawyer. When he whined that his career was in jeopardy, Ruth ran out of patience, accepted the job at Golden Years, and left the unhappy relationship.

"It's over." *Not my deep distrust of men, though.*

Her mother's face broke into a huge smile. "Thank goodness!"

Ruth feared her mother would burst into song, but Luke entered, carrying wine and glasses. He'd changed from his uniform into casual clothes. Ruth admitted to herself her mother had married a handsome man, despite his Green Bay Packers' T-shirt.

"I opened a Merlot. Good?"

"Perfect!" Her mother beamed at Ruth.

Luke studied the stovetop. "Are you making a stir-fry? Hang on. I'll get the extinguisher ready."

Mary Jo chortled. "You won't let me forget it, will you?" She turned toward Ruth. "The first time I cooked for him, the wok caught fire."

"Your mother almost burned down the trailer you're staying in." His smile dimple deepened.

"She's in Mr. Schultz's," Mary Jo corrected.

"Oh." Luke set the wineglasses by each place setting.

Tyler wandered into the room carrying a laptop. "I fixed this for you, Luke. Simple, the motherboard only needed a DC-in."

Ruth zoned out to the technical gibberish only her computer-genius friend understood.

"I checked the multimeter output of the power supply."

Luke appeared as confused as everyone else, but took the computer from Tyler. "Thanks. Whatever you did, we're good, right?"

Her mom interrupted Tyler's continued explanation. "Well, let's all have a seat. Ruthie, you sit there, and Ty is next to her." She served the dinner from the peninsula. "Enough?" She scooped a healthy serving of stir-fry.

French doors led to a redwood deck. Below were tall oaks and rolling hills, and a stream trickled through a ravine.

"The view is amazing. You can't see a soul."

Mary Jo said, "It's private. That's why we put the hot tub there."

Ruth made a mental note to call first before she popped in for a visit.

Mary Jo exchanged a charged look with Luke. The electricity between them triggered a memory of her parents sleeping in separate beds, even before her dad got sick.

"This is delicious." Tyler dabbed his lip with his napkin. "May I have seconds?"

"Of course." Her mom loaded more onto his plate. "Ruthie?"

"No, thanks." She side-eyed Tyler. "Some of us need to watch our carbs."

He caught her glance and shrugged.

Mary Jo turned toward her. "I'd like you to check in with Kathy at the office in a couple of days. She'll have your schedule by then."

Not only would Ruth have to work at the assisted living center, in exchange for rent, she'd agreed to help at the campground. "As long as I don't have to clean any bathrooms."

"No. My Workampers take care of the dirty work." She patted Ruth's arm. "You'll have the fun jobs like the Friday night wine and cheese tastings. And the Saturday bonfires."

Any hope of a social life away from Eureka evaporated.

"We'll post pictures of the events on our website." Mary Jo grinned at Tyler. "The internet's terribly important. Without Ty's technical advice, I would've gone bankrupt."

Tyler shrugged. "I helped. My mom would've kicked me out if I hadn't."

"You underestimate yourself. He is *so* talented, Ruthie."

When her mom stopped praising Tyler long enough to come up for air, Ruth changed the subject. "Luke, what was going on with Aunt Cordelia?"

"Now what?" Mary Jo asked. "Is it Rupert again?"

"Nothing that can't be ironed out." Luke rubbed his square jaw. "Pot isn't any worse than it's been, but there's a huge influx of illegal prescription drugs. When people can't afford those, they buy heroin instead. Or Fentanyl, which is killing people. It's an epidemic in small towns everywhere."

Tyler's face hardened. "Dad's been spending a lot of time at the ER lately."

Ruth recalled her patient's death, found sympathy in Luke's eyes. He knew. Howard might have told him. Or, since Luke was the police chief, the nursing facility might notify him. She also sensed he wouldn't bring it up this evening unless she did.

She glanced at the kitchen clock. "I have an early day tomorrow. Can I help you clean up?"

After clearing, her mom reached into the refrigerator. "Let me get you something for breakfast." She loaded a pile of supplies into a reusable market bag and then reached for brown-speckled eggs on the counter. "These are from my hens."

Ruth put up a hand. "No, thanks. I haven't made the ones you gave me."

Mary Jo narrowed her gaze. "You don't cook, do you? I figured you'd learned by now. I could teach you, honey."

"Thanks, Mom. When I get some free time. I heard your rooster this morning. Don't your guests complain?"

"They have, but then they love the organic foods we offer from our garden, as a promotion."

After saying their goodbyes, Ruth and Tyler strolled down the hill toward the campground. Smoke rose from fire rings, leaving a haze over the RV park.

Ruth rolled her eyes. "I see myself around the fire with kids and old people singing *Kumbaya*."

"You have a beautiful voice."

"Thanks." She remembered singing in the church choir with Tyler wailing off-key behind her.

He walked closer to her, and she smelled his familiar scent, a combination of starched linen and fresh-cut grass.

Ruth gazed upwards. The moonless night showcased the stars and planets. Orion hung in the sky, the Milky Way glowed as a smudge of light, Venus burned blue-bright.

Her dad had taught her about the constellations. Her throat tightened as she recalled him stretched out on the lawn with her, looking up at the stars.

Ahead of them, a white apparition emerged from the smoky haze. It crept closer and grew wider. The telltale hiss confirmed her fear.

"Holy crap! The flippin' goose!" She stepped behind Tyler. "*This* is what Mom calls posturing."

Tyler barely flinched as Gandalf neared, wings spread to their six-foot spans and waggling his tongue.

Ruth peered around his solid frame. "Do something!"

The gander drew nearer, viciously snapping its beak.

"I watched a YouTube video on confronting goose behavior."

"*Why?*" Ruth snorted.

"I was helping your mom."

"Oh, for goodness' sake." Ruth stepped from behind him. "Go away!"

The stubborn gander stood his ground.

"Let's see here." Tyler tapped his phone. "Avoid Altercations." The goose flapped his wings and hissed. "Too late." He continued. "Keep your shoulders square and using your peripheral vision back away slowly." The two of them did as instructed and tumbled into a bush.

"Ouch!" Ruthie rubbed a scrape on her arm. "So much for our side vision."

He helped her to her feet. "I remember now." Tyler held up his phone.

"What *are* you doing?"

"Videoing our encounter." He drew himself up and raised his arms. "Make yourself big and don't run away."

They stood side by side, waved their arms and hissed at the bird. After several minutes of their bizarre behavior, Gandalf cocked his head, lowered his wings, and waddled toward the pond.

They turned to each other, fist bumped and broke into laughter. Strolling toward Ruthie's trailer, they stopped and reenacted each other's goose-defense moves.

"You. Watched. The goose video. On the internet?" Ruth's side pained from laughing so hard. "Now you've made your own." When another snicker rose in her, she snorted instead, resulting in another fit of hilarity.

Tyler shoved her playfully. "Still snorting when you cackle, huh?"

"Some things never change." She grinned. "You're still my buddy."

He combed his thick auburn hair with his hand. "That's great."

They climbed the rental trailer's porch steps and stood at the front door. The outdoor light emphasized the planes on Tyler's strong features.

He moved closer to her. "Good seeing you again."

Ruth fiddled with the phone in her pocket. "I've got a busy day tomorrow."

He leaned forward and kissed her forehead. "I hope it's better than today."

"It couldn't be worse." She prayed she was right.

CHAPTER 4

On the way to work the next morning, Ruth drove behind a creeping John Deere tractor. Farmers had the right of way, and they knew it. She tapped the brakes and slowed to a crawl. The minutes crept by as she looked for a safe place to pass. Her stomach churned.

I can't be late again.

"Come on!" She beat her fists on the steering wheel.

In her rearview mirror, a black sports car gained on her, the sun glaring off the windshield. It neared, riding her bumper.

"Stop tailgating me, butthead." The tinted window in the sports car made it difficult to discern the driver, but she deciphered the model. Viper.

She tapped the brakes and slowed the Saturn.

Oh, no. The idiot's going to pass me in a no passing zone.

The driver laid on his horn, flew past her and the wide cultivating tractor. She fervently wished for a police speed trap to nab him.

Finally, the farmer turned onto a side road. Relieved, she gunned the engine and arrived at work with twenty minutes to spare.

A group of uniformed people chatted by the employee entrance. Ruth recognized one as an aide she'd met the day before, so she walked to the short, stout woman, and greeted her.

"Hello, Yolanda."

The others glanced away, but the Hispanic woman said, "Nurse Markson."

Ruth spoke in Spanish, asking the aide to call her by her first name, and inquired about Yolanda's background.

Yolanda beamed. "You speak very well, *Señorita.*" She told Ruth that she had several children at home, all of whom were doing well in school.

"You must be proud." Aides were often the underpaid heroes in nursing homes, struggling to house and educate their families.

Yolanda walked with her to the group and introduced her as "Nurse Ruth" to the others, who nodded in acknowledgement with unsmiling faces. Stanley, his scrubs stretched across his ample middle and thinning blond hair in a ponytail, finished his cigarette and ground it out with his heel. He moved towards the employee door and the other aides came behind him.

Yolanda apologized. "They are uncomfortable with new people."

"It's okay." Ruth forced a smile, but the aides' reactions stung. In Madison, she'd easily made friends with her coworkers. Automatically, she fiddled with the magnetized disk on the silver chain around her neck. It had been a graduation present from Aunt Cordy, who believed magnets cured a slew of ailments. Ruth didn't agree with its healing properties but considered it a good luck charm.

I need all the help I can get these days.

She told herself to shake it off and followed the aides into the nursing home, where Lillian directed her to the registration counter.

She handed Ruth a cup of tea. "We have to talk, but first, how did it go with your mom last night?"

Ruth sipped the hot brew and winced as it burned her lip. "Dinner was okay."

The older woman ran her hand through her hair, raising it up into a Mohawk. "What did Mary Jo say about your boyfriend in Madison? Or should I call him your ex?"

Ruth hated to admit her mom had been right all along. "You knew too?"

Lillian snorted. "We all did. The worthless, lying, S.O.B."

Ruth's cheeks burned, and she raised her palm. "Enough. It's over."

"You and Tyler are an item now?"

Ruth sighed, wondering if this was going to be a theme for the entire year that she lived in Dairyland.

"He's a good friend."

Lillian scrutinized her. "Friends with benefits?"

Ruth ignored her. "You mentioned we needed to talk?"

Lillian looked both ways and then leaned across the desk. "Residents are missing things, like clothes, money, even valuable jewelry."

Ruth remembered Mrs. Jankowski's dress. "Sometimes things get lost in the laundry."

"If you believe that, I have a bridge to sell ya."

"Have they reported these incidents to staff?"

Lillian said in a low voice, "They're scared." She paused as Debi entered the lobby with a hiss of the automatic door and strode by them with a quick wave. "The patients are afraid to make trouble. They write it off as forgetfulness, poor dears."

"Do you have any suspects?"

"Not yet. But I'm willing to help whittle down the field."

Ruth suppressed a grin. "You do that, Nancy Drew. I'll keep an eye out too."

Older people. They get bored. What's the harm in playing along with them? Since she had arrived early, she made her way to the dining hall where staff and residents enjoyed breakfast. She was spreading cream cheese on her toasted bagel when Miriam ambled to her table, clad in a T-shirt emblazoned with *Recreation GOT FUN?* A huge smiley-face covered the Activity Director's ample bosom.

"May I join you?" Without waiting for a reply, Miriam plunked down her tray of sprinkled donuts and a mug of hot chocolate. "Want one?" She held out a gooey specimen dripping in fudge.

"No, thanks." Ruth picked up her bagel.

Between bites and sips, Miriam described a litany of activities available to the residents that included luncheons, shopping trips, visits to the Old Wisconsin living museum, bingo, and casino nights at the facility.

"Our biggest event is our annual 'Fund Fair.' Lord knows we can use the money around here. Are you crafty?" Miriam pursed her lips.

"No. I can only sing."

Miriam put her mug down. "We can put together a talent show. You could star."

"Well, we'll have to see." Ruth scanned the room, searching for an escape route from the conversation.

"Or you can perform sing-alongs with the residents. Do you like *Under the Old Mill Stream*?" She hummed a few off-tune bars.

"I have to get the hang of my job first before I make any commitments."

"I won't take no for an answer." Miriam wagged her finger at Ruth. "I know talent when I see it."

Ruth glanced at her watch. "Time to get to work. Good seeing you." She stood and moved toward the door.

Miriam called after her, "How about *Let Me Call You Sweetheart?*"

A sea of faces twisted toward the recreation director, who flushed beet red.

Ruth strode down the hall to find Debi, wondering if Miriam was always so cheerful. Banners strung along the corridor read *Bettini—the man who can! Vote for change.* Scattered posters urged the residents to vote for Resident Council positions, including *All the way with Ethel J. for president!*

From around the corner, Yolanda rushed toward her, and Ruth grabbed the aide's arm. "What's going on?"

"Mrs. Jankowski's heart. We called 9-1-1."

They rushed to Ethel's room where Debi, with stiff arms and hands interlaced, rhythmically applied pressure to the patient's chest.

"Markson. Get the AED. Now!"

Ruth raced to the closest station, grabbed the automatic defibrillator, and rushed to the room.

Debi grabbed the machine from Ruth. After ripping open the woman's nightgown, she ran her hands over the patient's chest. "No pacemaker."

The unconscious woman's face was ashen. Debi applied the pads.

A male, mechanical-sounding voice announced, "Analyzing."

The patient's lips were turning blue.

"Analyzing complete. Stand clear." The eerie space-alien-like voice echoed in the room.

Debi pressed the button marked *shock.*

Ruth spotted a movement on the woman's face, but she wasn't certain.

"Continue CPR."

Debi resumed her rhythmic motions, the muscles in her arms tensing with exertion.

"Come on, Ethel. Stay with me, stay with me."

Ruth held her breath. Two paramedics swung open the door and ministered to the patient. Ruth stepped back and Debi joined her, both panting.

The men eased Ethel onto a gurney and wheeled it out.

"I'm going with them." Debi charged off.

Ruth picked up the AED with shaking hands and returned the machine to its station, cleaning it for the next use.

Yolanda joined her, her face creased with concern. "How is the nice lady?"

"It doesn't look good." Ruth ran her hand across her forehead.

"I make Mrs. J. tamales at Christmas. She loves them."

"Does she have a history of heart problems?"

"I don't think so." Yolanda frowned. "She complained of pain last night. It might be arthritis."

Ruth patted her shoulder. "You couldn't have known."

"*Dios mío,* my God." Yolanda crossed herself.

Head Nurse Steele cleared her throat behind them. "Don't you have work to do?"

As Yolanda hustled away, Nurse Steele turned toward Ruth. "I'll take Nurse Peterson's place."

"How is Mrs. Jankowski?" Ruth frowned.

"Nothing is certain yet."

As she went about her morning's duties, Ruth followed Tyler's advice and asked more questions about the outdated system, so she might give him specifics.

Nurse Steele narrowed her eyes and studied Ruth. "I didn't know you had such a good grasp of computers."

Ruth raised her brows, hoping to appear innocent. "I like to understand as much as possible."

Eventually, she discovered the system was old, with no budget to update to a newer version. At lunch, she sent Tyler a text with the information, but didn't see how it would help. As she sipped her vegetable soup, he responded with a quick reply, thanking her. A minute later, her phone sounded again. He'd sent the link to a video, "Funny animal buddies."

She laughed aloud as a Great Dane sniffed a tiny baby goose. Every time the gosling fluttered, the enormous dog jumped. Occasionally, the bird took a peck at the dog's nose, sending the canine running. Ruth sent a text, *Portent of viciousness to come.*

Setting her phone down, she spotted Luke's dad talking to a group of people. She caught his eye and gave him a small wave.

Howard held up his pointer finger. One minute. He patted a woman on the arm and walked toward Ruth, using his cane.

Close up, lines of fatigue crisscrossed his face. "How's Ethel Jankowski?"

"I don't know. Debi followed her to the hospital."

Howard sighed. "We have loads of medical emergencies here. Ethel was so healthy."

"Debi gave Mrs. Jankowski her medications yesterday. I entered them into the system, along with her vitals."

"Anything unusual?"

"No, nothing I noticed, though one of her aides told me the patient complained of pain later in the day."

Howard's gnarled hands gripped his cane; his knuckles whitened. "Something's not right. She's the second one this month to have an emergency."

Ruth recalled the banner she'd seen earlier. "Is Mrs. Jankowski running for president?"

Howard nodded. "At least she was."

The Head Nurse walked in the doorway and called out, "Nurse Markson?"

Ruth said, "I have to go."

Howard nodded. "Duty calls."

Ruth fought a wave of exhaustion as she plodded to the parking lot. Long shadows crossed the asphalt, outlining the few cars left. As she walked across the hot pavement, she neared her vehicle.

Something was wrong.

The Saturn leaned hard to the left, like an injured animal.

CHAPTER 5

"Dammit." A hot afternoon wind blew across the employee parking lot. Ruth knelt to examine the left front tire of her Saturn, as flat as leftover beer. Her dad had taught her how to put on a spare as soon as she had her driver's license. He was proficient in anything mechanical, from repairing RVs to restoring his vintage Corvette. She'd only had to change a tire once in high school, but the method came back to her. As she struggled to loosen rusty lug nuts, she wondered where she had picked up a nail.

Sweat trickled down her sides with the effort. Breathing hard, she examined the tire, but spotted nothing. There weren't options in Eureka for tire repair. Bobby McKay's garage was it unless she wanted to drive a far distance to Janesville.

Ruth drove to Eureka Automotive, parking beneath the sign that read *May we have the next dents?* The strident odor of diesel and spent motor oil assaulted her as she walked into the concrete block building.

"Hello?"

The waiting room, outfitted in orange vinyl chairs and a gray metal desk with matching dented file cabinets, was empty. A vending machine presented candy bars and fluorescent orange crackers and cheese. The tool company calendar on the wall displayed a photo of a scantily clad brunette.

"Pinups? In today's world?" Ruth asked aloud.

When a raspy voice spoke immediately behind her, she jumped.

"Good-looking girls never go out of style."

He was larger and more muscular, but his hair was still in a duck's ass cut with thick sideburns. There was no mistaking him.

"Hey, Bobby."

"What can I do you for, Ruth?" Cigarette smoke clung to him. His heavy-lidded eyes creased at the corners as he scrutinized her. A five o'clock shadow did nothing to hide the deep dimple in his chin. Her mom's saying came to her, "Dimple on the chin, devil within."

"I need my tire repaired."

He regarded the car. "Who put the spare on? Those rusty lug nuts must've been hard to get off."

"I did."

He chuckled. "You're still a tough cookie."

Crap. He remembered The Playground Incident.

Tyler had been a twig-skinny kid with red hair, earning him the nickname "Matchstick." A group of sixth-grade bullies continually tormented him at recess until one day Ruth had enough. She'd knocked Bobby McKay, the ringleader, to the ground until her friends pulled her off. Word circulated in the school that Ruthie could "kick the crap out of anyone."

As if reading her mind, he said, "It was a long time ago. I'm willing to let bygones be bygones if you are."

"Sure." Was he really going to let it go? "I called ahead and spoke to Dixie."

He read a daily planner calendar on the desktop. "It's marked here as a 1996 Saturn. SC1 or SC2?"

"I don't know. It's a sedan."

"And the mileage?"

She swallowed. "184,402."

Bobby smirked. "Yours?"

"Yeah." A flush crept up her neck.

"It doesn't exactly scream *you*."

"My mom gave it to me as a graduation present."

Bobby nodded. "Ah. From the campground." He pointed to the bumper sticker.

"I call it the Toad."

"Clever." He patted the hood. "Front-wheel drive will be good in the snow."

"How much will this cost?"

He pointed at the sign with the rate. "Okay?"

She winced inwardly at the price, but nodded. He bent over and got to work.

Ruth spent an hour leafing through old issues of *Sport Illustrated* and *GQ*, when Bobby reported he'd finished.

"You could do with an oil change and a tune up." He wiped his hands on a greasy rag. "Bring her over any time and I'll be happy to give you a reduced rate, for old time's sake."

"That's nice of you." Perhaps he *had* forgiven her for everything.

"How's the nursing home job?"

"Great." The fewer details, the better, as far as she was concerned.

He gestured toward the Golden Years recreation van, parked next to a shiny black sports car. "I service their vehicles."

"Oh, so you know the people well?"

"Sure. Miriam brings the van. She's a friendly gal."

"She is." Saccharinely so, she silently added. "And all the staff?"

"The place has a great reputation. If my mom ever needs more help than I can give her, that's where I hope she'll go."

A great rep?

His eyes narrowed. "Why do ya ask? Aren't you happy there?"

"Sure." She turned toward the black vehicle. "What a nice car!" She hoped her insincerity didn't show. "Did I see you going by this morning on my way to work out on Highway 14?" *Passing me like a madman, endangering everyone in your path.*

He shook his head. "No. I live in town."

"It's unique."

He beamed. "True. Few people can afford a Viper." He frowned at the Toad. "If you ever want to trade up to something sportier, call me. I have connections."

"Can you get me one like yours?" She almost batted her eyelashes but refrained.

"Hell no, sweetheart. I'm afraid it's out of a nurse's reach." He eyed her up and down, sending a wave of revulsion over her. "You need something more feminine, anyway. Like a cute little Miata convertible." He checked his watch. "Well. I got to get over to Mom's and cut her lawn before it gets too dark."

She recalled Mrs. McKay's town-renown garden overflowing with delphiniums and roses, complete with a white picket fence. Ruth glanced at the tattoo with a heart and *Mother* that decorated his arm. Everyone was someone's child, she reminded herself. Even this guy.

"I'll load the spare for you," he offered.

"Gee, thanks." She followed him and he hoisted it into the Toad's trunk.

"Nice and spacious." He slapped the lid closed and leaned on it. "You still singing?"

"Some." The two of them had starred in the high school production of *Grease.* "And you?"

Back then, Bobby's performances had sent most of the girls swooning. He'd appeared dangerous in his black leather and tight jeans. His off-stage antics reflected the musical and added to his mystique.

He reached into his pocket and pulled out a business card.

Beneath a picture of Bobby in sunglasses and gold chains, she read, *THE TRIBUTE TO ELVIS show by Bobby McKay. See him at nightclubs, restaurants, and festivals. Also at a variety of charity events.*

"You're an Elvis impersonator?" She fought down a giggle. Not surprising. In high school, he called her on the phone and sang "Hound Dog" and "Don't Be Cruel" in an excellent imitation of The King, way before she'd turned him down for Senior Prom. She hadn't been able to get past his earlier bullying, even if he'd reformed. He hadn't taken the rejection well.

He winked. "Next time I have a gig, I'll get you a VIP pass."

"Great." She put the card in her purse.

He took a step closer to her. "Want to hang out together? Do a duet like the old days?"

"Ah, I'm in a relationship."

He nodded at her left hand. "Not married, not even engaged."

She hesitated. "It's complicated."

Bobby dangled the key above her palm for a moment and then dropped it. "Either you're attached officially or not. Word has it you've been hanging out with Matchstick."

She bristled at the nickname, but held her temper in check. She glanced at the strong biceps beneath Bobby's T-shirt, his veins standing out on his forearms.

"Tyler's a good *friend.*"

"Right." He lit a cigarette with his Dunhill lighter.

She got into her car and started the ignition. "Oh, I meant to ask. Did I pick up a nail or screw to get a flat?"

He leaned on the open window. "I didn't find either. There was a puncture, though."

"From what?"

"Anything might've caused it. There are signs of general wear and age. You probably should put new tires on it." He hesitated. "You don't want to risk an actual blowout at speed. It would be a nasty accident." He tapped on the door. "See you around, Ruthie."

As she drove from the repair shop, he peeled away in his Viper. She noted the vanity license plate for future reference: THE KING.

Elvis has left the building.

When she passed by Rupert and Cordelia's motor home, she noticed the empty greenhouse. She wondered what he'd done with enough weed to keep a retired hippie stoned for months. Ruth slowed to follow a woman riding an adult-sized tricycle who blocked most of the road. Other campers lazed in folding chairs and waved their hellos.

As Ruth drove up to her trailer, she noticed packages on her porch. She grabbed her pre-packaged sandwich from Piggly Wiggly, as cooking supper tonight was beyond her. When she climbed the steps and neared the containers, a wave of warm gratitude filled her. The Post-It note on a salad read *Join the Walkie-Talkies sometime. Betty.* The aluminum-covered casserole's note told her to *Cook at 350 for 30 minutes. Love, Aunt Cordy.* Ruth sniffed and the aroma of garlic and tomato sauce greeted her. A bottle of Chianti was tagged *You may need this. Lillian.*

She'd finished Aunt Cordy's lasagna when a knock sounded on her trailer door.

"Come in," she called out without looking up.

Luke walked through the door, carrying a professional-looking meringue pie. He had changed from his uniform into shorts and a Green Bay Packers T-shirt.

"What did I do to deserve room service? Or should I call it 'trailer' service?"

She set the pie on the tiny dinette and took two travel cups from him.

"I didn't want to leave it out on the deck in this heat." His glance landed on the bag of kitty litter. "Do you have a cat?"

"No, my guinea pig, Oreo. Ah, you mean that. It's supposed to get rid of other odors." The former deceased occupant, Mr. Schultz, always wore a black suit and reeked of Bengay. The trailer held the musty odor of old age.

He asked, "Why did you take this trailer?"

"Mom's done enough. I figure she would get more money for the one next door."

He studied her long-haired pet. "Good-looking animal. You should enter it in the County Fair." He gestured toward the banquette. "Mind if I sit?"

"Please." She sat opposite him, the pie between them. "This looks amazing. Where did you buy this?"

"I made it from my mother's prize-winning recipe."

She cut two pieces for them and took a bite. "This is the best pie ever." No wonder her mom married him. Not only was he handsome, and a nice guy, but he could bake.

"The things I make best are restaurant reservations," Ruth said. They nibbled in silence for a minute. "So? You didn't come over only to deliver desert, did you?"

Luke regarded her. "No. I wanted to talk to you."

Ruth waited for him to continue.

"My dad told me you've had a rough two days."

"It's been challenging. Especially when one of my patients went into cardiac arrest."

"Do you know her status?"

She shook her head.

Luke took a deep breath. "I'm sorry. Mrs. Jankowski didn't make it."

Ruth's heart was awash with sadness. "That's too bad."

"Howard wants me to treat it as a suspicious death." He tapped his fork. "I can't go on his gut instincts, good as they are."

"Suspicious? As in criminal?"

"Yes. My dad insists people are passing away who are in relatively good health."

"Older people go without warning all the time. Howard might identify with his own mortality."

"Perhaps." He hesitated. "I've got my hands full with limited personnel to investigate something so vague. Our town is in a crisis, with cannabis the smallest part of it. It's heroin, fentanyl, Oxy. They ambushed us, and it's gotten worse. Without NARCAN, we'd have twenty people dying a month, minimum."

She was familiar with the overdose reversal drug. "What can I do?"

"Help set Howard's—and therefore my—mind at ease. Assure him everything's okay. He likes and trusts you."

After telling him she would, he stood.

"Oh, Luke. One thing. I had a flat after work. Bobby McKay thinks I need a new set of tires."

"He's the one you beat up once, right?" Luke broke out into a wide grin, showing off his smile dimple. "Tyler's always teasing your mom that she raised a hellion to be his bodyguard."

"No one forgets the incident, including McKay."

Luke's expression turned serious. "Did he threaten you in any way?"

"No, no. He claims he's forgiven me."

"Do me a favor." He rinsed out the empty cups and tossed the paper plates into the recycle bin.

"Like?"

He turned to her. "Don't be tempted to tangle with any grownups. Just in case, you might try kickboxing classes at the Y. Use our family membership."

"I'll consider it." They made their goodbyes, and she watched out the kitchen window as Luke studied the Toad. He took out a coin and spent several minutes measuring the tread on the tires.

A white blur approached him from the left and stopped with flapping wings. He bent to pet the goose's head, and then strode off, the gander waddling behind him, like a dog following his master.

Her phone chimed and the text from Luke read *Tires look fine but will keep an eye on them.*

A tingle of suspicion ran through her. McKay was the only person who'd seen the flat tire. Had it worn through or had something else caused it?

CHAPTER 6

The hallways of Golden Years were devoid of the usual morning bustle. Groups of residents and aides spoke in hushed tones. Campaign banners lined the walls, including those for Ethel Jankowski. As Ruth maneuvered along, she spotted Tony Bettini heading toward her, dragging a portable oxygen unit behind him.

"*Buongiorno,* good morning, Nurse Ruth." He squeezed the semi-transparent tube running from his nose.

"Emphysema or Bronchiectasis?"

"The first one. Guess I should've cut out the cancer sticks a long time ago."

She studied his labored breathing. "What can I do for you, Mr. Bettini?"

He fiddled with the gold religious medal around his neck. "I was wondering if you know who'll replace Ethel Jankowski in the race for president."

"No idea, but isn't it too early to worry about the election?" She crossed her arms.

"You can never be too prepared. My campaign team tells me it's going to be a close one."

She opened her mouth to reply, but before she said anything, a voice from behind her replied, "I am."

She turned to see Howard wearing a gloomy expression.

Surprise registered on Tony's face. "How so? You got term limits."

"I spoke to administration. Under the circumstances, they're allowing me to run again."

"Well." Tony looked at the banners lining the walls. "You better put your signs up." He shuffled away down the hall, towing his oxygen behind him.

Ruth turned to Howard. "Luke came by last night. He told me you're concerned about Mrs. Jankowski's passing."

"I am."

"Why?" She paused. "I watched Debi perform CPR and administer emergency treatment. I don't think there was anything more she could've done."

He stole a glance around them and leaned toward her. "Ethel's not the first. I'm in good shape still, thank the Lord, and well enough to be in the Independent Living section."

"So? I'm not sure I understand."

He pointed around the corridor. "These folks have to rely on the people here for their medications. I mail order mine, and it's only cholesterol and blood pressure meds."

A man glided by in an electric wheelchair, nodding at them.

Howard touched her shoulder. As soon as the other resident was out of earshot, he continued. "I'm asking if you see anything unusual—anything at all—tell Luke."

"I guess. I'm still learning the ropes. The only thing different here than the nursing home where I worked in Madison is the computer system." He was such a nice man, and he meant well. It wouldn't hurt to humor him. "Okay."

"And be careful. I wouldn't want anything to happen to you."

She imagined older people needed a little drama in their predictable lives. She played along.

"Sure. I'll be cautious."

He patted her arm. "Don't forget Ethel's service this after-noon."

She nodded and headed off to locate Debi. She found her in Mrs. Jankowski's room, seated next to a tearful middle-aged woman. Someone had sorted scattered possessions into piles. Yolanda bus-ied herself with emptying drawers.

"All of my mom's things, down to these." The woman studied two cardboard boxes. She pointed toward a dark blue shift with embroidered white flowers. "Her favorite." She visibly gathered herself. "I'll donate everything."

Yolanda handed over the clothing with a sad look on her face, tenderly stroking the material. "It is a beautiful thing."

At least the laundry had finally delivered the dress, and Ruth wondered if Ethel had worn it one more time. Ruth cleared her throat, sharing a look with Debi.

Ruth nodded. "I'll get to work without you."

She walked the empty corridor where an orderly removed Ethel's banners. As the morning passed, she continued to make a point of discussing Ethel's passing with the residents, some regis-tering a shadow of fear across their faces as they acknowledged the loss.

As Ruth recorded their vitals and mental health responses, she was getting the hang of the computer system. Only the unusually long response times continued to annoy her.

At lunch, she picked at a Greek salad when her co-worker, Mir-iam, arrived with her tray.

"Mind if I join you?" Today she wore the T-shirt: *Activities-the other best medicine.* Her graying brown hair formed a halo around her face.

"I'd love it."

"Everyone's depressed today, aren't they?"

Ruth scanned the dining room filled with small groups of som-ber-looking people in hushed conversations.

"You might say so."

"It's time to turn those frowns upside down. It's up to us to keep the morale high."

"Us?"

"You visit the patients every day. You can be a positive influence on redirecting their thoughts to happier things."

"Some of them are worried."

"Exactly what I mean. Negative thoughts equal negative results." Miriam slapped the dining table. "I bet you can help me out. I'm looking for therapy animals. Any pets you can bring?"

Ruth immediately discounted her mother's goose and noisy rooster. "I have a black-and-white guinea pig, Oreo."

Miriam grinned broadly. "What a cute name! Bring it next week. It'll help raise morale."

Ruth politely agreed, but she returned to work, doubting any therapy pet would change the residents' moods. After combing the corridors searching for Debi, she found her surrounded by a knot of male residents, with Tony Bettini standing in the center. As she approached, Ruth caught a few phrases.

Tony said, "It ain't right. It's against the rules."

"I'll look into it." Debi placed her hand on Tony's arm.

"Mum's the word." Tony spoke louder as Ruth neared. "Here comes an enemy spy."

The group of men regarded her with looks of curiosity combined with animosity.

"Hardly, Mr. Bettini." She addressed Debi. "Are we working together this afternoon?"

"No." Debi looked at her with unblinking blue eyes. "I'm busy putting Ethel's service together."

"Oh. Okay." No one spoke. Ruth turned on her heel and headed down the hallway, hearing laughter in her wake.

Mid-afternoon, Ruth finished entering the data into the computer system for a patient. As she left the room, she nearly collided with Nurse Steele.

"Charts, please." The head nurse studied the clipboard. "It looks like you catch on fast, Nurse Markson." She looked intently at Ruth. "You did well on your own today."

"Thank you." Ruth wanted to add, especially as she'd had only a day of training, but decided against it. "I heard there's a service here for Mrs. Jankowski."

"It's customary. We don't go to the funeral home as a group. Many of the residents would find it difficult."

The mention of funerals reminded Ruth of Tiedemann's parlor, where her grandparents, and most recently, her father, had their wakes and services. She remembered the air akin to a florist's cooler with fresh pink carnations, red roses in every corner, and white lilies blanketing her father's closed casket. The numbness of grief momentarily overwhelmed her.

"Nurse Markson?"

"I would like to attend."

Steele regarded her with narrowed eyes. "How good of you. You hardly knew her."

"A gracious woman, from her reputation."

"Then go ahead. The service is near enough to the end of your shift."

. . .

At four in the afternoon, Ruth went to the recreation hall. She estimated at least fifty people in wheelchairs encircled a card table. Behind them, ambulatory residents sat in orange plastic chairs. Next to Howard, a tall woman held his hand. Ruth remembered her from her mother's wedding as Gert, Howard's lady-friend.

Ruth walked to the group of staff and stood at the edge. Debi was stone-faced, and most of the aides and orderlies studied the floor. Yolanda shifted from one foot to the other. Lillian sat nearby, dressed in a black pantsuit, her magenta hair uncharacteristically flat against her head. Tears smudged her mascara.

On the table, a black-and-white photograph depicted a young Ethel posed in a one-piece bathing suit on a beach, beaming into the camera, confident and hopeful of her future. Miriam pressed a button on a boom box, and "Amazing Grace" filled the air.

Ruth recalled the same hymn at her dad's service where all of Eureka had filled the funeral home. Her mom had sat white-faced, clutching Ruth's hand in a vise-like grip as the strains of the music surrounded them. At his passing, Ruth vowed to become a physician.

The hymn ended, and residents and staff memorialized Mrs. Jankowski.

Yolanda stood. "Mrs. J. was always asking about my family, always remembering my kids' names." She wiped a tear.

Howard spoke of Ethel as a good friend who had run for president of the Residents' Council as a favor to him. Debi remained silent. Miriam recalled how the deceased had taken part in fundraising events.

Ruth's father had been buried on a frigid afternoon under a lapis sky. She'd spent most of the service breathing deeply and praying for the strength to finish out the day. When her father's coffin lowered into the ground, both mother and daughter clutched at one another, unsure who supported whom.

A resident's stutter interrupted Ruth's reverie. "Eth-eth. Ethel cared. She cared about ev-everyone."

Others in wheelchairs had difficulty speaking, their speech slurred. Ruth held her breath as one woman articulated how much Ethel had helped her when suffering the loss of a good friend. After the residents and staff had spoken, Ethel Jankowski's daughter stood up.

"My mother was a bullhead. She would tell you exactly what she was thinking. She spoke the truth, like it or not. At least it was her truth." Her face crumpled, unable to speak. Finally, she gathered her composure. "I don't know how I will go on without her."

Yolanda walked over to the sobbing woman and held her in her arms. "You were a good daughter, always visiting her. She knows that."

Sunlight bounced off the orange and gray linoleum, causing Ruth to squint. She inhaled the nursing home's scent of disinfectant and wax, so like the hospital where her father wasted away. Her mind raced to process the barrage of images flashing in her mind with doctors' visits, the bleak oncologist's face, her dad's nights of violent purging, the pointless chemotherapy sessions, and the never-ending sleepless nights. His skinny frame grew thinner, his face so gaunt she feared she would forget the handsome daddy of her youth and forever remember her sickly father in this emaciated state.

Ruth stared at the residents in wheelchairs surrounding her. She recalled Yolanda telling her that Mrs. Jankowski reported she was in pain, which was odd. Most of the residents were so heavily medicated they shouldn't have discomfort. Yet, some of the group here were shifting in their chairs and rubbing their limbs.

Ruth hadn't been able to help her father, but if something was wrong in Golden Years, she vowed to keep an open mind.

CHAPTER 7

The next day, Ruth discovered Howard in the dining room, surrounded by friends. She grabbed a bagel and cream cheese and waited at a table until he strolled over, carrying a cup of coffee.

Howard reached inside his breast pocket and handed her a folded piece of paper. "You'll need this."

Glancing at the list of five names, she stuffed it into the pocket of her scrubs. She might as well humor him. "I feel like Mata Hari."

Howard rested his hands on his cane and scanned the crowded dining room.

"Be careful."

"Oh, I will." She suppressed a grin.

Howard set his hand on top of hers and patted it gently.

A young patient, pushed by an aide, wheeled past them. His head lobbed to the side, and his mouth twisted in a grimace. A bumper sticker on the side of his wheelchair read *Single and Looking.*

Howard motioned to the man in the chair. "That's Mike. He's only thirty-two years old. He got his head bashed in with a pool cue in a bar fight. Permanent brain damage."

"You must be satisfied representing these people."

"I do what I can."

A loud burst of laughter came from the corner of the room. Ruth spotted Tony and Debi. "I wonder what's so funny?"

Howard snorted. "Who knows?"

"Catch you later."

Ruth lost herself in finishing her tasks for the day. She'd seen all her patients when she found an empty desk at a nurses' station. The green and black screen prompts took her to a main menu, where she searched for the names on Howard's list in the database. No results.

Ruth entered Mrs. Jankowski's identifier when someone spoke behind her.

"Earning extra credit, Markson?"

She quickly cleared the screen and turned around to find Debi. She attempted to quell her racing heart and hoped her voice sounded normal.

"Only trying to understand the computer system." Ruth held Debi's gaze.

Debi edged closer, peering at the home screen.

"What kind of technical support do we have for this?" Ruth found it difficult to stare sincerely into her coworker's gaze, but forced herself to maintain eye contact.

"Our help comes from a specialist in Janesville. He takes care of everything." She squinted. "Why?"

"I was hoping someone might explain why the software is so slow."

"I've been told there's no room in the budget for an upgrade."

She faked a smile. "I'm sure I'll get used to it."

"Anyway, I stopped by to tell you Nurse Steele says you can work on your own from now on."

"Well, that's great news!" She hoped her voice didn't betray her sarcasm.

Debi raised her eyebrows. "Good luck, Markson."

Throughout the day, Ruth listened for gossip about the five patients on her list. Some reacted with surprise at their passing, but most were fatalistic.

"When your time is up, your time is up."

As Ruth left, one of her patients stopped her. "Nurse Ruth, I think the doctor should review my prescriptions. My hands ache like crazy."

Ruth grabbed her chart, studying it. "Your pain patch should do the trick."

The woman shrugged. "It used to." She held up her twisted fingers. "But not so much now."

As Ruth's shift ended, she spotted Nurse Steele walking the corridor and caught up to her.

"Yes, Nurse Markson?" The older woman appeared as if she were being imposed upon.

"I've had a patient complaining of pain. She'd like to have the doctor review her meds. Who's the attending physician? I assume Doctor Kelly?"

"You assume wrong. It's Dr. Thompson." The nurse peered over her glasses. "And your point is?"

Ruth ruminated, but couldn't recollect a physician named Thompson in the area. "Where is he located?"

Steele harrumphed. "In Janesville. He's been the doctor here for over thirty years. Why do you ask?"

"The meds should work."

"I'll make a note on her chart."

Ruth struggled to think of something to add. "Thank you for signing off on my training."

"You've earned it. So far."

"Ah, thanks." Nothing like a strong vote of confidence.

As she walked away, she mulled over the latest information. There couldn't be many software support people nearby, so Tyler would find him with little trouble. She needed computer skills and only he would do.

After she logged out of her shift, she sent a text to Ty.

. . .

"B 12." Ruth suppressed a yawn, wondering how she'd ended up calling the bingo game at Golden Years. In her heart, she knew why. She was a people-pleaser. When Miriam called, whispering that she suffered from laryngitis and needed help tonight, Ruth had caved. Players filled the recreation room to capacity, and the air conditioning lost its battle with the crowd-generated heat. An elaborate pattern of bingo cards and bizarre good luck charms, including toys, rabbits' feet, and small stuffed animals, were placed on the long folding tables.

She'd gotten a bad vibe from the get-go. Before the game even started, Ruth had to referee a confrontation between two women residents. One of them had taken her "lucky" seat and demanded the other woman sit elsewhere. Beanie Babies had flown, along with bingo daubers, before Ruth intervened and prevented fisticuffs from erupting.

Golden Years invited residents and local townspeople to attend, Miriam had explained. "Makes the pot bigger." Ruth scanned the crowd. Tony Bettini's posse surrounded him. Howard was absent and had explained he had enough of gambling after being a farmer for many years. Many of her wheelchair patients lined the tables, bingo daubers in hand. The air crackled with expectant energy.

Amid the crowd, a woman with a ring of frizzy gray hair sucked coffee after coffee with the intensity of a crackhead getting a fix. She called out, "Bingo" regularly, which met with the murmuring of cusswords, mostly from Lillian, who had teased her magenta hair into a kind of feather headdress.

Ruth spun the bingo cage and balls, remembering her grandma calling out the numbers at the campground, using her bingo lingo to entertain everyone.

"I 29."

A honk rang out somewhere in the crowd, reminding Ruth of her mother's goose. She let out her breath at someone blowing his nose with the wallop of an air horn. Hisses and catcalls broke out around the hall.

"Repeat that!" Frizzy Hair demanded.

An older man in the corner called out, "I couldn't hear either."

"Turn up your hearing aid, you old coot!" Tony Bettini called out and laughter erupted.

"I 29." Ruth fought to recall Grandma's saying. "You're, you're doing fine!"

"BINGO!" Frizzy Gray Hair hollered and kissed a rubber ducky. This time, Ruth made out Lillian's swearwords above all the others' complaints.

When the room quieted, rumbles and wheezing came from the back of the room. Ruth spotted the bare pate of a man face down asleep on his bingo card. Everyone turned to stare, most with amused looks. Soon, people were laughing hysterically. The red-faced woman next to him tapped him on the shoulder. He jumped to his feet.

"Bingo!"

"Sit down, George." His wife blushed a brighter red. Now the group roared with laughter. Her husband's face was covered in blue dots from the daubs on the cards.

Ruth glanced at the schoolhouse-style clock. Seven o'clock at last. "Ladies and Gentlemen, that does it for this evening."

Guests glared at Frizzy Hair, who busied herself counting her cash. Ruth gathered up the bingo equipment and placed it in the labeled storage area. Some people slapped their cards on the tables and marched out, annoyed with the outcome of the game. The rest of them cleared their areas and dutifully separated recyclables from trash into the proper bins, accepting their fate at losing money or barely breaking even. The residents walked to their rooms or wheeled along in their chairs.

Lillian strode up to her. "You did good, even though I lost to that bi-bitty, June McKay. Nice to have a son who stakes you. Word is she starts out with a hundred bucks."

"Next time I'll wear a referee shirt and bring a whistle."

"Where there's money, there are soreheads."

Ruth recalled the wads of cash she'd put in the safe. "I should wear body armor, too."

"Or carry one of these." Lillian dangled a four-leaf clover encased in plastic. "Found it online. It's straight from the Emerald Isle, complete with the proper good luck spell."

"You don't believe in that, do you?"

"There's a money-back guarantee for a full year."

"How can you prove it worked?"

"If I win more than I lose." Lillian shrugged. "Everyone has something. Cordelia wears a magnet on a chain around her neck."

"I know. She sent me one for my graduation present."

"You should wear it. Never know when it'll help." Lillian made the sign of the cross.

"I do. By the way, when did you develop a stutter?"

Lillian grimaced. "I'm trying to give up swearing."

Ruth's eyebrows rose. "That so?" The older woman was notorious among the campers as having a mouth like a sailor on leave.

Lillian wore a sweatshirt decorated with transfer photos of *Grandma's Sweethearts*. She pointed to a young girl's image on her shirt.

"I was shopping at Piggly Wiggly with Kimmy when some bi-broad engaged me in a game of supermarket cart chicken. She told me to choose a side. I told her to go to hell. Then I let the f-bomb drop."

"Oh. That's bad."

"And expensive, too," Lillian said. "I had to bribe my princess-in-pink with a ton of candy not to tell her mother. Plus, I've gone through two swear jars this month."

Ruth looked at her watch. "I'll make one more round as long as I'm here."

Lillian nodded. "See you tomorrow."

Nightlights cast long shadows in the empty hallways. Without television background noise, there was only the sound of Ruth's rubber soles squeaking along the linoleum. An occasional snore broke the silence. Satisfied everything appeared well, she wondered if she'd turned off the lights in the recreation room. As she approached, the light flooded the doorway.

She peered into Rec Hall where she spied Miriam, who deftly unlocked the safe and reached in. She counted out a fistful of bills and placed them in her purse.

"Hi there," Ruth called out. "Everything okay?"

Miriam froze, then said in a raspy voice, "Oh. Great to see you, Ruth. How did it go tonight?"

"Fine. As you can see." Ruth nodded toward the safe. "We had a good turnout. Are you feeling better?"

Miriam shifted her weight. She pointed at her throat. "Hurts to talk."

"You should be home, taking care of yourself." And not sneaking around Golden Years after hours.

Miriam nodded and rasped, "Need to pick up supplies tomorrow." She lifted her purse.

"Remember to drink plenty of fluids and avoid talking."

As Miriam walked down the shadowy corridor, Ruth wondered what else happened at Golden Years under the cover of night.

On the highway, Ruth was stuck behind a truck covered in a black-and-white spotted paint job. The sign read: *Dairy Air Heating and Air Conditioning*. They rolled along the highway, well below the speed limit. She dared not pass with the Saturn's snail-like acceleration capability.

She drummed her fingers on the steering wheel after she parked. Leading a bonfire sing-along this evening was bad enough, and now she was late.

A battered minivan at the trailer next door caught her attention. She hoped her new neighbors weren't a couple of Baby Boomers who played their golden oldies at full volume. If she never heard the stupid song about the bullfrog again, she'd be delighted.

Ruth stopped short. Although the porch was piled high with boxes, she still made out the welcome mat. Resting on the mat were a pair of UGG boots.

CHAPTER 8

The next evening, Ruth said to Tyler, "Can you believe my mom rented the trailer next door to Debi? Her excuse is that there's a lack of affordable housing in the area."

"Your mom's right. Plus, keep your frenemies close."

"I appreciate you coming over tonight." She plopped next to him on the plaid couch. "There's something wrong with the software or hardware at work, and no one will listen to me." Ruth gave Tyler the details she'd been able to glean. "And there's a doctor in Janesville I know nothing about. You might find out something about him. No hacking, right?"

"Right." He grinned. "Only public information."

She recounted the bingo game antics of the night before. "And then someone tells him to turn on his hearing aid." She put her hand on Tyler's well-toned arm, aware of his proximity.

"Is it still warm in here?"

"Uh-huh." He held her gaze.

A thrill shot through her. She cleared her throat. "Afterward, I found the recreation director, Miriam, with money in hand from the safe. In my experience, that's not standard operating procedure."

"What's her last name?"

"I don't know."

"No problem." He took his phone and swiped it. "Got it. 'Jorgensen.'" He frowned. "You confronted her?"

"Why, what?"

He touched her shoulder. "I want you to keep a low profile until we find out more about everyone involved."

"You're being melodramatic, like everybody else." But at least he cared.

She wiped her mouth and put the dishes in the sink. "I need to deliver something to my mom. Want to take a walk with me?"

As they neared her mother's house, she stopped short at the sight of the goose standing stock-still on the porch.

"Oh my god, look! The darn thing is right next to the front door."

Tyler squinted and barked out a laugh. "It's one of those cement statues. You know, people dress them up seasonally."

"Geez. As if the actual monster wasn't enough." She glanced nervously around as they stepped onto the porch and knocked on the screen door.

Mary Jo welcomed them and gestured toward the wicker chairs. She smoothed her highlighted bob. "Did I hear a shout?"

"I feared it was your goose 'posturing.'" Ruth pointed to the statue. "I forgot to give you this the other night." She reached into her pocket and pulled out a thumb drive.

"What's on it?"

"Remember when I scanned all of our old pictures into my computer?"

Mary Jo's eyes filled with tears. "These will replace the photos I lost in the tornado."

Her mom's hug, coupled with words of thanks, overwhelmed Ruth. "You're welcome, Mama." She squeezed her mother, inhaling her mom's familiar scent.

Then something rustled in the foundation junipers.

Ruth jumped. "Oh my god, the goose is back!"

Mary Jo said, "Just the wind. This is a perfect opportunity to get over this phobia of yours, if you want to."

"I guess I might try to make friends with it. I mean him." Ruth hesitated and forced out the name. "Gandalf. I'd like to run in the mornings and stop looking over my shoulder."

"All right. I'll go get Luke. Gandy's my pet. Promise me you won't upset him too much." She went into the house.

"Upset *him*?" Ruth said. "What about me?" Her heart pounded.

Her mom and stepfather emerged from the farmhouse sporting wide grins.

"Hey." Luke nodded at Ruth. "This should be fun."

Really?

"He's usually down by the pond this time of night," her mother added.

The four of them strolled through the park, waving at campers as they passed. With each step forward, Ruth was tempted to come up with an excuse to back out.

They rounded the bend in the road where the pond-turned-swimming hole gleamed in the setting sun. The kids had gone home, and the lifeguard station stood empty. The reeds along the edge bent in the gentle breeze.

"Looks like he's not here tonight. We'll try another time." Ruth spun on her heel.

Tyler grabbed her arm and when she turned, she spotted the gander, dipping his head into the reflection of the sky.

"He looks so innocent." Ruth sighed.

Her mom stood at the edge of the water and called his name. The goose shook his head and swam toward them. The gander neared the bank, waddled up to her mother and then to Luke.

Both Luke and her mom made encouraging sounds to the goose as Ruth stood still. Finally, the goose noticed her. She held her breath as he stepped forward. Lowering his head, he stretched his snake-like neck toward her.

"Mom!"

"Don't move, honey." Her mom and Luke walked closer to her, flanking Ruth on either side. As the goose neared, she closed her eyes, steeling herself for the attack.

"Eye contact, Ruth!" Tyler called from the side.

Instead, she made eye contact with Tyler as a glare.

Gandalf clucked softly and smelled her Crocs. She tried not to flinch.

"He probably thinks your shoes look like eggs," Tyler said.

"Shut up Ty! Luke, if you don't want a murder in the campground, tell him to be quiet."

A kid rode by on his bicycle and let out a whoop. The goose turned his head toward him and hissed.

Ruth jumped from foot to foot.

"It looks like a Highland Fling." Tyler hummed an off-key Scottish tune.

Her mom rushed toward her pet, stroking him on his head. "There's a good boy. Calm down." Her goose cooed and closed his eyes.

Both Luke and her mom continued to placate the gander. After a full minute, Gandalf's feathers smoothed as he neared Ruth. He gave a last cluck and curled up on her feet. Tyler snickered.

"Now what?" She turned to Luke, whose face twitched. "Do you think he's trying to hatch my Crocs or what?"

Her mom chortled next to her. "He's accepted you, honey." She wiped the tears from her eyes and then held her sides.

Ruth tentatively stroked the white, smooth feathers atop his head. *Was he purring?*

"Great. Now get him off my feet, please." Unbidden, the laughter bubbled up in her, and they all shook with amusement until Gandalf arose, gave them what Ruth interpreted as a disgusted look, and waddled to the pond.

. . .

Tyler and Ruth stood on her trailer's deck, where she slipped off her shoes.

"My Crocs won't ever be the same, and they're never coming inside again."

"Didn't you trip on them, anyway?" He grinned. "The look on your face when Gandalf huddled on them was priceless."

"I'm glad you enjoyed it."

His green-eyed gaze held hers. "The stars are beautiful tonight, huh?"

"Yeah. Right."

"You're not even looking." He leaned on the door frame. "Did you know there's a nebula, Messier 42, in the center of Orion's sword? It's visible to the naked eye." He leaned a fraction of an inch closer.

She swallowed hard. "You silver-tongued devil, you."

"Why, because I said 'naked'?" The corner of his mouth lifted. "Well, good night. I'll let you know what I find out tomorrow."

"It's all probably legitimate." She prayed she was right.

CHAPTER 9

Ruth jolted awake in a cold sweat at 3:01 AM, the Witching Hour. She recalled the phrase her Grandma Ruth used—someone had walked on her grave. No specific reason for her panic came to her as she studied the maple's silhouette twisting behind the window shade.

At dawn, after a fitful sleep, she decided exercise might ease her apprehension. After throwing on her running attire, she started her phone's playlist and jogged to the tune of "Mamma Mia." The morning dew covered the grass around each campsite.

She neared a secluded corner where a vintage Bluebird motor home occupied a site with a carved wooden sign *The Kloppenheimers, Mabel and Abel Est. 1984.*

"Oh, boy." She didn't tear her gaze away fast enough and caught sight of the naked eighty-something couple behind the open shades. She had no choice but to wave to the nudists who toasted her with raised coffee cups.

As she averted her eyes, she spotted something unusual on the edge of a copse of sumac. Spiky plants covered the freshly turned earth. She inspected them and confirmed her suspicions. *Rupert has another garden. I wonder if this one's on the honor system too?*

Luke appeared around the bend, running in her direction. She jogged toward him, rather than draw attention to the marijuana growing on the property.

Ruth turned off her tunes. "Mind if I run with you?"

If it surprised Luke, he didn't show it. "Sure thing."

They took off at a comfortable pace through the cool June morning air. Luke was taller, but he adjusted his stride and they jogged in silence. Whenever they circled near the illegal garden, Ruth would automatically pick up speed. If Luke noticed, he betrayed nothing. After an hour of running, they arrived at the campground office, sweating but easily catching their breath.

Ruth checked her pedometer. "I worked off at least some of your pie I ate last night."

Luke studied his fitness watch. "I'm good too."

They were stretching out when Ruth noticed the scar on Luke's upper arm. She recalled his gunshot wound the previous year in the line of duty. Her early morning foreboding returned.

"Your dad may be right. Something's off at Golden Years."

Luke touched her arm. "Do you have any specifics?"

"No. Only a gut feeling."

"If there are people dying unnecessarily, it's a police matter."

"I can't prove anything." She straightened. "Besides, nothing much happens in Eureka, right?"

"This is a very small town, but very bad things can happen here."

A bubble of nervous laughter welled up in her. "Everyone is awfully melodramatic."

"If you find anything, please tell me."

A cool breeze raised goosebumps on her arms. The bare branches above her rubbed together like worry beads. "Sure."

. . .

Ruth recalled the morning's news story about nursing home abuse caught on granny cams as she drove to work. Entering the atrium, Lillian, her hair streaked in gold and magenta, waved her over.

Lillian leaned in. "News. More clothes and someone's wedding ring are MIA." She raised her brows. "And the natives are restless. There's been a crapload of shouting going on most of the morning."

"Thanks." Ruth hurried down a corridor. As she turned a corner, she discovered two ladies slapping at one another's wheelchairs.

"You old whore." The smaller woman with bones as fine as a pigeon swung her handbag at the other's electric wheelchair. "You're voting for him because you have the hots for him."

"You should talk." The stocky woman took an age-spotted hand and smacked the purse, sending it at her attacker. "You were a tart in high school, Nympho Nellie. I remember you and the football team."

"Hatty the Fatty." Nellie sneered. "You couldn't get laid to save your life."

"Then you should live forever."

Ruth placed herself between the two warring factions. "Ladies, please."

They both cast her venomous looks and drove around her. They hit each other and shouted out insults. The flurry of strikes was more like pats, but Ruth couldn't let it continue. She stifled a chuckle and pasted a firm expression on her face.

A crowd gathered in the hallway, and most of the onlookers had bemused looks. Two men goaded the fighters on.

"Go get her, Hatty. Nellie *was* a fast one in school."

"Well, Hatty was no angel."

"Oh, yeah?" The smaller man's jaw jutted forward. "You know this firsthand?"

Now the two men eyed each other menacingly. If Ruth couldn't get them all under control, a geriatric riot might erupt.

Miriam arrived wearing a T-shirt with a rainbow across it. "Peace, love, and understanding, ladies." She flashed a peace sign.

"Screw you, hippie." Nellie rushed Hatty.

Miriam glowered at the woman. "You need some downers, lady." She stomped away.

Ruth planted as stern an expression on her face as she could muster. "Enough! Both of you!"

The two women halted with their hands suspended in space. Yolanda, the aide, appeared from around the corner and spoke into the smaller woman's ear. Nellie extended one middle finger at Hatty, who responded with a hand under her chin and a flick. After a few seconds of staring, they wheeled down opposite hallways.

"What did you say to her?" Ruth asked.

Yolanda beamed, her bright white teeth contrasting with her warm brown skin. She spoke in Spanish. "An old Mexican proverb. A clear conscience is the sign of a poor memory."

"I haven't seen them all so worked up before."

The aide shrugged. "The elections. Already this morning I broke up two other arguments."

"Or they're off their meds."

Ruth paced the hallway where she counted approximately an even number of election posters promoting Tony Bettini or Howard Engel for the Resident Council President. If the voting outcome sparked this morning's confrontation, she couldn't wait for it to be over.

Throughout the day, she pondered the legality and cost of installing granny cameras in residents' rooms. If Tyler found nothing amiss with the computer system, it might be another avenue to monitor the patients' routines. She needed Tyler's expertise to achieve her plan. Howard would be happy if they protected his friends from mysterious deaths. She texted both, requesting a meeting after work. Howard replied immediately in the affirmative.

At lunch, Tyler responded with a message, confirming four o'clock. Before he ended the exchange, he posted the cryptic comment *It's gone viral. Congrats!*

As she replied, a shadow crossed her table.

Quickly, she turned her phone face down. "Hey. What's up?"

"Texts and calls should be limited to your personal time." Debi squinted at the table.

"It's my lunch break. You wanted something?" Irritation surged through her. How many times was Debi going to interrupt?

"Nellie Wilson wants you to stop by."

"Fine. I'll get there as soon as I finish."

"One other thing. Remember, rules forbid developing relationships with residents. It isn't professional."

"And yours with Mr. Bettini isn't personal?"

Debi's eyes narrowed. "You always have a comeback, don't you, Markson?" Shaking her head, she walked away before Ruth responded.

Just as well. If I come back with what I think, I might get myself fired.

.   .   .

After her shift, Ruth set off for the independent living area of Golden Years. She tapped on the door, prepared to see a larger version of the assisted living rooms. Howard broke into a welcoming smile.

Impressionistic paintings and black-and-white photographs lined the walls, each illuminated by spotlights. No stuffed La-Z-Boy recliners with accompanying sagging sofas, and curio cabinets filled with sentimental figurines. Instead, she found an apartment tastefully decorated and furnished in modern Scandinavian.

"Your apartment is delightful."

"Thank you." He gestured around the stylish surroundings. "After I left the farm, I needed to start over again."

He motioned at the sectional. "Have a seat. Can I get you something? Wine?" He gestured at the wine cooler under the granite counter. "Or fresh-squeezed lemonade?"

After choosing the non-alcoholic option, Ruth listened to the sounds of soft jazz emanating from a Bose sound system. She rubbed at the twin knots of tension at the base of her neck. Howard returned with a tray of drinks and soft chocolate chip cookies.

"I can't find any details for the patients you listed, other than Mrs. J. I don't know when patients' records are archived offline."

Howard snorted. "How's that for your tombstone? Born on a certain date, then archived for eternity."

Ruth agreed it sounded harsh. "You know they call it 'termination' when you're fired?"

"Sometimes life can be rough." He took a sip of lemonade. "Is this sweet enough for you? I went light on the sugar."

"It's perfect. Like my grandma used to make." Ruth took a bite of a cookie. "These are great too."

"Thanks. My lady-friend, Gert, makes them. She lives down the hall, for now."

"For now, huh?"

Howard's weather-worn face crinkled into a smile. "She grooms dogs. I'd rather not have a mess in my place, beautiful as Gert is."

Ruth quashed a chuckle at the image of his immaculate apartment defiled by tumbleweeds of dog hair blowing across the wooden floor. The soothing sound of jazz enveloped them, and Ruth's shoulders relaxed. Across from her, she spotted a collage picture frame entitled *Our Family Grows with Love.*

He pointed to the photos. "They're the only things I kept from the old place."

She studied the series from left to right that showed the progression of his life, with an old wedding photo, studio baby pictures of Luke and another young girl, a much-younger Howard and his wife next to him, proudly holding a blue ribbon at the Walworth County Fair.

"My wife Edna wasn't only beautiful. She was a talented baker."

"Oh. Now I know where Luke gets it from." Ruth stood and walked closer to the pictures where Howard joined her.

He pointed at a photograph of his son in uniform. "This is Luke graduating from the academy."

"You two look a lot alike."

"You resemble your mom. And your grandma when she was young."

"You knew her?" Her heartbeat quickened at the connection.

"Went to school with Fred. I remember when he brought his Ruth home from Up North. Met her on a fishing trip and always called her the catch of his life."

"I miss them." And my dad. "How did you meet your wife?"

"We were classmates, but I always figured her as a friend. Then one day, she was standing with a group of girls, and she turned and smiled at me."

"Just like that?" Ruth marveled at the naïve way people fell in love.

"No way. She made me court her for a long time. Finally, she let me give her a smooch behind her dad's barn." He grinned. "Two months later, we married."

"You must be some kisser."

Howard winked. "In my day."

He showed her more photos, the highlights of his long life. "Here's one of Gert and me at your mom's and Luke's wedding ceremony."

"Very nice." There was one open space. "What goes here?"

"I wanted to ask you." He retrieved two pictures from a cabinet.

They were similar photographs of the wedding last year. Her mom and Luke posed, flanked by Howard and Luke's daughters, and Ruth stood next to her mother.

"Which one do you like?" Howard held up the photos.

"Either." Her throat tightened with affection for him. "Both are great."

A knock on the door interrupted them. Ruth introduced Tyler, and he and Howard shook hands.

"This group deserves a name since we're committed to finding out what's happening here," Howard began as the three of them convened around his teak dining table. When the doorbell rang, he turned to Ruth with a puzzled expression.

She shrugged. "Another person wants to help."

He answered the door to find Lillian, whose bleached hair was stiffened into peaks tipped in red, resembling flames. Howard momentarily hesitated and then welcomed her in.

"You're our part-time receptionist, right?" Howard squinted at Lillian, who sported a T-shirt with the silhouette of a man smoking a pipe and wearing a deerstalker hat.

Lillian winked. "And part-time detective, my dear Watson."

Howard waved at the table and resumed the meeting. "Should we get a name for this group?"

"How about The No Ship, Sherlocks?" Lillian asked.

Ruth suppressed a chuckle. "I'm not sure we need a name, *per se*."

Howard cleared his throat. "Here's what we know. Some of my friend's deaths came out of the blue."

"And then there're more missing items from the residents," Lillian said.

Howard stared at her. "How do you get your hair like that? Never mind."

"I caught Miriam taking cash out of the bingo proceeds," Ruth said. "She claimed she needed the funds for supplies. People fill in expense reports or requests for petty cash, not take money out of the safe."

"Ruth says the computer system is slower than snails." Tyler stared at the group. "Anything else?"

Ruth said, "There are patients who are feeling pain. The attending physician is an hour away. He's the one who prescribes the medication. I hope to speak with him when he's here."

Howard frowned. "I don't see how any of these events connect."

"I don't know yet." Ruth stared into space, trying to see the larger picture.

"We need more data." Tyler took out his phone and swiped at the screen. "All I found out about the good doctor Thompson is his association with the nursing facility for over thirty years. My dad knows him a bit but doesn't have much of a professional opinion of him."

Ruth proposed her idea. "I read an article about granny cams. What do you all think of placing them in residents' rooms?"

"Are they legal?" Howard frowned. "And how much do they cost? My friends aren't rich."

"Oh yeah. They're legal, all right." Tyler studied his phone. "They can't aim at 'private areas' like bathrooms."

Lillian held out her hand. "Stop. We need not see *that*."

"Agreed." Howard grinned. "Our birthday suits are past our sell-by dates here."

Ruth recalled the naked Kloppenheimers toasting her with their coffee cups. "I second that motion."

Tyler continued to read. "It would be best if management was involved."

Howard snorted. "That would defeat the entire purpose, wouldn't it?" He took a long sip of his lemonade and the air filled with a John Coltrane riff. "I'll get a bunch of my friends to agree to the cameras. They'll even cough up the money for them if they're not too expensive."

Tyler spent a half an hour discovering a variety of granny cams disguised as everything from stuffed animals to coat hooks and power supplies. After much discussion, they agreed clocks might make the best choice. They were affordable and, once aimed at the doorway, they would remain stationary.

"It's not perfect," Howard pointed out. "We would direct the cameras at my friends."

"They can be motion-activated so we can see who comes into the rooms. They'll also be time-stamped," Tyler responded. "It might give us a clue what's going on here."

Lillian nodded. "At least for the missing items."

"And how will they get installed?" Ruth asked. Howard and Tyler looked at her. "Stupid question. Me."

. . .

As Tyler and Ruth walked into the parking lot, she turned to him. "*What* went viral?"

"Your encounter with Gandalf."

She stopped short. "Tyler Kelly, I could throttle you. You posted the video on your blog? Cut it out. I mean it, dammit."

He linked his arm through hers and pulled her forward. "That's no way for a star to react. You should read the comments from my geek friends who loved it. They posted you looked hot."

"Sure, I looked hot. I was broiling on a scorching summer's evening swathed in sweat clothes."

"Ruthie, you look amazing, no matter what."

Annoyance prickled at her, erasing the compliment.

They stopped near her car. As something caught her eye in the dim light, she rubbed what appeared to be a scrape. When she leaned closer, her breath caught. Someone had etched a six-inch word into the dark green paint of the back fender.

"What's wrong?"

With a shaky hand, she pointed at the scratch.

BITCH

CHAPTER 10

Tyler thumbed the screen on his phone. "What to do to fix my keyed car?"

Ruth stared at the offending scratch. "Do everything we can so my mother, and all of Eureka, doesn't find out." She didn't need her mom to worry about her.

"Says here we can try some shoe polish and sandpaper."

"Sounds like a scavenger hunt. Do we need TP too?"

"Or you can make an insurance claim and you'll need a police report to do so. It's vandalism, and technically a crime."

"No way. Luke will find out, and it's as good as telling Mom." She studied the mark. "What about green paint? Touch it up myself?"

He ran his fingers over the gouges. "It's deep. And we might have trouble buying automotive paint this late at night."

She wondered if any residents had spotted the jerk who'd defiled her car. She kicked a stone clear across the parking lot. "I am so pissed off. I want to beat the crap out of whoever did this."

"Whoa, down girl. We'll take this one step at a time, okay?" He put his arm around her. "Okay?"

She sighed. "Yeah. Let's go shopping."

. . .

They returned in full darkness to the deserted parking lot. Crickets chirped and the crescent moon had risen. Ruth held the phone, her flashlight app illuminating Tyler's handiwork. When he applied the white shoe polish to highlight the scratch, aggravation rose in her anew.

"When, and I mean 'when' not 'if', I find out who did this to my car, they're toast."

Debi's minivan had been parked in the lot. But why would she do it?

"Hold the light still, please." Tyler patiently sanded the area with some shoe polish and the surrounding green paint disappeared. He continued to wipe and lightly sand the section as Ruth leaned on the side of her Saturn. Her eyelids lowered, and she yawned after he had been working for what seemed like hours.

He straightened and surveyed the door panel. "We're lucky. It didn't get down to the base coat, only the clear coat and the first layer."

She studied the sanded block from different angles. "It's great, Ty." Relief flooded her. "Thanks for saving my butt. I can't thank you enough."

"It's one worth saving." He raised an eyebrow. "A dinner sometime would be a worthy repayment."

"Our annual campground luau is tomorrow night. It's dumb, but there's food if you want to come over."

"Sure. Love to."

. . .

Ruth spent a frustrating day at work wondering who might have keyed her car. The local kids sometimes vandalized, toppling rural mailboxes and occasionally, they threw toilet paper around people's front yards after homecoming games. Nothing major. Though her coworkers were far from friendly, she couldn't fathom why any of them would risk defacing her car. Nurse Steele had sent Debi away for the day to the local hospital, and Ruth wondered if she would show up at the luau looking guilty.

Once home, Ruth changed from her scrubs and reluctantly put on her ridiculous costume. Stealing a glance at Debi's trailer and parked minivan, she fervently hoped her nemesis wouldn't attend tonight. She trudged to the barnlike recreation center where her mom had saddled her with organizing the hodgepodge collection of potluck dishes. Hawaiian music played in the background and honeycombed tissue pineapples adorned the wrought iron chandelier. The aroma of grilled pork traveled through the open French doors, where a pig roasted outside. All the Workampers were theme-attired in Hawaiian shirts and artificial leis around their necks.

Lillian approached Ruth with two plastic cups in her hands. "How about a nice Hawaiian Punch?"

"Ha ha. That's an old one." She took the proffered drink and swigged.

Lillian pointed toward the front entrance. "Our Wahine of Bling has arrived."

Betty Fontaine sashayed by, accompanied by her fiancé, Bernie Feinstein. She wore a grass skirt and a coconut bra, with a frangipani lei nestled in her cleavage.

"Hubba-hubba," a male voice muttered somewhere in the crowd.

"She strips every year at the senior talent show," a woman hissed.

Ruth chortled. "Looks like Betty's bling is rubbing off on Mr. Feinstein." Her mother's accountant wore a crown of leaves on his bald pate, and a lei on his bare, gray-haired chest. "By the way, I like your muumuu."

"Thanks." Lillian's fuchsia hair matched her brightly colored garb. "We Walkie-Talkies take theme parties seriously."

Ruth remembered the group of walkers wearing costumes for Mardi Gras, Halloween, and for no reason at all. "That you do."

Aunt Cordy glided up to them in a diaphanous caftan. "Where do brownies go?"

Ruth remembered the weed growing on the edge of the woods. "Special recipe?"

Cordy put her finger to her mouth. "Shush. Don't tell anyone but—"

Ruth held her breath as the older woman whispered in her ear. "It's a store-bought mix."

Relieved, Ruth pointed toward the dessert table. "Put them over there."

"By the tart," Lillian added.

Ruth frowned. "I don't remember any pies."

Cordy craned her neck. "I don't see any either."

Lillian snorted. "Not that kind of tart. That kind."

Across from the dessert table, several of the men from the campground surrounded Debi, including Lillian and Cordelia's husbands. Her Hawaiian printed halter-top was low-cut, and the skirt was short.

"Oh, I see the tart now." Cordelia walked over to the table, placing the brownies with the other desserts. After whispering in Rupert's ear, he joined his wife, and then grabbed a brownie.

"The tart?" Ruth asked. "Is that what the Walkie-Talkies call her?"

"We will now." Lillian twirled the umbrella in her drink. "Is she wearing a dress, or a beach cover up?"

"Either." Ruth craned her neck. "I don't think I've ever seen her without her boots. She's wearing flip-flops."

Lillian grinned. "Hey, Tyler."

Ruth spun around and spotted her handsome friend.

"Sorry I'm late." He pointed at his loud Margaritaville shirt. "More Florida than Hawaii, but at least it's tropical."

Even in his silly attire, he looked great. The stuffed parrot on his shoulder wore an eye patch and pirate's tricorn hat. "The bird is a real swashbuckler, Ty."

When Tyler squeezed the toy, it squawked, "Argh, Matey!"

Lillian patted Ruth's arm. "I'd better rescue my husband before he makes a fool of himself." She winked. "Have fun, kids."

Ruth grinned at Tyler. "I'm surprised you bothered with the motif."

"Well, you look mar-ve-lous."

"Oh, come on." Ruth wore two fake leis, her Dairyland Acres logo golf shirt, and Bermuda shorts, with her grandmother's ancient grass skirt over them. Her neon running shoes completed the costume.

He threw his arm around her and murmured in her ear. "How about a lei?" Tyler nodded at her necklaces.

His whisper had sent a thrill down her neck. "Oh. You want to get lei'd. Sure." She took one of them off and put it around his neck, enjoying his startled response. Two could play this game. Ruth kissed him quickly on the cheek and caught the clean scent of his aftershave.

He grabbed her hand and kissed it. "*Aloha Nui Loa.*"

She didn't understand a word of Hawaiian, other than "Aloha." She'd have to look it up later.

Luke strode up to them and shook Tyler's hand. "Good to see you."

"I invited him." Ruth laced her arm through Tyler's.

"Oh, well, have a good time." Luke winked and left them to socialize.

Tyler peered at the tables heaped with covered dishes. "I love potlucks. It's like every grandma's best dish in one big party."

"They're usually heavy on the calories, but I admit, tasty." Men surrounding Debi let out loud guffaws. "My UGG-wearing buddy has alienated the women here, too." Lillian took her husband's hand and led him away. "Debi rarely deigns to attend our functions."

"She's entitled to as a resident, no?"

"I guess." Ruth hated to think she couldn't escape Debi, no matter the location.

He motioned at her now-empty cup. "Another punch?"

"They'll serve soon. Set it down at the head table." She called after him as he walked away. "Next to my ukulele."

Several campers approached Ruth.

"Are you the entertainment tonight, dear?"

She blushed. "Sort of."

Ruth noticed Debi was alone, staring at the table loaded with covered dishes. Seizing her opportunity, Ruth approached her.

"I noticed you stayed late last night." Ruth kept her tone light, but her heart pounded in her chest. "I spotted your minivan after I thought you'd gone home."

Debi gazed steadily at Ruth with unmade-up eyes.

"What of it?" Debi tossed her streaked hair and sighed.

"Something happened in the Golden Years' parking lot last evening. To my car."

"It's been a safe neighborhood." Debi poured some diet cola into her plastic cup.

Rage rose in Ruth like volcanic lava. "Ever had a problem with vandalism?"

Tyler's hand gripped her arm. "Honey, they're serving."

Ruth hesitated. "Right." She looked at Debi, who wore a smug smile. "Enjoy your evening." She hoped her sarcasm would come through.

In line, Tyler heaped his plastic plate with globs of every dish and several slices of roast pork.

"Are you sure you have enough, Ty?" Ruth smirked.

"They let you go for seconds, don't they?"

She piled iceberg salad on her plate and skipped the Thousand Island dressing. "Why did you pull me away from her?" she asked as they approached the head table.

"I'll tell you later."

Her mother glided toward them wearing a strapless maxi dress in a batik pattern and puka shells adorned her neck. "Welcome to our luau, Tyler. You're perfectly attired."

"Aloha, Mary Jo." Tyler squeezed the parrot on his shoulder that let out his greeting.

Her mother jumped and then laughed.

Mary Jo moved to the stage, and the music subsided. Speaking into a microphone, she welcomed them to the gathering and thanked everyone for their loyalty. She reported Dairyland Acres was fully booked for the first summer in years, causing a round of applause from the audience.

Her beautiful and confident mom had lost weight, accentuating her high cheekbones and chiseled jaw line. A stab of envy went through Ruth as Luke beamed at her mother with obvious admiration.

Mary Jo concluded her speech. "Now, everyone enjoy the wonderful food. Then the entertainment will begin, led by my daughter Ruth."

Ruth acknowledged the applause with a wry smile. Then she caught Debi's smirk from a corner table.

After clearing the plates, one of the Workampers turned up the music. The lights dimmed and Ruth stepped into the center of the room. She perched on a stool, half-heartedly strummed her ukulele, and sang "Tiny Bubbles." Soon, the audience joined in for the chorus. After the song ended, more Hawaiian instrumental music whined like plaintive whales.

Betty shouted from the corner, "Come on, everyone! It's hula time!"

The Walkie-Talkies rushed to form a line, including Cordy and Lillian, with Betty sandwiched in between them, center stage. Hips swayed somewhat rhythmically to the music. Their attempts at graceful hand movements reminded Ruth of either waving good-bye or trying to unroll toilet paper.

Ruth checked out Tyler playing with his stuffed parrot. She sighed with relief when there was no evidence of his videoing her in her dumb costume. Perhaps he had mended his ways.

The dance ended to wild applause and a few catcalls. Ruth strolled to the table for more punch and sat next to Tyler with a grin. "Watch this."

The lights dimmed. Women parted from Betty, who stepped forward. Drum music flooded the recreation center. Betty's hips swished first one side, then the other. As the staccato beat of percussion increased, so did her gyrations.

"She's solid." He squeezed his parrot, who squawked in agreement.

"Betty's been rehearsing all week."

The audience clapped, rose to their feet, and stomped in time with the beat. Bernie joined his fiancé with a shriek and a loud whoop. His knees rocked back and forth.

He circled Betty. Her movements increased to a blur, her skirt swished and hissed, faster and faster.

"Go, baby, go," someone in the crowd called out.

Then, a raffia string on Betty's bra snapped, and one coconut fell forward. She quickly placed the lei strategically covering her left breast, held on to the other coconut, and danced off the stage, Bernie following at her heels.

The music stopped, and for a moment, the room was silent. Then the applause reverberated throughout the barn. Calls rang out, begging for an encore.

Ruth turned to Tyler and burst out laughing. "Was that a wardrobe malfunction?"

"I don't know, but it sure was something else."

"At least you weren't videoing the complete debacle."

"Oh, I wouldn't assume not." He grabbed the parrot from his shoulder.

Ruth's eyes widened. "No."

He squeezed the stuffed toy. "Meet one of your new granny cams."

CHAPTER 11

Ruth checked Howard's list of friends who'd agreed to place cameras in their rooms. She recalled Nellie Wilson's catfight with Hatty as she rapped on the door.

A chipper voice called out, "Come on in."

The private room's institutional dresser was festooned in crocheted doilies. Multi-colored afghans covered two beechwood chairs. A crazy quilt in shades of yellow and green covered the single hospital bed. The television blared on the wall with a Food Channel program. It struck Ruth that most of the residents' sets played shows featuring home improvements, cooking, and travel, and yet they could no longer do any of those things.

"Hi, Nurse Ruth." Nellie nodded at the screen. "Do you like watching food shows?"

"I don't cook."

"Neither do I anymore. I love those competitions where they make food from all sorts of stuff."

Ruth looked at the television screen where a personality chef was sampling raw fish.

"I love sushi." She sighed. "I used to have it a lot in Madison."

"Never tried it. But you needn't go far. I saw a Japanese fellow making it on the last field trip we took to the grocery store in Walworth."

"No kidding. I'll check it out. I have something for you." Reaching inside her purse, she pulled out the pirate parrot and handed it over. "Your new granny cam."

"He's cute." Nellie squeezed the toy, and it let out a loud squawk. "I think I'll call him Petey."

"Good name choice." Ruth placed the bird among the teddy bears, pink elephants, and giraffes lining a shelf above the bed. "He'll make a great addition to your collection." She arranged it so the camera pointed at the doorway.

Nellie studied the angle of the parrot. "Uh. Am I able to turn the camera recording off? I mean, I occasionally have gentleman visitors."

"Oh. Sure." Ruth took the parrot down and was pointing out the features when someone knocked on the door.

Ruth hurriedly placed the parrot on the shelf.

Nellie called out, "Come in."

Nurse Steele entered the doorway. "Everything okay here?"

"Yes," Nellie answered. "I was asking Nurse Ruth about the availability of condoms for the residents."

The Head Nurse raised an eyebrow. "I'll see to it. We don't need an outbreak of STDs, do we?"

"We sure don't," Nellie said. "Some people in here shag and shag and shag."

The nurse's mouth formed a thin, straight line.

"Were you looking for me?" Ruth sidled away from the parrot.

"Dr. Thompson will speak with you at three o'clock this afternoon. I can't stop you from meeting with him, but I hope you will conduct yourself professionally. I understand you have theories fostered by Mr. Engel."

So, Steele was aware of Howard's suspicions. A rush of irritation washed over Ruth. "Of course. I'm always professional."

The Head Nurse nodded and then stopped by the doorway. "By the way, we have an open-door policy here."

After she left, Nellie mimicked the nurse's severe expression. "Don't let the open door hit your ass on the way out."

Ruth snickered. "Not too popular with the residents, is she?"

"I enjoy ruffling her prissy feathers." Nellie flicked her fingers under her chin.

"I don't have the luxury, I'm afraid."

Nellie leaned closer. "She'll be retiring soon. Can't wait. I think she's sucking on cough syrup to get through the next few months."

"Honestly?"

"I smell it on her breath. No one has a cold that long."

Ruth hadn't been close enough to her supervisor to notice.

"And how about the reference to your grandpa?"

"Howard's my step-grandfather, I guess."

"Don't matter." Nellie pointed to the photographs of kids lining her walls. "Some of these are my blood relations, the rest are my second husband's family. They all call me Grandma."

Ruth recalled Howard's obvious pleasure at adding her photograph to his family collage, and how touched she had been by the gesture.

"Let's get you your meds." She cracked open the plastic case marked "Nellie Wilson" that she'd prepared. The list of medications was long. Nellie dutifully swallowed each of the pills and then patiently waited for Ruth to put in glaucoma eye drops.

When Ruth finished wiping Nellie's eyes with a tissue, her patient winked. "Some inmates here keep a stash of pills. They pretend to swallow them. They're building a hoard, just in case."

"*What*? That's very dangerous."

Nellie shrugged. "Not as dangerous as being unable to go when you want out."

Ruth knelt beside Nellie's wheelchair. "Please tell me you don't sanction this practice."

"Nah. I've got a 'do not resuscitate' order." She cackled. "I've been a little depressed, but I'm better now that I riled up Nurse Pruneface."

"If you need to talk to someone, will you let me know?" When Nellie didn't respond, Ruth rose to leave. "Promise?"

"Thanks for Petey."

Ruth covered Nellie's hand, as fragile as a bird's wing, with her own. "You're welcome."

. . .

Ruth spent the morning overtly following her usual routine. Following lunch, she went out to her car and grabbed the granny cams she had stuffed into a duffel bag.

Furtively, she opened the trunk when a shadow glided across the Toad. She shoved the bag containing the cameras into the car and spun around. Debi stood with her hands on her hips.

Ruth faked a shiver. "I'm out here warming up. It's freezing in there."

Debi's eyes narrowed.

When Ruth noticed an electrical cord peeking out of the hastily closed trunk from the corner of her eye, she sidled close to it, hoping to block the view of it with her leg.

Debi smirked. "You should bring a sweater. Or a parka."

Ruth crossed her arms. A hot wind blew across the asphalt in the late June afternoon. Heat waves reflected off the parking lot.

"Some of my patients have complained of the cold."

"Personally, I prefer it cooler. I didn't think you were so delicate." Debi looked at her watch. "I came out here to remind you of your appointment with Dr. Thompson. If you're not too busy warming up."

Debi sauntered away to the group of aides, where a round of laughter erupted.

I'm not frickin' delicate. As the automatic door opened, she stepped into the entryway filled with bright fluorescent light. Residents crowded the orange Naugahyde couches and chairs. Red, white, and blue balloons decorated the dracaena plants and Ficus trees, giving the atrium a festive mood.

Ruth knocked on her supervisor's door and found an older man in a white coat who gestured her in. After introducing themselves and shaking hands, she took a seat. She had misgivings when his handshake was less of a grip and more of a gingerly grab of her fingers. *A man who thinks women are the fairer sex. He should see me kicking ass at kickboxing class.*

She plunged on. "So glad you could meet with me today, Doctor."

He glanced at his watch. "The Head Nurse mentioned you had some questions about the prescribed medications."

Ruth explained patients appeared to be over-prescribed and yet others complained of pain. When she gave him specific details, he raised an interrupting hand.

He peered at his notepad. "Nurse Markson, is it? I understand you graduated well placed in your class. This is, however, your first full-time position, isn't it?" He looked questioningly at her through his bifocals. Silver strands of hair covered his balding pate.

"Yes, but—" Ruth's stomach clenched at the patronizing look in his eyes.

The corner of his lips lifted, emphasizing the deep marionette lines from his nose to his chin. "I have a question for you. Why are you here?" He pointed around the room. Dust motes drifted in the weak light and settled on the Ficus plant, that looked like it was about to give up the ghost. "I don't mean this office. I mean this nursing facility. With your credentials, you might work anywhere and probably earn more."

Did he know of her plan? She fought down panic and came up with a plausible answer.

"I wanted to come back to my hometown to be near family."

"I see." He raised his eyebrows. His jowls sagged, and he stared at his vein-lined hands clasped on the battered desk. "Well, I will answer your questions about the medications. I've been associated with this institution for over thirty years." The color of his face deepened. She knew the medical profession suffered a high rate of drug and alcohol abuse, noting the network of capillaries on his nose turning purple.

"My goal, and that of this establishment, is the comfort of patients in their last years. Do you not agree?"

"Yes, but there are holistic approaches, including more natural means. Too much medication—"

"Would cause overdoses, and other issues. These haven't occurred." He fumbled with the papers. "And you followed procedures when warranted, did you not?"

"Yes." Her stomach sank.

"I reviewed the patient charts, issued the proper orders, and that is that." He shuffled through more papers. "Nurse Steele reported that Howard Engel has also complained. He's your relation, isn't he?"

"Well, yes. He's not the only concerned resident."

"Mr. Engel is over eighty. It's well-known that dementia is an almost certainty. He's likely paranoid, depressed, or at the very least, bored. We have put in place programs to address the latter, but nobody can stop the deterioration of aging."

Ruth bristled. "Dementia is not inevitable. In fact, in a recent study—"

He smiled with thin lips. "Nurse Markson, I appreciate and admire your diligence." He reclined in the chair with his arms linked behind his head. "You're not the first young woman, fresh out of school, to question authority and judgment. You will make an excellent nurse as long as you keep your opinions to yourself and support the people in charge."

As he continued to extol the virtues of subservience, she noted the yellow perspiration circles under his arms. *Those with hyperhidrosis should never assume the pose.* Praying this meeting would end before a career-ending explosion of her temper, she remained silent and chewed on her lower lip.

"Does that answer your questions?"

"It does." *There will be plenty of drugs available, regardless of whether patients need them.*

"Wonderful." He nodded, showing their meeting was over. He locked the desk drawer and put the key in a magnetic clip.

As she stood and headed toward the door, he said, "Oh, and there's nothing wrong with taking a position to be close to a wealthy future husband. Your predecessor left to marry an anesthesiologist."

It took every bit of willpower she had not to slam the door.

As soon as she spun around, she found Debi leaning against the wall. "I thought I'd catch you here." She stared into Ruth's eyes. "What were you doing in the software at 12:01 AM this morning?"

Damn Tyler. He must've figured out her password to hack into the computer. She'd have to tell him a thing or two when they met.

"I was practicing, familiarizing myself with transactions so I can do a better job." She hoped Debi didn't hear the anxiety in her voice.

Debi raised her brows. "Practicing? That's a good one." She tittered and then turned serious. "Listen to me. Whatever you're up to, stop it right now."

Ruth hoped to appear casual. "Don't have a clue what you're talking about."

Debi leaned in so close Ruth smelled the mint on her breath. "Markson, I mean it."

Ruth stared down at the gold linoleum and remained silent.

Debi sighed. "Don't say I didn't warn you." She turned on her UGG boots and strode away.

As Ruth waited for her heart to quit pounding, a thought occurred to her. How did Debi know she'd been in the Golden Years' computer system?

CHAPTER 12

Ruth drove from Golden Years to Dairyland, relieved to put the workday behind her. The fields raced by, and she lowered the Toad's window to breathe in the fresh afternoon air. She spotted a package on her trailer's deck. Lillian perched on a lower step, her pink-highlighted hair standing at attention.

Ruth hauled herself out of the Saturn and greeted the older woman.

"Well. Who are they from?" Lillian demanded.

Ruth studied the package from the local florist with its folded corners. "You tell me."

Lillian shrugged her wide shoulders. "They're not signed. They were from Tyler, no?" She paused at the frown on Ruth's face. "Hey, not much romance happens around here. The last good love story was when your mom and Luke were courting."

Ruth tore open the top of the paper to uncover a dozen red long-stemmed roses.

"Did you and Tyler have a fight? You're dating?"

Not rising to the bait, Ruth asked, "What brings you here?"

"I came here to see how you were. Since you're in such a mood, I take it your meeting with the good doctor didn't go well."

"Can you say a male-chauvinist-brick-wall?"

"I have another name for the son of a biscuit." She pointed toward Gandalf, nesting in the corner of her porch. "Who's your new buddy?"

Ruth shrugged. "He's incubating my Crocs." The goose honked softly and settled himself on top of her shoes.

Lillian studied the bird. "He's not been the same since his mate flew off with a Canada goose. Or so Mary Jo says."

"I thought geese mated for life."

"Apparently not. He connects with unattached females, like you *allegedly* are."

Ruth rolled her eyes in response.

Lillian pointed toward the flowers. "Well, if you won't enlighten me, I've got to run."

As Lillian flittered toward her fifth wheel trailer, Ruth called after her. "Try not to go through my packages anymore, okay?"

Without turning around, the older woman snorted, raised her middle finger, and continued walking.

Inside her trailer, Ruth set the expensive flowers on the counter. She didn't care for hothouse roses as their odor always struck her as funereal. Whoever sent them apparently didn't know her very well. Weird.

She changed into the coolest pajama set she had, fed Oreo, and selected a casserole for the microwave. At the dinette, she tucked into Aunt Cordy's signature lasagna. It was hard to recall a time when Cordelia hadn't been a part of her life, even though she technically wasn't her aunt, but her grandmother's best friend. Ruth's eyes went to the framed photo of her grandparents, a studio portrait her mother had saved from the tornado. They'd passed away two years before her father died.

About to dig into the lemon meringue pie from Luke, a knock on the trailer door interrupted her.

She glanced down at her thin camisole and silk boxer shorts. *Oh well, it's probably one of the Walkie-Talkies or Mom.* "Come on in."

Tyler filled the doorway with his masculine presence. "Hey." He stopped. "Nice flowers."

"They're not from you?"

"No." He inspected a rose. "And you don't know who sent them?"

"Don't have a clue."

"That's hard to believe." A muscle twitched in his jaw.

Oh, my god. Was he jealous? "I figured you sent them as an apology for nearly getting me fired."

He cocked his head and frowned. "I'm clueless."

"Debi found someone with my password in the system early this morning. And it wasn't me."

Tyler set his phone on the counter. "Interesting. She shouldn't have rights to read archives." He explained the system logged all transactions into a file, with an ID of who did what. He'd signed in first with Ruth's password, but now he would be a ghost administrator.

"So, you're not here to apologize?"

"Your mother called me because there's a problem with this quadrant's Wi-Fi signal."

"News to me." She lifted a forkful of pie. "I've been busy having dinner. And dessert."

"Mind if I get to work?" He stood with crossed arms.

"Not at all. Campers get upset without their emails." She resumed eating her pie as he walked through the trailer, apparently measuring the signal strength. With one sidelong glance, she found him staring at her ultra-short boxers. She crossed her legs to their best advantage. Served him right, showing up with no warning, and refusing to say he was sorry.

He waved his phone, muttering about the Wi-Fi. His masculine presence filled the small trailer. He moved close enough for her to smell his familiar scent.

"Have you had any problems with the signal?"

"Nope." *It's getting hot in here.* "But, then again, I wasn't on the Internet." She looked pointedly at her food.

He nodded and stopped in front of the kitchen window. "I don't understand. The signal should be good here since you're right across from the office." In his fitted jeans, the rear view of him was oh-so-fine.

His attitude sent a rush of annoyance through her. "Do you realize hacking into the system with my sign on and password might be more than a job killer? I'm talking about career-ending!" Oreo curled herself into a ball in her cage.

"Not my fault you used such a simple password." He pointed toward her pet. "I mean Oreo01?"

"What?" She sprang to her feet. "It's *my fault* you screwed up?"

"I've told you to be careful. But you keep ignoring me."

He grew closer and stared down at her, his green eyes stormy. She was aware of how few clothes were between her body and his. His angry glower went from her face to lower, where her treacherous breasts responded with tightening nipples.

"I can take care of myself."

Tyler sneered. "I'm sure you can. It's about taking the proper precautions. You've always been impetuous."

"What's it to you, anyway?" Her hands clenched.

His eyes hardened. "Nothing." He spun and stormed toward the door. "I'll tell them to reboot the damn router."

The trailer door slammed shut.

With trembling hands, she sat down. He'd always been her friend. Now she found him a mixture of irritation and attraction, as if he'd morphed into a total stranger.

"What just happened, Oreo?"

Her pet raced round and round her cage, going nowhere.

. . .

A couple of hours later, a knock sounded on her door. *Welcome to Grand Central Station.*

"Were you having sex?" Lillian looked pointedly at Ruth's attire, or lack thereof. "If not, we used to call teasing a PT a pr—"

"I know what it means. And no, not that it's any of your business."

"Maybe you should've. Tyler's wearing his crabby pants today."

Ruth sighed. "You're here because?"

"Kathy the Workamper told me she had to leave for a family thing. Can you go close up the office?"

She groaned. "All right."

Lillian pointed to the drooping bouquet on the counter. "If you don't want 'em, at least bring them to the Home."

After Lillian left, Ruth filled a mason jar with water and tore open the roses' wrapping. A small piece of paper floated to the floor.

A VIP pass invited her to the next Elvis impersonation at Mars Resort, compliments of Bobby McKay.

Ruth had finished closing out the office cash register when the side door slammed open, and Tyler strode in.

"Now what?" She crossed her arms.

"Your mother says the Wi-Fi is down again. I can't understand how it keeps happening."

"Wow. Mr. Computer Genius doesn't know everything." Ruth slammed the cupboard door. "What do you need to do here? I have to lock up."

"The repeater's out." He walked over to the equipment and fiddled with the device. After a full minute, he sighed. "I signed into Golden Years when I thought no one would notice. I underestimated their expertise." He turned toward her and placed his hand on her shoulder. "You trusted me with your plan, and I may have jeopardized it. I'm truly sorry."

Mollified by his apology, she knew what it took for him to admit a failing. "I'll change my password to whatever you suggest."

"Good. I'll text you one that'll be hard to crack. Use it for work and your home computer."

It was overkill, but she agreed, tired of arguing with him. Her grandmother had always told her to pick her battles, and this one didn't seem worth the win. She'd missed Tyler all evening, missed his silly texts, missed her friend. She showed him the pass as a peace offering. "This was in the bouquet."

"You're kidding me. McKay thinks you'd enjoy his performance as The King?"

They both chuckled. The soft glow from the overhead chandelier was the sole light in the darkened building. He stepped closer and her heartbeat quickened. He put his hands on her shoulders, drawing her nearer.

His green-eyed gaze mesmerized her. "That's a date."

She nodded. "I guess it is." Her heart raced.

His phone buzzed, and he grabbed it. "I have to run. We're good, right?" Without waiting for an answer, he said, "Looks like the Internet's back up."

CHAPTER 13

Ruth spent the next day avoiding Debi, occasionally catching her nemesis giving her long looks. She did her best to ignore her and prayed something would show up on the granny cams she'd installed earlier. She also texted Tyler, asking him to access the security cameras.

He'd responded: *I thought no hacking,* followed by a smiling face.

Things have changed with a poop emoji.

When her shift was done, she went to see Nellie.

"I'm doing fine, but I could use a push to the beauty parlor. Would you mind?"

Ruth wheeled Nellie into the salon where several other residents were lined up along the wall under helmet-shaped hairdryers.

Abigail from Hair on the Square greeted her with a hug. "Great to see you, Nurse Markson." The heavyset woman's hairstyle was a classic Mohawk and streaked with metallic silver and gold. "I come here once a week to do the ladies' hair." She began shampooing Nellie. "Stick around if you can. I bet your ends need a trim. It's on me."

"I'm fine." She didn't want to impose on her mother's long-time friend.

"Get yourself some style," Nellie advised. "You probably clean up real nice."

Ruth relented and leafed through a catalog targeted at seniors desiring comfortable shoes and clothes.

"Check out the vibrators in there." Nellie rolled under a hairdryer. "They say there're for sore joints and tense muscles. They'll relieve tension all right."

Ruth repressed a chuckle as Abigail shampooed her hair.

"You could use a good conditioning while we're at it."

"Whatever." Ruth relaxed with the scalp massage. When the hairdresser finished with warm water, then rubbed in the conditioner, she wrapped a towel around Ruth's neck.

"This has to set for a bit." Abigail, wielding tweezers, crossed over to the women, who one by one, lifted their chins. "Their families have me on retainer, so I do their hair once a week, perm and color as necessary, and keep chins hair-free."

Ruth said, "Seems like a plan."

The beautician returned to Ruth and began rinsing her hair. "Some ladies need facial waxing. You know, the more Mediterranean types." She leaned closer to Ruth. "And Nellie over there gets a Brazilian."

Ruth opened her eyes and looked at the ninety-something woman who was reading the latest "Cosmopolitan."

"Honestly?" Ruth's eyebrows raised.

"TMI? I hope I care about my hoo-ha at that age if I live that long."

The hairdryers shut off, one by one.

"I'm done cooking," a lady volunteered.

"Be there in a minute." Abigail motioned Ruth to the chair and snipped a tiny amount of hair from the ends.

One woman announced, "I spied an aide last night going into Mable's room."

"Who was it?" the resident to her left asked.

"That's the problem. The nice one. I didn't think she was still on duty."

A tingle went through Ruth. *Please don't let it be Yolanda.*

"And then I spotted Tony Bettini late at night roaming the halls." The blow dryer in Ruth's ear made it impossible to catch the rest of their chatter.

"It will take you a long time to dry it," Ruth told Abigail. "My hair's thick."

"Don't worry. It'll thin out after menopause." The stylist lifted sections of Ruth's locks into sections.

Aging would be a matter of losing the hair she wanted and getting rid of others.

"Thanks, Voice of Doom."

"Don't mention it."

The ladies tittered, and Nellie's dryer stopped. Abigail took a curling iron to Ruth's long tresses, sending a nimbus of steam with each press.

When she finished, Abigail gave Ruth a hand mirror to show her hair falling in golden waves down her back and across her shoulders. "She looks great, doesn't she?"

Nellie glanced up from her magazine. "She sure does. That'll drive the former Mrs. Wisconsin nuts. Debi's jealous already."

"She doesn't have custody of her children. What kind of mother could she be?" one of them sniffed.

"I wonder if there's an Ex-Mrs. Wisconsin contest," another cracked.

"Do you like it, Ruth?" Abigail beamed.

"Yes, thank you." The girls in Madison wore their hair ironed or natural, but this style must be *chic* in Eureka.

"Any plans this weekend?" Abigail ran her hand through a long wave.

"I'm seeing Bobby McKay perform Elvis at Mars."

"I'll bet his mother will be there. You realize, she and Miriam go to Potawatomi Casino regularly," Nellie said.

"No, I didn't." Ruth hesitated as four faces turned toward the doorway.

"Working late, Nurse Markson?" Debi wore a phony smile. "Or getting to know more staff?"

How long had she been standing there?

"Ruthie and I go back a long way. I've known her for her whole life." Abigail covered Ruth's face with a towel and sprayed her hair. "Isn't she beautiful?" She unveiled her masterpiece.

The ladies all nodded with loud sighs all around.

That's right. Rub it in. Our relationship isn't bad enough.

"You're late for your meds, Mrs. H." Debi doled out pills, eye drops, and patch. As she waltzed out the door, she said over her shoulder, "Have a nice evening. I hear Bobby's good."

.   .   .

Ruth drove to her trailer and saw packages on her deck, with Lillian waving to her.

"Wow. Are you hot or what?" The older woman eyed Ruth's newly coiffed hair. "I hope you're going out tonight." She took a seat on a step and set a covered dish next to the parcels.

"Tyler's coming by. I invited him to go to see Elvis at Mars."

"At least have him buy you dinner. Don't give them anything for nothing, I say." Lillian gestured toward the boxes. "What did the handsome UPS driver deliver?"

Ruth sidled toward the door of the trailer. "Some stuff."

"Ah, come on, show me."

Ruth sighed as she opened the large box. "New work shoes." She held up the sturdy oxfords. "They're supposed to be slip resistant. I had to replace those, anyway." Gandalf had covered her Crocs in goose down in his effort to hatch them.

Lillian frowned. "Those old-lady shoes are so ugly, they should sell them as a method of birth control. What's in the other one?"

Ruth sighed and opened the second package. "My new seat covers." The stretchy fabric had a zebra stripe pattern.

"Sexy. Not like the shoes." Lillian stood and pointed to the covered dish. "Those are brownies. I can't bake like Luke, but these are yummy."

Ruth recalled the marijuana stash she'd uncovered and wondered if her Aunt Cordelia ever made baked goods with it. "Will they give me the munchies?"

Lillian smirked. "You found Rupert's not-so-secret crop, did you?"

"I can't imagine Luke hasn't noticed, but I don't want to get Rupert and Aunt Cordelia in trouble in case he hasn't."

"Simple. Talk to Cordy and hear what she has to say. Back when I drove a school bus, I had a herd of cows block the road. One heifer kept bashing the front of my bus with her head. The cops reported the suckers had been eating wild marijuana."

"I'll talk to Aunt Cordy when I get time to." Ruth peeked at her phone. "I'd better get ready."

"Have fun." Lillian added, "Whatever you do, don't wear those clodhoppers tonight."

. . .

Lillian needn't have warned her. Ruth rummaged through her closet to find an outfit. She located her spaghetti-strapped sundress, patterned in flowers and ending mid-thigh. From a jumble of shoes, she pulled out a pair of high-heeled sandals. She fluffed her hair and surveyed the results in the full-length closet mirror. After applying a brush of mascara and a whiff of perfume, she was ready.

Outside, car tires crunched on gravel, announcing Tyler's arrival.

Ruth sprinted to the bathroom and put on lip gloss. "Come on in. It's unlocked."

The front door creaked open.

"Did you know many break-ins occur in broad daylight?"

"Dairyland Acres is hardly an epicenter of crime." She glided into the living room.

His eyes darkened. "You look amazing." He handed her a bouquet.

"Daisies, my favorite." She stuffed the drooping roses into the garbage and replaced them with the Shastas.

"They're from my mom's garden."

"Thank you." She took in his knit shirt and pressed khakis. "You clean up pretty well yourself." She gave him a quick kiss on the cheek where he smelled of lime and fresh-cut grass.

He opened the door for her and followed her out.

"Aren't you going to lock up?"

"Nah. No one ever breaks in here."

Once they were in the car, Ruth looked at her phone. "We're early. Would you like to tour the campground to kill some time?"

He shrugged. "Sure. Why not?"

Tyler drove slowly through the RV park. When Ruth waved at Lillian, the older woman walked over to them. She motioned them to a stop and frowned as she studied Ruth's feet.

"Have fun tonight, kids." She winked. "And don't do anything I wouldn't do."

Ruth snorted. "That gives us free rein."

"If you can't have fun, why bother living?" Lillian headed to her fifth wheel trailer. Her husband, Chuck, sat by their fire pit in a folding chair. Their Chihuahua, Taco, raced in circles under the picnic table.

Tyler drove off with a purr of the Triumph's engine. "She seems to think we're on a date."

"With her mindset, it's easy."

"Why was she studying your feet?" His brows knitted together.

"She must have a foot fetish among all the others."

Tyler continued to drive along the winding road, nearing the far corner of the campground. Ruth glanced at the time on her phone to find it was Happy Hour.

"Avert your eyes!" Ruth warned Tyler.

Too late. The Kloppenheimers, dressed in their eighty-year-old birthday suits, stood in full view of the roadway. They raised their wine goblets and toasted the young couple.

"Geez, I forgot about them." Ruth returned the wave.

Tyler peered into the woods. "Holy crap, is that Rupert's crop?"

"Yep. I'm worried. What if something eats the marijuana plants, like dogs or wild pigs? Lillian told me about stoner cows attacked her school bus."

Tyler barked out a laugh. "Dirty socks. The scent repels many animals."

"Where did you get that idea?" Ruth stopped. "Never mind. I know. The internet. I could put old socks in my Crocs."

"Your scent might keep attracting Gandalf." He wiggled his brows. "He's bonded to you at a deep, unbreakable level."

"Just my luck."

He nodded forward. "Shall we blast off to Mars?"

"Sounds like another planet."

"It is." Tyler shifted into a lower gear and the convertible leaped forward into the softening light.

CHAPTER 14

"I can't wait for the fish fry at Mars. It's all you can eat." Tyler smacked his lips.

"I remember the relish tray!" Ruth's mouth watered.

"Wouldn't be right without one."

Ruth was excited to revisit her local favorite supper club. She recalled the heaping platters of food and the friendly ambiance of a "club" with no required membership. All anyone needed was a hearty appetite and the ability to savor the nostalgic. Mars coupled large quantities of food with rural lake view ambiance and entertainment.

They drove the short distance to Mars Resort with the top down on the convertible. Evening swallows swarmed above them in the deepening dusk.

Tyler turned down the pine tree-lined road leading to the restaurant. Pickup trucks and SUVs filled the parking lot of the low, white clapboard building.

As Tyler escorted her up the restaurant's walkway, they stopped in front of a life-size poster.

Bobby McKay PRESENTS:

A TRIBUTE TO ELVIS

They squinted at the photo of Bobby dressed in the white, fringed jumpsuit embellished with rhinestones and studs.

"Looks like the comeback-Elvis." Tyler tapped on the poster. "Bobby's put on a few pounds. I wonder if he photoshopped this."

"Me-ow, Ty." Ruth grinned.

At the door, a bored-looking guy in a Wisconsin T-shirt sat on a stool. "There's a five-dollar cover charge. Each."

Ruth whipped out the VIP pass, and he nodded. "Go on then. You got a table by the windows."

"At least Bobby was good for something," Tyler muttered.

Inside, a packed horseshoe-shaped bar held center stage. The locals were out in force, perched on barstools as they sipped Korbel brandy Old Fashioned cocktails, the quintessential Wisconsin concoction. Heads turned as they walked through the crowd. Ruth's long, golden hair touched her bare shoulders. In her high heels, she was nearly as tall as Tyler, who was well over six feet.

He murmured in her ear, sending a chill down her spine. "The other guys are eating their hearts out."

The table by the window had a reserved sign, and a setting for one with a single rose in a vase.

"Oh boy. I think Bobby will be disappointed," Ruth said with a sidelong grin at Tyler.

"Too bad. He can croon 'Heartbreak Hotel.'"

The stocky waitress who doubled as the restaurant's hostess ambled over. "This is usually Elvis' date's table."

"Not this time. He's an old acquaintance," Ruth said.

It may have been her imagination, but the woman's face seemed to brighten. "I'll get ya another place setting. Fish fry or menu?"

Tyler lifted his brow at Ruth.

"I'd like the fish fry with broiled cod. And a glass of white wine, please."

The server tapped her pen on her order pad. "And you, sir?"

"I'll have the same, only the fried walleye, and a beer. Whatever you have on tap."

The waitress shrugged. "No offense, but I will need to see some ID, please."

Ruth reached for her purse. Tyler grabbed his wallet from his back pocket. When the server read their driver's licenses, a hint of a smile flashed across her face.

"You're Mary Jo's daughter, aren't you?"

"I am."

"Should've recognized the resemblance since I heard you were moving back." The woman studied Tyler. "And you're Doc Kelly's son?"

"Guilty as charged."

"I'm Melinda. All your parents are regulars of mine." She studied him. "Anyone ever tell you that you resemble Prince Harry?"

"I make my living as a double for the prince. When he doesn't want to be seen in public, I substitute." His attempt at an English accent was terrible.

Melinda turned to Ruth. "Is he always like this?"

"Usually. It's why it took a long time before I agreed to date him."

Melinda studied Ruth. "And you might be Grace Kelly." Ruth flushed at the compliment. "Wait till I tell them in the kitchen Prince Harry and Princess Grace are here." Melinda chuckled and ambled away across the crowded restaurant.

Unwrapping his paper napkin, he removed the silverware. "You think this is a date, huh?" He gave her a wicked grin.

"You're not wearing a Comicon T-shirt, for starters."

His smile dimple appeared. "I like to get dressed up once in a while."

Two could play this game. She leaned forward enough to show him the top of her lace bra. "Me too."

The corner of his lip lifted. "Like in the little pajama set you had on the other night?"

"Sometimes." She smiled as his gaze hardened, sure it wasn't the only thing that did.

"Ruthie, I need to tell you something—"

Melinda interrupted with their drinks and a classic supper club relish tray filled with raw carrots, celery, radishes, and breadsticks. They munched on the crispy vegetables, dipping them into the homemade cheddar spread.

"You were saying?" She unwrapped a breadstick and stuck it into the whipped cheese.

"Yeah." He cleared his throat. "I contacted the guy who supports the computer system." He reached for a celery stick and crunched down on it. "He says they refuse to pay for the latest upgrade."

"Does that explain why it's so slow?"

He shrugged. "It might be the hardware. I don't know yet."

"What you're doing isn't legal, is it?"

"Probably not, but if you think something dangerous is going on, I'm in."

"I do." She filled him in on the latest gossip she'd heard in the beauty salon and her successful distribution of the granny cams.

"We should get images from them shortly."

She leaned forward. "I can't tell you enough how much I appreciate your help."

Melinda cleared her throat, prompting Ruth to sit up. The waitress set a huge tray of food on a nearby stand and then served their meals.

Ruth piled applesauce onto her potato pancake. "I haven't had a meal this good in a long time."

Tyler's face creased with bliss as he chewed on the fish. "I'll have to learn to cook. There's a school in Lake Geneva."

"The Walkie-Talkies are always delivering care packages. I don't think I'll bother until after I move back to Madison."

"And then?" Tyler set his cutlery down. He stared out the window and Ruth followed his gaze. A family sat at one of the picnic tables on the beach. The calm lake glistened silver in the twilight.

"I want to be a doctor. After that, who knows?" A mother outside wiped her baby's mouth and then kissed the top of his head. "What about you?"

"What about me?" The sky had darkened outside.

"Marriage? Kids?"

He shrugged. "When I find the right woman, yes. I'm old-fashioned enough to believe in families."

"What would Ms. Right be like?" She hoped she sounded nonchalant.

"Intelligent, strong, talented, beautiful." He leaned forward and touched her hand. "Probably too good for me."

"Oh, I don't know. You're—"

Melinda whisked by to clear the table. "Want any dessert or coffee?"

Tyler released Ruth's hand. "No, thanks. Just the check, please."

A raspy voice sounded behind them. "Hey, Ruthie." Bobby McKay wore a white bell-bottomed jumpsuit fringed along the front and sleeves. He'd piled his dark hair into a pompadour, and with his golden aviator sunglasses, he made a good impersonation of Elvis.

"I see you got the VIP pass." Bobby barely nodded at Tyler and returned his gaze to Ruth. "You're looking sweet, darlin'."

Tyler smirked. "How're they hanging, McKay?"

"Real good now *she's* here." He winked at Ruth.

She compared the two men. Her class had voted Bobby the cutest boy in high school, but there his good looks peaked. He was gaining the bloated look of Elvis in his later years. "Hillbilly handsome," her mom called it. Tyler had become anything but a scrawny "Matchstick."

She gave him a Midwest-nice smile. "Thanks for the pass, Bobby."

"It's Elvis from now on tonight," he drawled and shimmied his shoulders. "Gotta keep in character."

"Well, *Elvis,* shouldn't you swivel your way up to the stage?" Tyler smirked.

McKay gave him an Elvis-sneer, then turned to Ruth. "See ya up there, sugar."

Tyler whistled a few bars of "Hound Dog" as McKay strode to the piano bar, fist bumping patrons along the way.

"He *is* popular," Ruth said.

Melinda arrived, set the check on the worn table, and pointed to the piano bar.

"Enjoy the show, kids."

When she waddled away, Tyler set a wad of cash next to the bill.

"What's my share?" Ruth reached into her purse.

"Never mind. We're on a date, right?" Tyler nodded toward the group surrounding the musician and McKay. "Shall we? This ought to be good for a laugh."

"Sure, why not? I could use a glass of red wine first."

Tyler laced his arm through hers as they circumvented the crowded room packed to capacity. He pulled out a barstool for Ruth marked by a VIP card and sat next to her. He ordered a Merlot for Ruth and a non-alcoholic beer for himself.

A woman with long gray hair in a ponytail set up her sheet music and prominently displayed her tip jar. She played a few bars of "Jail House Rock."

"Good evening, ladies and gentlemen. We're lucky tonight to have Elvis Presley in the house!"

Scattered applause broke out. "We have a VIP, invited by Elvis. Your name, honey?" The piano player grinned as Ruth blushed and introduced herself. "And we also have another celebrity tonight. Prince Harry's double has deemed to join us."

This time it was Tyler's turn to redden as Ruth snickered and lightly jabbed him in the side with her elbow.

"And now, introducing Mr. Elvis Presley!"

Bobby swiveled his hips and rubber-legged his way through "Jail House Rock." Hoots and catcalls accompanied the applause when the song ended. He plowed through the rest of his set, shimmying, snarling, and curling his lip when appropriate. The audience went wild.

After a vibrant rendition of "Hound Dog," McKay wiped the sweat from his brow and tossed his hankie into the crowd. Women leaned to catch it, and several struggled to stay on their barstools. One of them tossed something to the stage, and Ruth shuddered to think it might be a pair of panties.

He walked over and implored Ruth, "Join me, sweetheart?"

She sat frozen until Tyler propelled her gently forward. "This'll be great," he said.

Downing the rest of her wine in a gulp, she handed the glass to Tyler, and joined Elvis on stage.

"This purty little girl and me go way back. Don't we, honey?"

There were a few catcalls and whistles. "Talk about great gams," an older man called out.

Tyler shot him a dirty look.

"Ready?" Elvis grabbed her hand.

Whenever there was music, Ruth had to sing. She usually restrained herself, but if she knew the words, the song would burst from her. As soon as she took the microphone, her reticence disappeared. She nodded, and the piano played "Love Me Tender."

She remembered enough of the words to perform a decent duet with him. His voice hadn't improved with age, but together they were credible. All the chatter at the bar ceased. The servers stood in silence, watching them perform. Women near them were swiping tears from their eyes. As they sang the love lyrics, McKay kept his heavy-lidded gaze on Ruth's face.

When they sang the last stanza, proclaiming they would always love each other, Ruth looked straight at Tyler.

A burst of applause followed a moment of stunned silence. Tyler rose, leading people in the supper club to a standing ovation.

She was shaky as she left the stage, embarrassed at the compliments she received. "No, I will not try out for any talent show." One person thrust a placemat toward her and requested her autograph.

Ruth fanned herself with her hand. "Let's get some fresh air."

Tyler took her arm and led them out the side door, past the patio and deck, to the small beach.

"Hold me up." She leaned on him and removed her heels. The cool sand tickled her bare feet. They settled on a picnic bench side by side, staring at the moonlit water. The air held the tang of fish and outboard engine fuel.

"Your performance was something else." His voice was low and deep. "I knew you could sing, but I loved your voice tonight."

"I didn't make too big a fool of myself, huh?" she teased and put her head on his shoulder.

He turned toward her. "Anything but, Ruthie." He leaned closer.

Her heart thumped. The moonlight highlighted his handsome features. He reached and took a strand of her hair and put it behind her ear.

"Just friends?" McKay stood a few feet away, smoking a cigarette. "Bosom buddies more like it." He snorted, crushed the cigarette butt with a booted heel, and turned into the building.

"Good night to you too, Mr. Buzzkill," Tyler muttered.

She smacked a mosquito. "We should probably head home."

Ty grasped her hand as they walked through the parking lot, and she pointed at the black sports car with its identifying license plate. "That's Bobby's."

Tyler swiped his phone. "His business must be good." He studied the sleek vehicle. "The Viper's list price is over one hundred thousand dollars."

.   .   .

Tyler insisted on walking her to her door. To her relief, Gandalf wasn't in the corner of her deck.

"Alone at last." She moved closer to him, the heat of his body warming her.

He grasped her shoulders, pulling her to him. "Finally."

Certain this wouldn't be another forehead kiss, she'd almost closed her eyes when she noticed something unusual.

Her voice shook. "I'm sure I shut the front door when we left."

CHAPTER 15

Tyler spun around. "Stay here." He kicked the door, and it easily swung open. He turned on his phone flashlight and crept into the trailer. Ruth followed, peering around his shoulder.

"Anybody there?" Tyler shouted.

"Like they'd answer," Ruth said in a low voice.

"I told you to stay put." He shoved her behind him. The beam of light cast eerie shadows on the wall.

She reached around him and hit the switch, flooding the place with brightness, and gasped.

A snowstorm of white feathers floated in the air. A lampshade tilted thirty degrees and her books littered the floor. She rushed to the overturned cage.

"Oreo!" Her pet let out a small *wheek* when Ruth reached in and cuddled her. "I don't think she's injured." She focused on the feathers. "Did they cut a pillow?"

Tyler inched toward the bedroom, following the trail of down. "Stay there! I mean it."

With shaking thumbs, she texted Luke, imploring him to come to the trailer as soon as possible. Then she joined Tyler, who was illuminating the bedroom with his phone.

Something stirred in the corner. Ruth's heart raced. They jumped and slammed the door. "Luke's on his way!" They retreated to the hallway.

A soft sound from behind the closed door lured them closer.

"Did you hear that?" She held her breath.

"I did." He leaned forward.

A honk filtered through the door.

"Oh my god, it's Gandalf." She pushed past Tyler and flung open the door, turning on the light. The gander sat in the corner, with feathers ruffled. He stretched his neck out to her and let out a feeble call.

She carefully set Oreo on the bed and reached out to the goose. Running her fingers across his disheveled feathers, he closed his eyes.

Tyler knelt next to her. "Is he wounded?"

"I don't think so."

He pointed to the feathers that littered the bed and floor. "He must've put up a hell of a fight."

"I'd hate to see the other guy." She laughed shakily.

"Ruth?" Luke's voice boomed.

"In here."

He rushed in, his eyes surveying the situation, his police weapon in his shoulder holster. "Are you two all right?"

"We are," Tyler said, answering for both of them.

Luke helped Ruth to her feet. "You've had a shock. Let's go into the kitchen."

She picked up her guinea pig and cast a worried look at Gandalf. "What about him?"

Luke's lips turned up at the corners. "We'll get him checked out by the vet, but he looks okay." He patted the goose as he looked around the room. "I want to see the other guy."

"That's what I said." Ruth giggled. "I'm sorry. I'm afraid I'm a little hysterical."

"It's all right." Luke helped her into the dinette. "If you're dizzy or nauseated—"

"I know. Put my head between my knees. I'm a nurse, remember?"

Tyler took Oreo and placed the guinea pig carefully in her cage.

"You like tea, right?" Luke went about making three cups. "Is there anything missing?"

She surveyed the room. "This place is a mess. But I don't think so." She had nothing of much value. She was wearing her only prized piece of jewelry, her peridot necklace, a present from her dad. "I have my phone and my computer is still there."

Luke set the steaming cup in front of her. "Was the door locked?"

She flushed with embarrassment and shook her head. She was afraid to look at Tyler, who had warned her.

Luke sighed. "I know most people don't bother here in the campground. Do you have any idea who did this?"

"No."

"Anything else unusual happen to you lately?" Luke's mouth formed a straight line.

She side-eyed Tyler. "Someone keyed my car a couple of days ago."

"Where did *this* happen?"

Ruth felt a wave of guilt at keeping the secret from Luke. "In the parking lot of Golden Years while I visited your dad."

Luke frowned at her. "Did you report it?"

She shook her head. "I didn't want to make a big deal about it." Tires crunched the gravel outside. "Mom?"

Luke nodded. "Couldn't stop her. I asked for a few minutes with you first."

Mary Jo rushed in. "Are you all right?" Ruth nodded. "What happened?" She sat next to her daughter and held her in a tight hug.

Luke answered. "It looks like someone came in the unlocked door." He pointed to the trail of feathers. "Gandalf probably followed them through the open doorway."

"Will you dust for fingerprints?" Tyler asked.

"Since there are no signs of forcible entry, and nothing stolen or damaged, there's not much of a case. It's a matter of trespassing, and without a witness, my hands are tied." He looked at Ruth. "I'm sorry. You can file a police report."

"Is Gandy all right?" Mary Jo's grip on her daughter tightened.

Ruth swiped away a tear. "We think so."

As if hearing his name, the goose appeared in the hallway, and waddled to the dinette.

"There's a good boy," Mary Jo cooed, and then turned to her daughter. "We'd like you to sleep at our house tonight."

"I'll stay with Ruth," Tyler volunteered.

"We'll be fine, Mom." Relieved, she wanted to reclaim her home. "And Gandalf can guard the front porch. I doubt anyone will want to tangle with him again."

"Well, okay. If you're sure." Mary Jo turned to Tyler. "Put in whatever surveillance cameras you think are necessary. Discuss their placement with Luke and send me the bill."

"Also, get a good quality deadlock for this door," Luke added. He needn't tell Ruth to use it. Message received.

Mary Jo gave her one last hug.

Luke patted Ruth on the shoulder. "You'll text if you need anything, right?"

After they left, Tyler said, "Is it okay if I stay? It seemed like you didn't want to be alone."

She nodded. "I'd enjoy the company. If you don't mind." Replaying the evening's ending gave rise to a wave of nausea, a precursor to her migraines.

Without asking, Tyler helped her clean the trailer. As she was vacuuming the feathers in the living room, he stood by her computer.

"Did you password protect this?"

"Like you told me." She turned off the vacuum. "I feel violated, Ty. Someone was here in my house, looking at my things, meager as they are." She teared up. "They didn't even consider them worth stealing."

He walked over to her and embraced her. "Hey. Hey." She sobbed into his shoulder until she slowed into hiccups.

"You're beat, honey." He stroked her hair. "I'll sleep on the couch."

"You're too tall for this sofa. It'll kill your back."

"I'll be fine. I've slept on worse."

She grabbed a comforter and pillow and made up a bed for him. "Are you sure?"

"I've got work to do. You get some rest."

Ruth's eyes grew heavy as she headed toward her bedroom. Despite the niggling anxiety, she fell asleep, secure in the knowledge Tyler was close by.

. . .

The next morning, Ruth tiptoed into the living room. Tyler must've given up on the couch, and he lay snoring, sprawled on the floor. He'd let Oreo out of her cage, and her pet guinea pig slept in the crook of his arm, purring with contentment.

His eyes fluttered open. "Morning, Ruthie."

The kitchen window was open, and a soft breeze blew through.

"Are open windows allowed? Couldn't someone climb in?" she teased.

"It was stuffy in here." He massaged his neck.

"Oh, the Bengay. I'm sorry. I'm nose-blind to it now."

"Did you sleep okay?" he asked.

"Thanks to you."

"No problem." He held her gaze for a long few seconds.

Aware she'd slept in her makeup, her mascara probably made her resemble a raccoon. She cleared her throat. "I have extra toothbrushes and razors in the bathroom. And spare towels if you want to shower."

He ran a hand over the stubble on his chin. "Sounds like a plan." He took Oreo and placed her gently in her cage. She let out a *whoomph* and fell asleep.

Ruth put water on to boil for tea. After a few minutes, Tyler opened the door, wearing only a towel wrapped around his trim lower frame.

"Razor?"

"Top vanity drawer, left."

He closed the bathroom door, but not before she'd treated her eyes to his six-pack abs.

She couldn't resist imagining him without the towel, and then she stopped herself. She was leaving in eleven months, and she had rigorous years of school and residency ahead. Last night, he'd made it clear he wanted to settle down and start a family here in Eureka with Ms. Right. Hadn't he expressed his love for the small-town life?

Who was she to impede his dreams? The moonlight and two glasses of wine had contributed to her selfish wish to make this relationship more than friendship. Blushing, she recalled how she flirted with him, sang to him, and played at being a couple instead of only friends.

Thank goodness fate had interrupted them, not once, but twice—twice! That time on the porch could have changed everything. Without the mood-altering home invasion, their kiss might have ignited into romance. Their clothes might have replaced the trail of feathers scattered behind them. They might shower together after a night of talking, laughing, and making love over and over.

Tyler returned with wet hair, smelling of Dial soap.

He sure looks tasty.

"Breakfast of champions?" she asked.

"Huh?" He took the cup of tea and the granola bar she offered with shaky hands.

She needed to have a heart-to-heart talk with him soon. He should find Ms. Right instead of wasting his time with her. Opening the window shades to the morning park, all the chaos of the night before seemed forgotten. People in jogging suits strode along the street, some of them walking dogs. Others greeted each other with travel coffee cups held high.

"Oh boy, it's the Walkie-Talkies." Ruth pointed out the window. Betty Bling led the women, speed walking and swinging hand weights. The group stopped in front of her trailer, studying Tyler's sports car. Lillian, sporting a crimson-streaked hairdo, and the two other women marched to the deck.

She groaned. "They're coming here. They must've heard about last night through CNN."

"What? The news channel?" he asked.

She grinned. "The Camper News Network."

The door rattled and voices muttered, followed by a series of knocks.

Lillian called out, "Ruthie, it's us."

She unlocked the door, and they stormed in. Nodding at Tyler, they embraced Ruth in a group hug.

"Tell us all about it," Lillian demanded, settling her sturdy frame on the dinette bench. As Ruth recounted the story, the others sat with jaws agape.

"How could this happen here?" Aunt Cordy asked, dragging her long, white plait of hair across her Greenpeace T-shirt.

Betty adjusted her sequined baseball hat and answered. "It's not the same world we grew up in. We've been living in a bubble of innocence."

"The question is, who did this? Strangers or someone we know?" Lillian looked out the window. "Her nibs isn't home."

Ruth hadn't looked for Debi's minivan last night.

Tyler spoke up. "We were at Bobby McKay's show until around ten."

"Who knew you were going?" Betty dangled a pink sneaker-clad foot.

Ruth grimaced. "I announced it at Golden Years' beauty salon. I might as well have put a notice in the *Eureka Gazette*."

"Plus, you two were driving around beforehand, all gussied up." Lillian smirked. "It wouldn't take much to put two and two together."

Aunt Cordy nodded. "So basically, everyone knew."

"Or an overnight camper knocked on doors pretending to be lost, and when no one answered, tried the door." Betty drummed the table with French-manicured nails.

"But no one here saw or heard anything?" Ruth asked. All shook their heads no.

"I heard your goose got into it with the perp," Lillian said. "We should look for signs of the conflict. There may be bite marks, broken fingers, bruises."

"I hope so." Anger coursed through Ruth. She couldn't wait to see if Debi had any injuries.

Tyler explained he would install several security cameras around the campground, per Mary Jo.

Lillian snorted. "Great. Nothing like locking the milk barn after the cow got out."

"But they took nothing?" Betty frowned.

Ruth said, "Maybe they didn't have a chance. Though there's not much here of value."

Betty looked at the trailer's interior with raised penciled brows and nodded in agreement. Ruth cringed inwardly. Not everyone had a half-million-dollar motorhome like the Bling on the Block.

Lillian banged her fist on the table, causing them all to jump. "Then what in the hell were they doing?"

"Maybe they weren't here to take anything," Tyler mused, staring at Ruth's computer. "Just look at something."

CHAPTER 16

After the Walkie-Talkies left, Tyler sat at Ruth's computer, tapping on the keys. Eventually, he turned to her. "I downloaded software to protect you."

"Like a computer condom?" A blush crept up her neck. Bad analogy.

"Yeah right." He cleared his throat. "Anyway, a public Wi-Fi network is vulnerable. I've asked your mom to add cable internet to this site."

She groaned. "She's spending too much on me."

He shook his head. "It's okay. She told me she was planning on installing the cameras anyway to catch the drive-aways."

A few campers arrived in the dead of night after office hours, hooked up, used the utilities, public bathrooms, and left early in the morning without paying. Honor and honesty were gradually eroding.

"And the cable internet? She wasn't planning on the expense."

"Mary Jo is Mama Bear-protective right now. Money is no object. I also want you to change your password daily."

"What would anyone want with my computer?"

He shrugged. "You tell me. What's on it? Do you access work from here?"

"Yes, I have a few times. My emails." Her eyes widened. "My plan. My spreadsheet."

"Any of those might have been of interest." His lips formed a grim line. "From now on, don't use the work system remotely. Leave it to me. Don't deviate from your routine." He explained he would install the campground security cameras the next day.

"How can I help?"

"You can study the granny cams' footage. The app is on your computer." He showed her the software. "You'll get motion sensitive alerts with video clips. We're looking for anomalies."

He checked his phone. "I have to run. Are you free tomorrow night? I have a surprise for you."

She resolved to tell him then that they were only friends. "Sure."

He strode out the door without his usual hug or a kiss on the forehead goodbye. He probably knew how close they'd come to stepping over the friendship line last night and was also regretting it.

She wouldn't have to put into words how they should ratchet down their relationship. Relief at not having to say aloud the bad news mixed with sadness. Their former friendly physicality seemed strained ever since the near kisses.

She sat at her computer and studied the images as they flashed by. Residents wheeled their way to and from their rooms, aides entered and left, and cleaners wiped floors and made beds. By nightfall, the lights dimmed as residents fell asleep.

She paused a video and studied it. A door opened, and a man's head peered in. He hesitated and then retreated. A few minutes later, another camera registered the same thing. The lighting in the room was better and this time, she identified him. The white pompadour and the gold chain around his neck glistened in the nightlight. Tony Bettini had been checking in on people, but why?

More images flashed by. Aides, probably responding to a call button, helped residents to the bathroom. One resident grabbed a small bottle from his bedside table and took a swig. He wiped his mouth on his pajama sleeve and waved at the camera.

Ruth grinned. "Cheers, Mr. Tibbets. Enjoy your tipple."

One camera identified as "Petey" registered activity with a time stamp after ten at night. An aide knocked on the door. When Nellie didn't respond, Yolanda walked out of view toward the closet, carrying a bundle of clothing.

. . .

The next morning, as Ruth pulled the Saturn into her parking space, a black Viper with "THE KING" license plates arrived at the Golden Years entrance. She sat agape as Debi exited the passenger side and strode toward the door. Her right arm wore a sling.

The sports car squealed out of the lot, and Ruth hurried toward the automatic door, following close behind Debi.

"What happened to you?" Ruth eyed the bandaged arm and underneath her right eye, a bruise showed on her cheekbone. Debi, who never wore makeup, had smeared concealer on it.

"A minor fender-bender over the weekend."

"Still, enough to get injured."

"I bumped into a tree at a friend's place. No actual damage, only a deployed airbag, and my front fender. Not worth reporting to my insurance company."

She probably hadn't filed a police report confirming the "accident." Or had a certain goose taken on her nemesis?

"I noticed your van wasn't around."

Debi shrugged. "My car's at Bobby's garage for the repair. He gave me a lift."

"My, what service!"

"It beats paying Uber." With that, she turned and limped away.

Limping? From an airbag?

. . .

Ruth studied Yolanda from a distance. She was so sweet, so nice. Why would she steal? And how best might Ruth approach the issue? No one outside their circle knew about the cameras. She hated to have to catch her red-handed. Her stomach knotted whenever the aide neared.

Then, in the afternoon, as Ruth administered Nellie Wilson's medications, Yolanda walked into the room.

"Hi, Yoli," Nellie greeted the aide. "Would you be able to help me into my favorite dress? I'm going to the ice cream social and want to fit in." The theme of the evening was "Adventures in Paradise." Paper pineapples and streamers decorated the recreation hall. Why tropical-themed parties were popular in Wisconsin was anyone's guess.

Yolanda removed a Hawaiian muumuu from the closet. The aide hadn't asked which dress was her favorite.

Nellie gave a coy smile. "Back in the day, people told me I resembled Dorothy Lamour."

Ruth studied the ninety-something woman. "I can see it."

Yolanda nodded. "She was a beautiful lady."

"Funny. I couldn't find this dress yesterday." Nellie said. "I must be finally losing it. Can't keep track of my clothes anymore."

"Not missing anything else?" Ruth attempted to sound casual. Was it her imagination or did the aide look guilty?

"Nope." Nellie pointed to her head. "Only a few of my marbles."

"Hardly." Ruth left the room and stood in the hallway with crossed arms until the aide exited.

Yolanda stopped short. "Were you waiting for me?"

Ruth dreaded the response. "Someone spotted you last evening going into patients' rooms as they slept. Why?"

The aide paled, and her hands shook. "I-I wasn't doing anything wrong." And then, to Ruth's dismay, Yolanda burst into tears.

She guided the aide by her elbow into the closest unisex washroom. She waited until Yolanda's sobs subsided. "What is it?"

"I wasn't taking anything. I was returning them." She looked hopefully at Ruth. "You believe me?"

Ruth looked questioningly at her. "Go on."

"Stanley, in the laundry. His house burned down a few weeks ago. His family lost everything. When I spoke to him, he told me he thought the ladies here wouldn't miss a few clothes. We argued, and I convinced him he was wrong. So, he returned the dresses."

"And you knew where each belonged?" Yolanda nodded, and Ruth asked, "You were taking an enormous risk. Why?"

Her features softened. "We heard you and the lady at the front desk talking. You may have found out and got Stanley fired. They don't pay him much, and he wanted to help his family. He is sorry." Her tears started anew. "Please don't tell the Big Nurse. It is hard for us to find jobs."

Overcome with sympathy, Ruth said, "Does any of the staff steal other things, like money or jewelry?"

"No!" Yolanda's jaw clenched. "If this is happening, it is not one of us."

"And you are sure Stanley will never do this again?"

The aide sniffed and swiped a lingering tear. "He swears he will not."

Ruth made a potentially career-ending decision. "If nothing goes missing again, I will keep it to myself."

Yolanda gave her a grateful hug and thanked her in Spanish.

"And tell Stanley I have an idea that might help him."

. . .

Ruth went to the reception area, where Lillian sorted through the day's mail.

"What's up? You look like the cat who swallowed the canary."

Lillian resembled a bird herself, yellow hair styled into soft feathers. Ruth explained she'd solved the mystery of the missing clothes but kept names out of it. She might as well have published the information in the *Golden Years Ears* newsletter if she hadn't.

"I guess I don't need all the dirty details." Lillian shrugged. "I wish I helped solve the case."

"But you can now."

"No shit, Sherlock." Lillian stopped. "Dammit, I have to put another quarter into my cuss fund."

"Does that account for two swear words?"

"No, I guess that's fifty cents' worth now. I'd better just quit talking."

As if it were possible. Ruth reached into her pocket and took out a precious twenty-dollar bill. "Next time you go to Goodwill, I want you to find nice clothes for men and women. Some kids' things too."

"I see where you are going with this. I've got a lot more money in my cuss fund. I'll be happy to donate."

"Since the residents' families check in here, would you mind advertising the charity?"

"I'll put a box on the desk." Lillian frowned. "Shouldn't you run it by the Head Honcho first?"

. . .

"You propose a room for staff to take donated items?" Nurse Steele frowned.

"And residents. A take one, leave one exchange." Ruth attempted a confident smile. This was the tricky part. Did Steele know of the thefts? The rules stated everything missing worth over twenty-five dollars needed to be reported to management, and over one hundred dollars to the police.

"For those living on a limited budget, it would provide some extra incentive to stay here. Turnover is expensive." She hoped it sounded believable.

"What prompted this humanitarian effort?"

"We had a similar program in my last place of work." *Not really, but I doubt she'll bother to check..*

Steele nodded. "Good thinking, Nurse Markson. I'll leave it to you to organize it in the storage room next to the beauty salon. Off the clock."

"Thank you." Ruth walked away, smiling. For the first time, Petey the parrot granny cam had helped her win a minor victory at Golden Years.

CHAPTER 17

That evening, Ruth sat in Tyler's Triumph convertible. "Still not ready to tell me your secret?"

As he grinned, a smile dimple appeared on his cheek. "This is a show and tell."

He turned out of the campground, and Ruth recognized the minivan entering Dairyland.

"Looks like Debi got her car back from the shop already."

Tyler snorted. "That was quick. Must not have been much of an accident."

"Agreed. I still wonder if it happened at all. A deployed airbag might have caused the injuries. Or Gandy." She told him about her discoveries using the granny cams.

"One mystery down." Tyler shrugged.

"But several more to go. Like Tony Bettini poking around late at night." A chill shivered down her arm, covering it with goose-bumps.

"Want the top up?"

"Nah." She tied her hair back and closed her eyes as the warm breeze whipped her ponytail. The lowering sun warmed her skin.

They drove the short distance toward the center of Eureka.

"Are you going to tell me where we're going, or do I have to play twenty questions?" She twisted the end of her ponytail.

Tyler grinned. "We'll stop at Ed Foo Young's and grab some takeout. Good?"

Her stomach answered with a low growl. She covered it with her hand, as if to quell the sound. When she caught his smirk, she smacked his arm.

They parked by the familiar Chinese restaurant. The interior hadn't changed since her tenth birthday. The last time she'd dined here, her dad had been in a wheelchair. They walked into the scent of stir-fry and hot jasmine tea. Eddy Fong, the owner, greeted them from behind the counter.

"Heard you were in town. I remember you as a little girl." He held his hand a few feet from the ground.

"Not so little now, Mr. Fong."

He looked at Tyler. "You, I see all the time. I'll see even more of you soon, huh?"

Tyler nodded and placed their order.

They waited for their takeout at the table near the window where her family had celebrated many dinners. Her parents had always ordered the same dishes, Chicken Chow Mein and Egg Foo Young for her mom, and a hamburger for her dad.

"Are you okay?" Tyler placed his hand on hers.

"Yeah. Just remembering."

"Your dad?"

Ruth's throat tightened. "I can't help thinking about him everywhere I go in this town." She tried to lighten the mood. "He refused to try anything 'not American.' I teased him about liking pizza."

"Pizza is a ubiquitous favorite."

"Thanks, Mr. Fountain of Information. Anyway, he admitted he liked it and other 'Eye-talian' food. I'd tell him, 'It isn't Eye-taly, Dad.'"

"Your family came here a lot, didn't they?"

Ruth frowned. "Most celebrations. Except the last time."

Tyler's face flushed. "Oh. I am so sorry. I didn't realize."

She patted his hand. "Don't worry. I was bound to eat here, eventually."

Tyler glanced down at the Chinese Zodiac placemat. "Let's see how our birth sign reads."

Ruth squinted at the paper. "We're rabbits. Wonderful. I suppose we're supposed to be shy and retiring."

"Chinese philosophy attaches other meanings than our Western view. 'Gentlemen with this sign are polite,' not timid."

She snickered. "And 'ladies are pretty and demure with a pure heart.' I don't think so." She read further. "But it says we'll be successful in our careers, especially medicine."

"There you go. It also says rabbits are lucky in love."

"Right." She snorted. It hadn't been true for her lately, and not likely soon.

Eddy arrived with two large brown bags and recited the long list of contents. "And extra fortune cookies." He rang up the total. "You're lucky you two have good metabolisms."

As they walked out toting the hot bags, Ruth asked, "What did he mean about seeing you more?"

Tyler gave her a mysterious smile but didn't answer. As she veered toward his car, he grabbed her elbow and steered her along the sidewalk.

"Close your eyes. I won't let you trip."

"What the?" She obeyed, although she felt vulnerable and more than a little foolish.

He draped his arm around her, pulling her so close she smelled the laundry detergent on his shirt. She relaxed with him, and they walked for a few more minutes. He pulled her to a sudden stop. "Ta-da!"

She opened her eyes and stared at the three-story red brick building. "Waal's Department Store?" Frowning, she looked up at him. "I don't get it."

He dangled a set of keys. "It's mine. Well, and the bank's."

Waal's in Eureka had gone out of business before Ruth went away to school, driven to bankruptcy after the discount stores opened at the edge of town. When she'd been a little girl, her mom had taken her shopping for Villager wool sweaters and matching skirts. A million years ago.

"Are you going to become a retail magnate?" Ruth peered at the large picture windows covered in brown butcher paper.

"Not exactly. Come on, let me show you." He unlocked the heavy front door and followed her into the cavernous interior. The musty, dark room closed in on them until he switched on an antique light fixture.

She recognized the high pressed-tin ceiling, the maple floors, and empty display cases shoved against the walls. Wooden horses and stacks of lumber littered the area. Dust covered everything like a light snowfall.

Ruth pointed to the corner. "Does the freight elevator still work?"

"Ah, probably. We'll take the stairs just in case."

They climbed the elegant, wide staircase with carved mahogany finials that led to the second floor.

She paused on the landing. "You still haven't answered me."

"Junque in the Trunk wants to lease the first floor."

They crammed their current store with antiques and shabby chic furniture.

"There'll be plenty of room for all their stuff."

"There's four thousand square feet on each of the first two floors, and the top floor is half the size."

The second floor had lower ceilings but was less cluttered than the main floor. She recalled racks of clothing, the displays of matching skirts and blouses, and sturdy bras enormous enough to hold up the largest dowager bosom, coupled with white cotton panties the size of small continents. The department store catered to the local clientele, but still hadn't kept them from going out of business.

"Did they leave any creepy mannequins, especially the disembodied arms they had for showing gloves?"

"No, thank God. Not in my office space."

"Office?"

He gestured around the vast space. "I have a few of my buddies already interested."

"Doing what?"

"Developing apps. I won't quit my day job yet. But I have some ideas."

He pulled her toward the arched ceiling-to-floor windows overlooking the barren square. Many of the stores wore *For Lease* signs.

"We're losing our town center and without small businesses, there'll be no community."

"What can we do? I mean, the big discount stores are taking over. And then there's the internet."

"Sometimes, I feel like I'm barking at the moon. I'm talking about more than buildings—it's an entire way of life in danger of disappearing."

"There's no hope?" Eureka's shopping district had been going downhill for years.

"I've been volunteering with the Historical Committee. If we can get Main Street approval, there's a strong chance we can rejuvenate our downtown." He explained the Wisconsin state program was in place to help small towns attract business.

With a stab of guilt, Ruth acknowledged she had paid little attention to her mom's committee to preserve Eureka's historic buildings.

"Over here is space for the Main Street Executive Director. Volunteers run the program, but we need one paid full-time position when applying. Mostly, I've been fundraising and scrounging for money."

A smaller staircase continued to the third floor.

"There'll be a door here." He stopped at the top. "And all of this will be an apartment." He stopped and wiped his brow. "With a separate HVAC system."

"Translate, please."

"Heating and air-conditioning."

The bottled-up June afternoon heat on the top floor sent a blast of warmth into her face.

"We could use some air-con today." She took in the exposed brick walls, the large windows in the front and back, the old maple wooden floors.

"It's a loft!"

"Exactly. With a city view. Well, a town view anyway." He pointed to a large section of wall. "This will be the kitchen, open to living and dining areas." He walked a few feet. "Here's the counter, with a big breakfast bar, lots of stools."

"Cool. What kind of material?"

"I'm thinking granite or concrete, but I'm open to suggestions."

She studied the area, trying to imagine his new apartment. "I don't have any experience in design."

"But you know what you like."

She folded her arms. "I like marble, but it stains. How about quartz? It's clean, modern, and impermeable."

"I'll check it out."

They walked across the expansive room toward the rear windows.

"Here's the best part." He pointed out an open area above the second-floor rooftop. "This'll be a terrace. Decking, a railing, plantings, even a hot tub."

"Where will the grill go?" She smirked at him.

"I *will* learn how to cook on it."

"Sure. And I'll learn how to use a stove and oven someday."

"In the meantime, let's open this window. It's scorching in here." Tyler tugged at the handles. Nothing happened.

"Maybe it's painted shut." Ruth stifled a snigger as he continued to yank at the casement. She reached to the top of the frame and unlocked the hardware. With his next heave, the window slammed open.

"Well, that was easy enough." Tyler coughed as a plume of pollen blew in through the cool breeze.

"Easy peasy." Ruth stifled a laugh.

Below them, the rooftops of the Historic District merged with deep green trees and fields in the distance, forming a crazy quilt design.

"It isn't a cityscape, but it *is* beautiful," Ruth said, taking in the view.

"Thanks. I like it."

Next to the window, two folding chairs flanked a makeshift table. As they feasted on their Chinese dinner right from the containers, Tyler sketched a few drawings of his proposed layout.

"An enormous building like this must have cost you a fortune."

Tyler crunched on Chow Mein noodles. "The bank sold it to me for one dollar."

Ruth raised her brows. "No way."

"Way. It's part of the Save Historic Eureka."

"Our moms *do* something on that committee?" Mary Jo and her best friend Joy spent hours every month attending meetings.

"It didn't hurt to know someone." He opened a fortune cookie and read it aloud. "'Help. I'm being held captive in a fortune cookie factory.'"

"Seriously?" She opened one of her cookies. "'One who admires you greatly is hidden before your eyes.'" She flung the fortune down on the table. "These apply to anyone."

"Yeah. Especially when someone is a talented singer." He grinned, and she caught herself warming to the compliment. *Stop it.*

As they ate, a cool breeze blew in from the open window, bringing with it the sweet scent of blooming catalpa trees. The sunset painted the horizon with shades of crimson.

"Can you tell me more about this deal?" She expertly lifted a water chestnut and balanced it on two chopsticks before plopping it into her mouth.

"I have to meet two conditions. One, I must bring it up to code. I took out a loan for the amount from the bank. The second is I need to live in it for at least two years."

Two years? "This'll make a great bachelor pad." Her heart sank. Any hope of a long-term relationship vanished. Although Madison was only two hours away, with a schedule like hers, they would hardly see each other. Why bother with a speech about how they should stay just friends?

"I want to design three bedrooms, two baths, for a couple or a small family. More future marketability." He opened a fortune cookie, looked at the message, and crumpled it. "I want your input on the design and decor. You know, get a woman's perspective."

"You need to ask my mom or yours. I decorated my apartment in Madison every year at Hippie Christmas. In late August, everyone puts out their unwanted stuff and people can take what they want for free." She reached for the rumpled paper. "Hey, what did it say?"

Tyler's face colored. "Like you said, these sayings are generic."

She grabbed the fortune and unfolded it. "'You will have love and wealth beyond measure.'" She looked around the immense space. "Sounds like you've got it wired. Now you have to find your true love." She tried to sound light, but another woman would eventually live here with him.

A pained look crossed his face. "There was someone once at Stanford. We were pretty serious."

"What happened?"

"When I said I wanted to move back to Wisconsin, she flipped. She was a California gal, all the way."

One more nail in the coffin. Fully committed to this town, it was enough for him to give up a woman he cared for.

"I'm sure you'll find Ms. Right-for-you."

"I may have already." His strong profile was in shadow, difficult to read.

"Really? Do I know her?"

"No, and it's way too early in the relationship to introduce you."

"Oh." An irrational flash of jealousy passed through her like a lightning bolt. *Deep breath.* With an effort, she forced a smile and opened the next cookie. "'Count your blessings by thinking of those whom you love.' Wow. Even good grammar." Her hands tremored as she set the fortune on the table.

The silence stretched between them.

Tyler cleared his throat. "Would you mind reviewing my contractor's plans after he's finished?"

"No prob." The sunset was a faint orange glow in the west. She stretched and pretended to yawn. "Love your new digs, but I should get going." The sooner they got out of this awkward situation, the better.

He paused from packing up the garbage. "Do you like it? You're not just being polite?"

"Of course not, Ty." She patted his arm. "I never go out of my way to be polite to you."

He rolled his eyes, and they headed downstairs.

They barely spoke on the way home. Well, at least there'd be no big goodnight kiss dilemma. Ty had probably brought her to his place to show her why they couldn't be a couple.

In front of the trailer, she practically vaulted from the sports car, leaving him with a puzzled look.

Sleep eluded her. *I give up.* All she thought about was Tyler's bombshell that he had found Ms. Right and was staying in Eureka, no matter what. She jumped out of bed and walked into the trailer's living room.

"I know you like Tyler, Oreo." Tonight's revelation confirmed that Ruth's goals of med school and a career in a big city were at odds with Tyler's aim of raising a family in the small town of Eureka, Wisconsin. "But you and I will move wherever I can find a prominent position. It might be Madison, Milwaukee, even Chicago."

Her pet's ears twitched. Ruth took a sip of Sleepy Time tea, studying the small space where she'd become comfortable. The '70s décor reminded her of her childhood, retro and filled with warm memories. No longer did the faint odor of Bengay bother her. Instead, it reminded her of her grandparents.

Her gaze focused on a framed photograph from the 1950s of Mr. Schultz and his fiancée. She'd discovered it in a drawer the other day, recalling how he'd lost the only woman for him. He lived by himself for the rest of his long life in Dairyland Acres. As she dragged herself to bed, she wondered if he'd been haunted by what might have been.

CHAPTER 18

Ruth took her morning run, relishing her Sunday off from work. As she neared home, she spotted Tyler on a ladder by the office.

"Hey, Ty." She tried to quell the thrill of viewing him working in the sunshine. There was nothing like a competent handyman, someone good with his hands. All he was missing was a tool belt.

He grinned down at her. "Three down, one to go. You can help." He pointed to the sign *Security Cameras in Use.*

Her heart quickened. "Sure." She handed him the tools as he asked for them. She stood below him, uncomfortably close to his jean-clad legs, eye-level to either his rear or his crotch. Both were equally unnerving.

He climbed down the ladder and then draped his arm around her shoulders. "The way you tore off last night, I was afraid you might have food poisoning or something."

"I was tired." *And scared of what we might do.*

"It was only eight o'clock." He cocked his head. "Did you hate my new digs?"

"No, no. Nothing like that. I'm sure it'll be beautiful."

He scratched his neck. "If you have a few minutes, I have something to show you."

That piqued her curiosity. "I have the day off. Want to come in?"

He walked to his car and retrieved his tablet. As she unlocked her front door, he said, "Good, you're following precautions."

"The cameras will help too." One of them pointed at Ruth's trailer, giving her a modicum of security.

"The signage alone will deter some people." He booted up his tablet. "You'd better have a seat."

"What?" Goosebumps rose on her arms.

"I hacked into the Golden Years' security camera history." He pointed at the screen. "I found the video of the night somebody keyed your car."

Her heart was in her throat. "And?"

"Come see for yourself."

She plopped down on the couch next to him. The video quality was poor and grainy in the half-light, but she made out the familiar shape of her car. The time stamp counted forward until Tyler paused it.

He pointed behind the Saturn. "There's someone there."

"Let me see." She grabbed the device and peered at it. The figure wasn't discernible at all, a mere shadow, silhouetted by the streetlamps. One thing was obvious, however.

The person wore UGG boots.

"That does it." Ruth stood and her hands balled into fists. "I'm going over there right now." She moved toward the trailer door.

Tyler jumped up and grabbed her arm. "*No.* You can't tell her I've hacked in."

Ruth hesitated, panting. "I'll lie and say a resident reported her keying my car."

"Who? Howard? And get him in trouble?"

"You're right. I can't stand that bitch."

"Calm down."

Ruth marched to the window and spotted Debi's minivan. Bobby McKay's shiny black Viper pulled in.

"Oh, my god. What's he doing there?" She imagined the two of them enjoying a romp. Her stomach churned.

"It's kind of early for a date." Tyler crossed his arms.

Luke appeared around the bend of the road, running at an easy pace. He slowed near Tyler's sports car, then picked up speed and jogged away. Ruth noticed Luke hadn't stopped by for their usual morning run.

"We can't tell Luke either, can we?" Ruth asked.

"Not if you don't want us to get in trouble."

The nanny cam video, the security camera footage, and the mysterious computer system were all illegally obtained information, and useless to anyone but Tyler, Howard, and herself.

A movement caught her eye. Debi and McKay walked arm and arm out of the trailer next door. Debi pulled a suitcase behind her, tossing it in the minivan's rear. They spoke for a minute, both making hand gestures. Though their voices were raised, Ruth couldn't make out what they were saying. McKay hopped into his sports car and took off down the road, with Debi following.

"Hopefully, she won't return today. I can't handle seeing the bitch."

"Be careful." Tyler laid his hands on her shoulders. "Okay?"

She looked down. "Sure."

He lifted her chin. "Promise me?"

They were so close she might count the freckles across his nose. *Kissing distance.*

She asked, "Would you like something to drink?"

"Water would be great. It's hot out there."

And in here. She lowered the thermostat, set the sweating bottles on the coffee table, and they settled on the couch.

"After I got home last night, I remembered I hadn't shut the window. When I returned to the apartment, I found a bat flying around." He tapped on his phone and showed her the video he'd taken. "I hate bats. I chased the sucker for the better part of an hour with a broom. As far as I know, it's still there."

She laughed at the image of Tyler flaying away at the poor thing. "Bats aren't dangerous. They're a necessary part of the ecosystem. They eat mosquitoes."

"Yeah, easy for you to say. The flying rat wasn't swooping at your head."

"They aren't part of the rodent family." She sipped her water. "Imagine a big muscular man like you, afraid of a little mammal." She patted his firm biceps and instantly knew it was a mistake. She drew her hand away as if she'd touched a hot stove. "Sorry."

He turned toward her. "About what?"

Her mind swam as the heat from his body pressed alongside her. Through the brain fog, she asked, "Huh?"

He stroked his thumb along her cheek. "Sorry about what?"

"Touching. We shouldn't be touching so much."

He put a strand of hair behind her ear, sending a shiver down her side. "Why not?"

"I'm going to school next year. You're looking for Ms. Right to settle down here. I don't want to waste your time."

A corner of his mouth lifted. "Very altruistic of you. Noble even." His green eyes twinkled. "I'm only in my twenties, no rush to start a family. I figure I have some time to waste."

She cleared her throat. "And I know we're not the friends-with-benefits types."

"Speak for yourself."

Her eyes widened. "What?"

"You can have a year of self-imposed celibacy, or this." He cupped her face in his firm hands and tilted his head.

She closed her eyes, half-believing it would be a friendly smooch with no more impact than kissing the back of her own hand.

He pressed his lips to hers, gently at first, then with more passion. His mouth sought hers with surprising urgency. He held her tightly, pulling her against his solid chest. When he stopped, she wondered if the kiss had lasted forever or between heartbeats. In his embrace, his heart pounded, matching the thrumming in hers.

"Whoa." She struggled for words. "This is not a good idea."

Ty stroked her hair. "No, it's not. It's a *great* idea, one I've had for a long time." He drew her to him again. After another lengthy kiss, she leaned forward and nuzzled his neck, relishing his familiar scent. His arms encircled her, and she entangled her hands in his thick auburn hair.

After a few minutes of cuddling, he said, "I have to warn you though, if you accept my offer—"

"Oh?"

"I can demand my benefits. Sometimes, twice." He kissed her neck. "Or three times a night."

Her pulse sped up. "Oh."

"Eventually, we can spice things up a bit. Mutually agreed upon pleasures."

"Oh?" How spicy? Her imagination took off.

"And I want other benefits. Time at the beach, walking the lake path, hiking in the Kettle Moraine, binge watching our favorite shows."

"Oh," she sighed as he kissed her again.

Footsteps on the deck?

He placed his hand under her chin. He trailed his warm lips along her neck, sending shivers down her side. Then he dragged his lips across her collarbone. She gasped as he took his thumb, lifted the strap of her running shirt, and kissed her there.

He murmured, "God, you taste fantastic."

She returned his kisses, savoring the sweet saltiness of his skin, then placed her hands inside his shirt, dragging her fingers across his neck and shoulders. She kissed his earlobe, his neck. He moaned, deep in his throat.

His face was flushed, and she assumed hers was too. They sat looking at each other, breathing raggedly. Ruth had trouble forming a cohesive sentence. Finally, she spoke.

"I heard something outside."

They listened for a second.

"Probably Gandalf." He framed her face again. "Ruthie. I—" He stopped and kissed her instead.

Her long hair formed a golden tent around them, sheltering them from the world. She had never felt so safe, so accepted, so real.

Someone tapped on the door. They jumped apart, startled.

"Is it locked?" When she nodded, he said, "Maybe they'll go away."

She sprung up, peered through the peephole, and groaned. "Not likely."

He shifted on the sofa. "Take your time. Give me a second to cool down before I stand."

"Be right there!" she called out and counted to ten. She opened the door where Lillian stood holding a casserole.

"I brought this for you. Oh, hi, Tyler. I figured you might be here. Kathy in the office says the Wi-Fi's down again."

"No problem." He walked out the door, adding with a grin, "Don't forget my proposal, Ruthie."

"Marriage?" Lillian asked after he left.

"Not exactly. He's offering friends with benefits, no strings attached."

"What are you going to do?" Lillian asked.

"I'm not sure. There're lots of reasons it's a bad idea."

"Well, I know one thing for sure." Lillian winked and handed the casserole to Ruth. "Tyler's gone up a couple of notches in my book."

. . .

Ruth awakened in the middle of the trailer's lumpy double bed, hugging her pillow like a lover. She cursed when she read the clock radio next to her displaying 3:15 AM. Her mind filled with Tyler's proposal.

She turned over and fluffed her pillow, attempting to mold it into something comfortable. No such luck. All she thought of was how his kisses thrilled her.

She hopped out of bed and wandered into the trailer's tiny living room. She switched on a lamp and nuked some water for Sleepy Time tea. From her cage, Oreo blinked in the light.

"Sorry, girl."

Her guinea pig squeaked and nibbled at a raw carrot in her feeder. Ruth settled in at her computer and looked at Tyler's blog. She clicked on his video link, showing him chasing the bat around his apartment, and chuckled at his antics. He wasn't afraid to make a fool of himself.

"Tyler's hot, Oreo, even when he's acting goofy." Her pet wiggled its whiskers in assent. "And I know you like him."

But she knew their romance would only flourish until she moved away. He had committed to living in his building for at least two years. Long-distance relationships didn't appeal to her. Now he wanted to be a friend with benefits. Until now, the keyword had been "friend." She recalled the past weeks, and how he had her back whenever she needed him, but she worried about risking their friendship for an allegedly no-strings-attached relationship. She Googled "friends with benefits, advantages and disadvantages."

On one site, Numbers 13 and 14 had the same title, both pro and con:

You might fall in love.

CHAPTER 19

Early Monday morning Ruth stepped into the fluorescent light-filled entryway of Golden Years. Dracaenas and Ficus trees, festooned in red, white, and blue balloons, gave the atrium a holiday air. The signboard read *Don't forget to vote by 3:00 today!*

At the reception desk, Lillian was a vision with her patriotic-colored hair and wearing a stars and stripes sequined tunic.

Ruth nodded toward Lillian's top. "Did you borrow it from Betty Bling?"

"Ha ha." She sniffed. "Mine is much more tasteful."

"If you say so," Ruth teased.

Lillian pretended to scratch her left cheek with her middle finger.

"I caught that. Pay up." Ruth pointed to the donation box marked *Greatwill of Golden Years*. "Greatwill?"

"It's one better." Lillian threw in coins from a stack of quarters. "Speaking of which, I've started hitting on patients' relatives to chip in. I also bought a bunch of stuff at Goodwill to donate."

"Thank you. We'll work on the room after we get this election behind us."

Debi hustled by.

Lillian said, "I noticed the bitch isn't wearing her bandage anymore."

"And I thought you weren't swearing anymore."

She threw in another quarter. "It's for a good cause."

Ruth spent a frustrating morning playing cat and mouse with Debi. The hallways formed a labyrinth where she caught glimpses of her arch-rival, only to find Debi had disappeared. The longer the game went on, the angrier Ruth got. She hadn't promised Tyler she would keep her cool, but he was right. It wasn't the time to disclose their discoveries.

At lunch, Ruth picked at her chef's salad.

"Hello, Ruthie."

She turned to spot Howard's warm face. "Did you get my text?"

He slowly lowered himself into a chair. "You think Debi vandalized your car?"

Ruth's mouth formed a harsh line. "I do."

"Why would she do such a thing?"

"Neither Tyler nor I have any ideas." She moved some lettuce around on her plate. "What do you think?"

His face lined with deeper grooves. "Let it go. You've fixed the scratch."

She dropped her fork. It clanked so loudly, several residents at nearby tables turned and stared. "I give a rat's ass about the car." Her heart thumped. "I don't understand why."

"Is she jealous of you?"

Ruth snorted. "I can't imagine why. Debi doesn't know." She stopped herself.

Howard's kind brown eyes studied her. "Know what, honey?"

She wanted to hold back, keep everything to herself. Then, like a dam breaking, she told him in a torrent of words about her acceptance at UW med school, worries for her mom, her fear of not paying off her debt in time for the next term.

"It explains a great deal." Howard steadied his hands on the table. "Is there any possibility Debi found out about your plan?"

"No way. The only people who know are Tyler, my sponsor at UW, and now you." She hesitated. "There's a possibility she came into my trailer."

"I heard about your break-in from Luke. What would have caused her to do that?"

"Tyler thinks she wanted to look at my computer."

"How does all this fit into what's going on with my friends' deaths?" Howard's right eye twitched.

"I don't have a clue." Something niggled at the edges of her thoughts, as if she'd forgotten an answer to a question in a test.

"One thing a farmer learns early. Everything is interconnected." He patted her hand. "By the way, I'm proud of you, future Doctor Markson."

"Thanks, Howard. I can use all the support I can get."

. . .

Ruth was studying her phone in the break room when Debi breezed in, redolent of coconut suntan lotion. A wave of annoyance washed over Ruth as she imagined the wonderful day her co-worker must've enjoyed while she'd stewed at home.

"Peterson." Ruth's tone was as cold as her iced tea.

Debi held her spoon suspended in midair. "Is there a problem?"

"Perceptive of you." She steadied her shaking hands. "Yes. I have a problem. With you."

Debi swallowed a spoonful of yogurt. "Indeed."

"Because I think you have a problem with me. And I don't know why." Ruth worked hard to keep her hands on the table from clenching into fists. "You've treated me like crap since the day I started here."

Debi stirred the fruit at the bottom of the cup into the plain yogurt. She looked up with cold gray eyes, but remained silent.

"I take your silence as an assent." Ruth tried another tactic. "Look, we're stuck working together. Can't you be professional?"

Debi snorted. "For how long?"

A tingle of apprehension shot through Ruth. "What do you mean?"

Debi threw her spoon down with a clang. "You're a lot of things, but stupid isn't one of them. Why do you assume I am?"

"I don't understand."

"Here's the deal." Debi leaned over the table. "You graduated second in your nursing class. Sure, you have loans. But why here? You could find a job anywhere."

Ruth held her breath, wondering if Debi had figured out her plan to go to med school.

Debi continued. "Steele's retiring at year's end. I'm next in line for the Head Nurse position." She glared across the table. "Then you come along, sleeping with Doctor Kelly's son."

Ruth wanted to protest Tyler wasn't her boyfriend, but kept her mouth shut. Debi must have seen his car parked by her trailer.

"Or there's another possibility. This is only a steppingstone for you."

She opened her mouth to protest, but Debi interrupted.

"Either way, you don't fit into my plans. If you want the top job, forget it. It's mine. I'll fight you tooth and nail for it. I need the post more than you do."

"Why do you think so?"

"My ex ruined my life." Debi scoffed. "And the rest is none of your business. When I'm Head Nurse, I want a team I can count on, not someone gunning for my job or using this place for a temporary stopover on her way to marrying into a wealthy family."

"None of what you're saying is true." Ruth stood. "*None* of it."

Debi smirked. "Know why I have a problem with you? You're a spoiled brat who has the world by the short hairs, but whines and complains about everything from the computer system to her car."

"I don't have to take this from you."

"You asked, Markson."

"You have borderline personality disorder." Ruth gritted her teeth. "Deeply rooted in your childhood. You hate women, *all* women. It's *your* problem and has nothing to do with me." Debi opened her mouth, but Ruth ignored her. "Maybe it's your poor relationship with your mother. I don't know and I don't care."

Debi's sardonic laugh rang out. "Whose idea is that? Your shrink's?"

Ruth's stomach clenched. Did Debi know about her ex, a psychology professor?

"You need a good year or two of treatment." Ruth panted.

They glared at one another.

"I don't need advice from you, Markson." Debi resumed eating her yogurt, licking the spoon after each bite.

Fury coursed through Ruth. "I care about this job. I care about every one of my patients and nurse them to the best of my ability. If you bothered to ask any of them, they'd tell you this." Ruth turned toward the door, and then stopped. "And I have a title in front of my last name. Use it from now on."

Debi tore her gaze away from the yogurt. "Okay, *Nurse* Markson." Ruth was by the door when Debi added in a singsong voice, "The Head Nurse wants you."

. . .

"I believe you needed to see me?" Ruth asked from the doorway of Steele's office.

"You'll help tally the election results today. Voting is over at three." Nurse Steele narrowed her eyes. "I'm sure you'll stay neutral, despite your relation to Howard Engel."

"Of course." A rush of irritation drove through her.

Ruth went about her afternoon, making sure each patient had their medications before she counted ballots. She was especially happy to visit Nellie Wilson.

"You look chipper today," Ruth said.

Nellie sported a button that read *I voted* and red, white, and blue clothing. Perched on her blue-white curls was an Old Glory top hat.

"I hope your grandpa wins." She leaned over with a conspiratorial wink. "Tony Bettini takes the cake. He must've figured I was asleep, and stuck his head in my room, the nosey numbskull. I hear he's been asking all of us for his vote."

Did that explain his nighttime forays into patients' rooms?

"And did you know he was Mafia?" Nellie sniffed. "He says he's connected and related to the Naples Camorra. I think he has a Godfather Complex. He's a little man with a big badge. Still, I'm thinking of reporting him to the Head Nurse for coming into my room uninvited."

Ruth peered at the granny cam where this conversation was being recorded, but fortunately, only she and Tyler would view it.

"Here are your medications." Ruth opened the plastic case labeled "Nellie Wilson" she'd prepared.

The ninety-two-year-old asked, "Has Petey been of any help?"

Ruth hesitated. She couldn't divulge Yolanda's foray into Nellie's room captured on the granny cam.

"We're watching all the cameras. I'm sure they will."

"Good." She patted Ruth's hand. "If anyone can figure out what's going on here, it's you."

Ruth left, hoping Nellie's trust wasn't misplaced.

.　.　.

She walked the hallway lined with Resident Council election posters until she arrived at her supervisor's office. They had emptied the ballot boxes on a long table where Debi was already seated.

Nurse Steele pointed at the paperwork. "I'll tally the pink ballots. You two do the others."

Ruth wondered what the colored ballots had to do with anything and began marking the columns for Tony Bettini and Howard

Engel. Every time she spotted a vote for Howard, she silently cheered. Occasionally, she stopped and did a rough count. Her heart sank; the total was a fifty-fifty split.

"When you're done," Nurse Steele said, "switch and tally each other's ballots."

Ruth stifled a smirk. Steele was treating this election as if it were the Academy Awards. She detected a slight rolling of Debi's eyes and caught her glance. For a moment, there was a small sense of comradery.

"We have a new staff representative to the Resident's Council." Nurse Steele ruffled through the fuchsia papers. "Congratulations, Nurse Markson."

"What?" Ruth looked at the two other women, who appeared nonchalant. "You entered me in some kind of election?"

"We all are, automatically," Nurse Steele said. "We've each had our turn in the barrel. Now it's yours. The residents have voted for you."

Ruth tried to grasp what had just happened.

With a final click of calculator keys, Debi announced with a wide grin, "Looks like we have a new president."

Ruth fought disappointment. She was trying to think of something to say when Yolanda rushed into the office. She attempted to relate something in Spanish. Ruth jumped up, putting her hands on the aide's shoulders.

"Slow down, please," Ruth asked in Spanish. "I cannot understand."

Yolanda's eyes filled with tears. "It is Miss Nellie."

"Mrs. Wilson?" Ruth's breath caught. "What's happened?" She fought the urge to shake Yolanda's shoulders.

"She's down. On the floor in recreation." Yolanda looked pleadingly at Nurse Steele and Debi. "I called 9-1-1."

The three nurses rushed past the aide into the hallway. Ruth sprinted ahead. Residents lined the recreation room walls. In the middle, Nellie lay crumpled on the linoleum, where Howard knelt next to her. At Ruth's arrival, he stood and moved aside.

"Nellie?" Ruth breathed a sigh of relief when she found a faint pulse. After ensuring Nellie's airway was clear, Ruth undid a few buttons on Nellie's blouse and placed her on her side.

The other two nurses hurried in, pushing past the group of residents staring at the spectacle.

"Why was she out of her wheelchair?" Nurse Steele asked as she knelt down.

"She wanted to practice a victory dance if Howard won," someone in the crowd volunteered.

As the Head Nurse monitored Nellie's pulse, Ruth asked, "Does Mrs. Wilson have a history of fainting?" She made a mental list of all the meds she'd given Nellie. With so many drugs, any difference in dosage might cause an interaction contributing to the condition.

"No. But then, we keep her in her chair except for physical therapy," Steele answered.

Ruth doubted standing up alone would cause a fall. Before she voiced her opinion, the paramedics arrived in a flash of red uniforms and bright equipment.

"How long has she been out?" one of them asked as they lifted Nellie onto the gurney.

"Several minutes," Nurse Steele answered. "No history of heart problems. Mrs. Wilson's list of medications is on file."

They wheeled her to the door. "Stay with us, Mrs. Wilson."

Ruth's throat tightened. "Her name is Nellie." She picked up the top hat from the floor.

Steele addressed them. "We're all here. Might as well make the election announcements."

Ruth gaped at a stricken Howard, who stood against the wall as if it were holding him up.

"Now? After this?" She looked at Debi, where a shadow of distaste crossed the other nurse's face.

"I don't see Tony here," Debi pointed out. "Why don't we give the results when we always do, at dinner?"

"I suppose you're right." The Head Nurse straightened her starched white uniform. "See you both in an hour."

Ruth trod to Howard, wondering if she should break the news about Tony's victory. Instead, she patted his gnarled hand resting shakily on his cane.

CHAPTER 20

In the evening dusk, Ruth knelt by the green and white hosta plants outlining her trailer. It occurred to her someone walking by might think she was praying. In a way, she was. Nellie had died during the insufferable dinner amid the self-congratulatory ruckus raised by the winner, Tony Bettini. Howard had sat stoically by her side. Neither had spoken much. The food tasted like cardboard, overcooked and dry.

Debi was elsewhere tonight, her trailer dark and the parking pad empty. To her credit, she seemed subdued, and rather than toasting Tony Bettini's win, she wore a wan smile. Howard had squeezed Ruth's hand whenever his opponent let out a loud *whoop.*

Ruth contemplated the variegated leaves with holes eaten into a filigree pattern by some unknown vermin. The plants were doomed. She imagined the detachment people might feel right before they died rather than clinging hopefully to unfulfilled dreams.

"Ruthie. Need help?" Aunt Cordy stared down at her, her white plait flung over her shoulder. Her tie-dyed T-shirt read *Recycle or die.*

"What?" Ruth was as foggy as a Wisconsin March morning.

The older woman knelt next to her, holding a can of beer. "I have the solution."

"Sorry, Aunt Cordy. I don't want a drink right now."

The kind woman's face crinkled in amusement. "Not for us." She gesturing toward the struggling plants. "This is to drown hosta-eating slugs. No pesticides, no harmful chemicals."

"Oh. Whatever."

Aunt Cordy poured the beer into a bowl and began setting the traps. "What's wrong, Pookie?"

Her throat tightened. "I can't even talk about it yet."

"Well then. Let me tell *you* a story about Joe Schultz, who lived here for the last years of his life." She spoke of the bachelor, working for decades as a tailor on the south side of Chicago. He'd lived alone and left no family. "Only us." Aunt Cordy pushed a mound of mulch around the base of the shaggy plants. "Mary Jo was the daughter he never had." She plucked a brown leaf. "These plants gave him purpose."

"Mom saved his life during the tornado." Ruth glanced toward the new office recalling where the campers had huddled in its basement as the twister ripped off the roof of the old A-frame building.

Aunt Cordy sat on her heels. "At risk to her own life."

Her mother might have died. Losing both of her parents filled her with dread and fear. The tears that had been threatening overflowed. "I'm sorry," Ruth snuffled as Aunt Cordy embraced her. "I lost a patient today."

Ruth clung to her friend, who held her and stroked her hair. When the sobbing subsided, she spoke of the details, how she had placed the nanny cam, and her stunned reaction to finding Nellie on the floor of the rec room. She'd retrieved the camera after dinner but was too heartsick to even play it.

"If the medicine I gave her harmed her, I couldn't live with myself." Ruth breathed deeply. "She was on so many meds."

"You won't be that kind of doctor, will you?" Aunt Cordy's smile reached her eyes.

"What?" Ruth's hand froze as she scooped a clump of mulch.

"You needn't hide your dream from me, Pook. As a young girl, you never played the nurse, only the doctor."

A ripple of fear swept through her. "You won't talk about my plans, will you? I haven't mentioned it to my mom, and I can't let the Golden Years' staff find out."

"Of course not." Aunt Cordy pointed at a particularly bedraggled hosta. "Mulch here."

Ruth did as she was told, even though the plant wasn't likely to survive. "I will consider the drugs I prescribe."

"I don't take any pills. Not even cholesterol medication." Her face hardened. "I agree with you. Too many of us are puppets of the pharmaceutical companies."

"Speaking of drugs." Ruth studied Aunt Cordy's face. "I was wondering if you could tell me about the plants growing on the edge of the park."

She raised her brows. "Okay. Shall we sit at your picnic table? My knees aren't what they used to be."

Ruth gave her a hand. The sunset was a watercolor wash on the horizon, the burr oak's silhouette a pen and ink drawing.

Cordy continued as they walked to the picnic table. "Rupert was in the Vietnam War. He was a successful cosmetic dentist afterward." She ran her hand over the scarred wooden table.

"Then he began having horrible nightmares. Once, a truck backfiring set him off. He didn't recognize me."

Ruth imagined the terror. "Scary."

Aunt Cordy nodded. "At first, the Veteran's Administration diagnosed 'combat fatigue.' Now it's called Post Traumatic Stress Disorder."

"PTSD," Ruth said.

"No prescribed medication worked. He'd always led a healthy lifestyle."

Ruth nodded. Rupert and Aunt Cordy ate healthily and had a glass of red wine occasionally. They both exercised and maintained their weight.

"Then one of his army buddies suggested marijuana. It's the only thing that helps."

"Luke must know about it."

Aunt Cordy sighed. "We've reached detent. Rupert is to harvest it in the fall. Then we'll travel to states in the winter where it's legal."

"And afterward?"

The older woman shrugged. "Who knows? We'll play it by ear, biding our time until Rupert's stash runs out or we'll find a dealer here in the spring."

"That can't be an option." Ruth imagined a furtive deal in a back alley with the couple buying their cannabis from a criminal.

"I've looked it up on the internet. Apparently, drug dealers aren't only in inner cities anymore."

Ruth remembered Luke's growing concern about illegal drugs the first night she'd arrived home. People were dying from heroin and prescription drug overdoses. It seemed impossible as she and Aunt Cordy sat comfortably in the growing darkness. Evening fires in the campground sent the aroma of wood smoke through the air. Soft laughter came from the surrounding campsites. Some kids were playing chasing the fireflies dotting the meadow, as she used to with Tyler.

"I guess you're right. No place is truly like it used to be."

.   .   .

Inside the trailer, Ruth's phone had a missed text. She read the message where Tyler asked her to call him.

He answered on the first ring, his voice filled with concern. "I'm so sorry, honey."

"You know about Nellie?"

"Dad was at the hospital when they admitted Mrs. Wilson."

"Cause of death?"

"A suspected stroke. Will they do an autopsy?"

Ruth sighed. "Only if they consider the death suspicious, or the family demands it. Not likely with a ninety-two-year-old."

As she told Tyler the emotional story of her day, she had to stop several times to compose herself. "She was a feisty lady. I'll miss her. I haven't been able to even look at the nanny cam recording."

"I've already gone through the computer logs. Nothing unusual." He paused. "I have to work late tonight. We should look at Nellie's granny cam now."

Might as well get it over. "Do I need to get the parrot?" She'd left it in the back seat of the Toad.

"No. You can use your computer, and I'll access it from my tablet." He tapped a few keys and Nellie's familiar room filled her computer screen.

From the timestamp of the video, shortly before noon, Nellie rolled from the room in her wheelchair, presumably for lunch. One of the housekeeping staff came in, turned on the television to a Spanish station, swept the floor with a few dance moves thrown in, and shut off the television.

Tyler fast forwarded the recording to when Nellie returned to the room. She then rang for help and Yolanda arrived minutes later and helped her into the bathroom. After the aide left, Nellie stood and reached toward the camera. Her face filled the screen with a close-up of her grin, a big kiss, and then a wink. At that point, the screen darkened.

"That's the end." Tyler's voice filled with disappointment.

"Damn it. She asked me how to turn it off if she had a 'gentleman caller.' I didn't understand she meant this afternoon."

"You can't blame yourself."

"Now what?" She rubbed her temples. "Did her visitor have something to do with her dying?"

He paused. "I don't see how."

"Was it only bad luck then?" she asked.

"We'll keep watching, searching for a statistical pattern."

"In the meantime, more people might die. And if Howard's right, unnecessarily." She studied the orange shag carpet as she traced her toes through it, creating an infinity pattern. "Heart attacks and strokes can occur in the older population, seemingly without warning."

"What do the victims have in common?" Tyler asked.

Ruth noted his choice of words. "The patients are fairly healthy. But they're all on loads of meds." She hesitated. "There's a problem with blaming the drugs. I was the one who gave them to Nellie."

. . .

The next day, Ruth strode toward Nurse Steele's office where she'd been summoned. Surprised to find the door shut, she knocked.

"Come in."

Steele sat behind her metal desk. Light shone in from the tall window, onto a weeping fig plant. Dust motes danced in the air.

"Sit down, Nurse Markson." She pointed to the opposite chair. "I'll get right to the point. Someone noticed that you took an item from Mrs. Wilson's room last night."

Ruth's heart thumped, remembering the parrot nanny cam. "Oh, a toy I gave to Nellie. I wanted it as a memento."

"But you didn't know she was deceased."

"I figured if Nellie recovered, she would want something comforting in the hospital." Ruth frantically tried to recall who might have spotted her leaving with the parrot.

Steele leaned over the desk. "I don't care if you gave the item to Mrs. Wilson or not. Removal of anything from a resident's room without their permission is theft. And it's a reason for dismissal and possible criminal charges."

The blood rushed from Ruth's face. "I would never steal from anyone, let alone a patient. The toy was my gift. I swear."

Nurse Steele opened a folder with Ruth's name printed on the tab. "I'll speak to the family. If they don't want to press charges, I will only make a record of this incident in your personnel file." The shadow of a smile crossed her face. "*Any* new infraction will be a sufficient cause for your immediate termination. Do you understand?"

Ruth only nodded.

. . .

She drove home on autopilot as she replayed the evening of Nellie's collapse. Who had spotted her with the parrot? All the staff had been at the dinner, along with most of the aides. She cycled through the people one by one, trying to imagine a motive for reporting the missing stuffed animal. Ruth and the aides were friendly and joked in Spanish with each other. She doubted they would report her. Had Debi noticed her leaving Nellie's room?

Barely noticing the world surrounding her, she mulled through her options to save her job. She might offer to return the parrot to the family but would have to remove the camera beforehand. Her lips curled into an ironic smile. It would be the first life-saving surgical procedure she would perform.

Maybe the episode would blow over. "Who am I kidding?" she said aloud. Nurse Steele wanted her to step over the line so she could fire her. It was only a question of when, not if. Ruth didn't know why exactly but had felt Steele's hostility from the day she started work.

The real problem would be a black mark on her record as "terminated," haunting her forever.

She pulled up to her trailer and saw Lillian waiting on the top step. Ruth sighed, in no mood for company this evening. On the deck, Gandalf perched on Ruth's discarded Crocs. Ruth crawled out of her car and trudged toward her home.

"Hey, Lillian."

"You look like you've been rode hard and put away wet." The gold glitter in Lillian's white hair glistened.

"Just dealing with my pain-in-the-butt boss." She told her about the parrot.

"I came by to invite you to the Stitch 'n Bitch meeting."

"I'm not in the mood."

"Aw. Come on. It'll be fun." Lillian stood. "I finished knitting Taco's doggie sweater. Took me long enough."

"I can't knit." Ruth headed toward her doorway.

"There's food. Lots of chocolate." Lillian grinned as Ruth hesitated. "That's my girl."

Drinking alone, no. Staring at the television, forget it. But chocolate called its Siren Song to Ruthie.

"All right. But there better be lots of the dark stuff."

"There'll be plenty." Lillian intertwined her arm through Ruth's, and they strolled to the office. Inside the recreation building, heaps of brightly colored yarn decorated a long table.

"Hi, Pookie." Aunt Cordy nodded as she knitted from a huge cone of yarn.

Ruth kissed Cordy and greeted Betty Bling, who, like herself, didn't knit. As promised, chocolate in all forms decorated plates as centerpieces. Ruth studied a container of Trader Joe's Dark Chocolate Peanut Butter Cups.

"Ah!" Ruth lifted the plastic tub above her head as if it were the chalice of the Holy Grail.

"Have at it, honey," Lillian said, as Ruth devoured a few cups. She addressed the group. "Ruth's had a few tough days."

Ruth swallowed the bittersweet peanut goodness. "An understatement."

Cordy set her work down on the table and stretched her fingers. "More than losing your patient?"

"My boss has it in for me."

"Why on earth?" Betty asked. "You are such a sweet girl."

Her comment surprised Ruth. Betty never appeared to have particularly liked her.

"She's wanted me out since the get-go."

Aunt Cordy crossed her arms. "People sometimes have their own agendas."

"Maybe." Ruth bit into a mouthful of chocolate-covered raisins. "These are delicious."

Lillian continued. "We're calling this meeting of the Walkie-Talkies to order." She outlined the mysteries. "And I take it Nellie's granny cam was inconclusive?" Ruth nodded and noted that the Walkie-Talkies were in on the plan, thanks to her blabbermouth friend.

Lillian finished chewing a piece of fudge. "Anyway, we're going to help."

"More actively," Betty said. "Vella Easton, a resident, was a friend of mine. She passed away suddenly earlier this year."

"I attended church with her," Aunt Cordy said.

Lillian frowned. "If the cameras show nothing, we have to search for more information. That's where we come in." She explained most of the nefarious activity occurred at night.

"And your point is?" Ruth struggled to understand where the three of them were going.

"The Senior Talent Show is at Golden Years with a Las Vegas theme," Lillian said. "Bobby McKay will be Elvis, and you will sing a duet with him."

"What?" Ruth asked. "No one's mentioned it to me."

Lillian ignored her. "And Betty here will do her Las Vegas show-girl dance. Guaranteed to keep the men occupied."

Betty swung a gold lamé loafer from her foot. "The video Tyler took of me at the luau has gone viral." She stood and did a few swift hip shakes back and forth. "It won't disappoint my fan base."

Ruth kept a straight face, but her lower lip twitched.

"You were never one to hide your light under a basket." Cordy resumed knitting.

"If you've got it, flaunt it." Betty winked.

Lillian cleared her throat. "Betty's, ahem, special talents will keep the likes of Tony Bettini occupied. While doing so, I will roll Cordy in a wheelchair, positioning her as a lookout."

"And then?" Ruth crossed her arms. "Let me guess. I search rooms looking for clues when I'm not on stage."

"Exactly right!" Lillian clapped. "See girls? I knew she would be game."

"Of course." Ruth gave an eyeroll. "What could possibly go wrong?"

CHAPTER 21

Nurse Steele summoned Ruth the next day. She knocked on the doorjamb with a trembling hand, fearful she was in trouble again.

"Come in." The nurse lifted her head. "The Resident Council meeting is today at ten this morning. You'll be there as the administration's representative." She grabbed a three-ring binder from a shelf. "Here's everything you need."

Ruth took the book and breathed a quiet sigh of relief. "Is that all?"

Nurse Steele glanced down at her paperwork. "Yes. For now."

"Yes, Nurse." Ruth fumed as she headed down the long hallway toward the recreation room. *What a waste of time.*

President Tony Bettini sat at the head of a long card table, with Miriam to his right.

"Welcome Nurse Ruth." Tony straightened in his chair. "I was mayor of a Chicago suburb for many years. Modesty prevents me from specifics, but let's say I understand how to run things. There's plenty of room for improvement, but it is a wonderful community."

Ruth recalled Nellie's comments that Tony claimed to be "connected."

"You'll find we get a lot done here," Miriam said. "I represent the Recreation Department and am secretary, following the strict guide for Parliamentary Procedure."

"Great to be here." *Not.*

Ruth hadn't slept well and fought to keep her eyes open as the meeting progressed. To keep awake, she drew doodles in the margins of the notebook Steele had given her. Daisies followed by abstract squares and circles intersected, and arrows pointed in different directions. She tuned in to the discussion of the temperature of the dining room and other common areas. If this was how the meetings went, it would be better to spend the time with her patients. To keep awake, she focused on the glint of Miriam's pen as she scrawled notes. A thought niggled at the edge of Ruth's mind as she doodled check marks and X's.

"We need better Italian food. I hate the gravy." Tony frowned. "It tastes like something out of a can."

Miriam tapped her pen. "Gravy? Like in Italian beef sandwiches?"

Tony traced his hand along the sides of his silver pompadour. "No, no, no. It's what we call the red sauce you put on spaghetti." He placed his hands together, rolled his eyes, and implored heaven, or perhaps his sainted wife.

The late afternoon sun glinted off the gray linoleum, reminding her of the memorial service she'd attended only a short while ago for Mrs. Jankowski. Weary of losing patients, the discussion sounded mundane, superfluous.

Miriam flourished her Mont Blanc pen and wrote in her notebook. "There. I've noted your request to Food Service. Reasonable." She batted her eyelashes at Tony. "Mr. President, might I add something to the request?"

"Sure." He swept his hand, as if enjoying his Godfather role.

"How about they play some Italian music at dinners when they serve the gravy?"

"*Bella,* beautiful." His face crinkled into a grin. "I enjoy all the classic artists, Dino, and, of course, Old Blue Eyes."

Ruth fought to keep from laughing. Forget opera, Verdi, and Rossini.

"*Fantastico,* fantastic!" Miriam beamed. "I have some knowledge of the most beautiful of languages."

Ruth hated it when someone used a sprinkling of foreign words to impress others.

Tony waved his hand, dismissing any further discussion of the subject. "I don't have no more to ask."

And double negatives were as bad.

"Good." Miriam scribbled away. "I'd like to update you with the latest plans from Recreation. I need Pet Day volunteers." She looked directly at Ruth.

Ruth remembered Miriam's request to bring Oreo. She briefly toyed with substituting Gandalf and the ensuing fireworks *he* would create.

"I'll consider bringing in my guinea pig." Not a chance. "When is it?"

Ruth dutifully recorded the date, knowing she'd never bring her shy pet to Golden Years. Her doodles had shifted to geese and guinea pigs. She didn't have her mother's artistic ability, but Gandalf was a pretty good likeness, snapping his vicious beak.

Miriam continued with the list of recreational activities, including Bingo and planned shopping trips. She droned on and on, her dangling cow earrings jiggling as she spoke. Her T-shirt read *Wisconsin: Smell our Dairy Air.*

"And the most exciting announcement is our Viva Las Vegas fundraiser!" She practically squealed with delight before she continued. "This is our first Eureka Senior Talent show. Bobby McKay will charitably headline as Elvis. Lillian, our vivacious receptionist, has arranged another act." Miriam looked at her notes. "Ms. Betty Fontaine as a Vegas showgirl and her poodle, Pucci. She apparently has rave reviews from previous performances."

Oh, you have no idea. Ruth fought back a snort-laugh. Wait until Betty does her striptease or her horny dog gets a hold of your leg. Betty should bring *him* to pet day.

She peered at Ruth over her rhinestone-studded readers. "Lillian has also recommended you for a duet with Elvis. Preferably one from the film."

Ruth attempted to remember any of the musical numbers and only recalled the title tune, where showgirls surrounded Elvis.

"I have to look at my work schedule. Rehearsals take time."

"No problem there. Nurse Steele has already approved as much leave as you need. This fundraiser is terribly important to Golden Years."

"I'm honestly at a loss for words." *Until I give Lillian a dressing-down for suggesting me.*

"Well." Tony appraised her. "I can see a resemblance to Ann-Margret."

If I was six or seven inches shorter and a redhead.

"I think there's a duet where the lady is in love and denying it," Miriam said.

Interesting.

Soon, the buzz of conversation lulled Ruth, and her attention drifted to kissing Tyler. She missed him last night. Her latest drawings of flowers and hearts crowded the margins, making bigger and bigger blobs on the stationery.

Tony's loud voice broke her reverie. "Why hasn't the recycle bin been emptied? It's an eyesore."

Miriam sighed. "We have changed contracts to save money. We'll get back on track in a couple of days."

Ruth zoned out. Worrying about garbage was the least of her concerns. Miriam's voice demanded her attention.

"Our notes will be in the newsletter Nurse Ruth will prepare for us."

Ruth glanced up to meet Miriam's bland gaze. "Sure." The editorial position offered a glimmer of opportunity.

"After administration approves it. We must adhere to proper procedure to support our president." Miriam tapped her pen.

Ruth noted a tiny crack of hostility beneath the Midwest-nice façade of the Bettini supporter.

"Of course. We must support the residents' *elected* leader." Ruth gave a sweet, fake smile. "I'll get right on it."

.   .   .

Ruth struggled to make it through the day with her eyes open when Yolanda flagged her down.

"Come with me."

She motioned Ruth to follow her into Nellie Wilson's former room. Stripped of everything personal, it smelled of fresh paint. Desirable private rooms were never empty for long.

The aide reached under the mattress. "I found this." She handed a leather-bound book to Ruth.

Ruth leafed through Nellie Wilson's daily journal. "Thank you, but we both might get in trouble if they find out we took it."

Yolanda regarded her with steady brown eyes. In Spanish, she said, "Big troubles require big remedies."

"You heard about the parrot? The toy?"

"*Si*, yes. We all talk." Yolanda nodded toward the Head Nurse's office. "She doesn't treat us badly, just like we're not there. She forgets we speak English."

Ruth debated for a moment. "What do you think is going on here?"

Yolanda frowned. "I heard *Señora* Steele on the telephone, the other day, yelling."

Ruth's heart quickened. "Do you remember exactly what she said?"

Yolanda nodded solemnly. "It has to stop. Now."

A swell of disappointment washed over Ruth. "That's it?"

"Sorry." The aide bit her lip. "One more thing. The recreation lady rushed into the office. They noticed me and slammed the door." She looked at Ruth. "Did I help?"

Ruth studied the empty wall that once held so many photos of Nellie's grandchildren. She slipped Nellie's journal into the waistband of her scrubs.

"Very much so." She patted Yolanda's arm. "Thank you, my dear friend."

.   .   .

An hour before Ruth's shift was over, she went to a small cubbyhole she'd set up as an office. Located off the main corridor, she'd discovered the mostly unused visitor's area at the dead end of one of the offshoot hallways. It held a small table, an orange plastic chair and a large Rhododendron plant, partially hiding her from view. She took the journal and her laptop out of her bookbag. Reading through the most recent entries, she searched for clues. Three days before she died, Nellie had written *M. coming over the day after tomorrow. Can't wait!*

Ruth read the next day's entry. *Pretty nurse Ruth brought me Petey. I love it almost as much as M.*

The day she died, Nellie wrote the poem about the supposedly golden years, humorously bemoaning her old age, ending with the line, "The golden years can kiss my ass!"

Once Ruth stopped laughing, she took the notebook Miriam had given her and dutifully began transcribing the notes.

The head of recreation's handwriting was as elaborate as her decorated T-shirts and dangling earrings. The fountain pen made it even worse to decipher the words since splotches and "i's" dotted with hearts peppered the pages.

Give me a break.

Ruth stretched her neck after she'd hit *send* to email the newsletter to Nurse Steele. She was closing Miriam's notebook when she spotted a scrawled to-do list: *Get the word out about the Recreation Fund Fair. Schedule pet day. Van serviced. Check, check, check.* The check marks were as annoying as the rest of her elaborate scrawls, with little curly ends ending in blobs of ink. Unique. Where had she seen these before?

Energized, Ruth straightened. The answer to what had been niggling at her since the election appeared before her. Several of the ballots had the distinctive check marks. Ruth wrote them off as a fad of various people.

But what if a single fountain pen had made them?

. . .

At ten o'clock, Ruth stood with Tyler outside the Golden Years' recycling dumpster. Outfitted like cat burglars, they wore headlamps, courtesy of Aunt Cordy. Ruth had spotted them hanging on the greenhouse, surmising they were used to tending to the marijuana garden at night. Ruth asked to borrow the lights, providing the excuse she and Tyler were on a scavenger hunt. The disbelief had been clear on her friend's face, but she'd handed them over after warning Ruth to be careful.

Tyler gave Ruth a leg-up, and she tumbled into the container.

"Everything all right?"

"Yeah, I'm fine." She'd landed on a pile of plastic milk containers, cushioning her fall. "You coming?" She peeked over the side of the dumpster.

"Be right there." He eyed the contents. "Kind of tight quarters, huh?"

She rummaged, and still no Tyler. "What the heck is wrong, Ty?" She stood and faced him eye-to-eye.

"It looks confining."

It all made sense. The open windows, the top down in his sports car.

"You're claustrophobic."

He nodded. "Got locked in a closet by accident once as a kid. Hard to get over it."

She gave him her hand. "We won't close the lid. Come on in, the water's fine."

After one more glance into the dumpster, he scaled the side, landing with a thud. "Only for you." He lifted the cardboard boxes and moved them aside. "I'll scrub the security video from tonight."

"You think of everything." Ruth pushed her braid aside. Sweat poured from beneath her black wool cap since the metal box was hotter than Hades. "The hope is they didn't bother shredding the ballots."

"And hope they're committed to preserving the environment." He dug around, turning his head to light up some papers.

Ruth grabbed his arm. "Watch out!" A pair of headlights glared from across the street.

They dove deeper and shut off their headlamps. Crouched next to each other amid the recyclables, they remained silent. A rush of affection for him washed over her. He'd jumped in for *her.*

He seemed to sense her mood. "Romantic place, isn't it?" He squeezed her shoulder.

Headlights crawled across the yellow brick above them. When she and Tyler peeked over the dumpster, she imagined they resembled Minions.

She stifled a laugh. "We have to stop meeting like this."

He grinned, highlighting his dimples. "Only you could get me to spend an evening dumpster diving."

God, he's cute. She returned to her task with shaky hands. Dammit, why had they ever kissed?

He reached down to a pile of papers. "What're these?"

She studied the sheets. "Nope. Good try though."

After another half an hour of digging, she spotted a ballot. "Ah ha!"

Tyler crawled over and together they collected the contents of the ballot boxes.

She tapped the papers. "Now all we need to do is to find how many of these babies have the Miriam-style checkmarks."

"And what will you do with the information?" Tyler's brow furrowed.

"I'm not sure. But everything we learn counts."

. . .

In her trailer, Ruth spread the ballots on the dinette, and sorted them into categories, those marked with a pencil, others with ink, and the few with crayons. The fountain pen ballots were in a separate category. She counted and recounted the votes. Had the Miriam-styled ballots not been included, Howard would have won by twenty-five votes.

She rubbed her temples. "Why would they want Howard out?"

Tyler took a sip of pop. "It's possible Miriam was helping those with disabilities."

Ruth contemplated the theory. "Doubtful."

"I'd better scrub the security camera video." Tyler stretched on the couch and typed it into his phone. "Done."

He patted the seat next to him.

She sat, marveling at her attraction to him. His T-shirt and jeans accented his lean frame.

"You look good in black." Why had she blurted that?

He chuckled. "You should talk." He lifted the tail of her braid. "It sets off your beautiful hair." He licked his thumb, reached over, and dragged it across her cheek.

"Bit of recycle dust. There. Now you're perfect."

"Ty, I'm out of here in a year." She ignored her pounding heart.

"Can't we cross that bridge when we come to it?" He leaned closer.

"We can, but what about finding Ms. Right?" Her thoughts muddled as she breathed in his aftershave.

"I promise you'll be the first to know."

He cupped her face, kissed her forehead, nose, and lips. She closed her eyes and returned his kiss. She wrapped her arms around his neck and pulled him closer to her.

The kiss lasted and was so good, lights flashed behind her eyelids.

She pulled away, opening her eyes. "Something's *wrong.*"

The lights were real, strobing across the walls of the trailer. She and Tyler leaped up as Luke's police car tore through the park. Tyler grabbed his phone. The sound of a scanner came through. They paled as they listened to the call.

"Fire at Golden Years."

CHAPTER 22

Tyler raced his car to the nursing home. They drove in silence as his phone app reported Luke and the fire department's arrivals.

"No ambulance call yet." Tyler gripped the steering wheel, his jaw set.

"I guess it's a good sign."

Streetlights blurred as they sped down the highway toward the edge of town. Ruth fiddled with the end of her braid. Were the residents safe? Would they become homeless? Would she still have a job if the place burned down?

As they approached, strobe lights painted the familiar building in blood red flashes, and firefighters held hoses spraying water in vast arcs. Luke and other uniformed officers milled about.

"Is everyone safe?" She scanned the groups of pajama-clad residents standing outside the assisted living section. With a sigh of relief, she counted heads and spotted Howard hugging his lady-friend, Gert.

Ruth and Tyler stood behind the police tape. She craned her neck, trying to determine the exact spot where the flames originated. As the firefighters disbursed, she asked, "Is that—?"

Tyler nodded. "It's the recycle bin."

Ruth swayed, and he embraced her and held her tight against him.

Firefighters theorized the blaze had started either from "hoodlums" or "juvenile delinquents."

A shiver of fear slithered through her. If the fire was set in the recycle bin, then perhaps someone had figured out they should burn the ballots. She and Tyler had been lucky.

Nurse Steele strode between the clusters of residents, holding a clipboard. Ruth turned as a minivan drove up. Debi sprinted toward them, wearing a worried frown.

"What happened? Is everyone okay?"

Ruth nodded. "The residents are fine."

"What a relief." Debi looked around. "Where did it start?"

"It looks like the recycle bin." Ruth studied Debi's expression, which hadn't changed.

"Do they have any theories?" Debi asked.

"They say kids might've done it." *But I don't believe it for a moment.*

Debi didn't reply and strode toward Nurse Steele.

Luke surveyed the area. His gaze narrowed and lingered on Ruth as he strode toward them.

"Oh, boy." Too late, Ruth realized she and Tyler were dressed in their burglar-black getups.

Luke asked, "How are you two?"

"Fine, fine," Tyler answered, his arm around Ruth.

"Looks like vandalism to the recycle bin." Luke raised his brows.

Ruth let out a breath. "I'm glad no one was injured."

Luke regarded her, his gaze steady. "Me too." He looked toward the building. "The security tapes should show us something."

Tyler flinched next to her. Anyone examining the tapes was sure to notice the scrubbed video during their evening's exploration of the dumpster.

After giving Tyler a last hug, Ruth accepted Luke's offer of a ride home. As they drove toward Dairyland, she worried he might question her further, but he remained silent.

After they arrived home, he asked, "If you're coming to dinner tomorrow, would you like to shoot some hoops beforehand?"

"Sounds good."

Luke drove off. As she got to the front door, she froze. She'd forgotten to lock it in her haste to get to Golden Years.

She looked around. No Gandalf on the front porch. She grabbed her phone and slowly turned the handle. She kicked the door, and it creaked open. At least she'd left the lights on.

Ruth crept in. Nothing appeared amiss. Oreo uncurled from a ball in her cage and let out a *wheek* of greeting. After a sigh of relief, an idea occurred to her.

What if the person who'd invaded her trailer had been too busy setting a fire at Golden Years to repeat the act?

. . .

The next evening, she found Luke warming up at the basketball hoop. Ruth was ready to rumble in her UW T-shirt, running shorts, and high-top sneakers.

"I hope you're not intimidated. I was a star point guard." Ruth grinned.

"So was I. You're on." Luke passed the ball to her. "You start."

Ruth dribbled the ball, missed the shot, recovered it, and made the basket. "Easy peasy."

"We'll see about that." Luke took possession, ran the ball, and dunked it.

They continued to play as the momentum swung like a pendulum. Ruth lost herself in the flow, watching only the ball, the hoop, and the plays until Luke won by a point. Panting, they sat on the stoop of the farmhouse porch. Next to them, the cement goose sported a Packer's jersey.

"That was a good game." Luke took a swig of water from his water bottle.

"Yes." Ruth gazed at the expansive view of the campground below.

Luke's phone chimed, and he looked at his screen. "My girls. Ashley isn't coming home for the Fourth of July. She'll be in Chicago with her mother. I don't know about Leslie."

His disappointment was obvious. She, too, had spent little time with her dad as she grew older. Now, she regretted the lost opportunity.

"Do you visit with them often?" His daughters were at UW-Green Bay.

He shifted his weight on the step. "They've been busy. And they spend all their holidays with their mom."

"Right." There was pain in his eyes. She barely knew his daughters, and they were now related by marriage. She wanted to know them better and hoped she would have the opportunity.

"Do you want to talk about last night?" Luke's eyes were kind, so much like Howard's.

"About what?"

His firm expression spoke volumes. "Start at the beginning and end with your cat burglar outfits."

She studied the scar on his arm. "Okay." Everything about Golden Years poured out, the suspicious deaths, Howard's concerns, her unease with her supervisor, Debi, and Miriam.

She winced. "I even set up granny cams."

"And what did you find? Or should I say, what did Tyler find?"

She decided not to deny Ty's involvement. Instead, she recalled Nellie kissing the camera, then turning it off. "Not much. Only that the residents need some privacy when they have dates."

He frowned, looking toward Dairyland, where campfires made a haze in the distance. "Is it nursing home abuse?"

"I'm not sure. But something's wrong."

"And the fire last night? Was it set for a purpose?"

"Might've been. Tyler and I took the ballots from the recycle bin right before it started. I think they rigged the election. Your dad should've won by twenty-five votes."

"I'd like the evidence, even though it's not admissible. And the granny cam."

Ruth nodded. "And you'll probably find some missing video from the security cameras around the time we were in the dumpster."

Luke sighed. "Tell Tyler to stop screwing around with those, will you? And the computer system too, while you're at it."

"I'm not sure what you mean, but I'll let him know."

Luke half-smiled. "I'll step up extra patrols at Golden Years. In the meantime, please don't get all Nancy Drew on me, okay?"

Ruthie shrugged. "Who's she?"

He explained, stopped, and passed the ball to her, which she easily caught. "Come on. Your mom's expecting us for dinner. It's lasagna tonight."

Mary Jo grinned as she loaded Ruth's plate with the casserole. Luke poured a glug of Merlot into a large, stemless wine glass for his wife. He sipped a club soda.

"So, I want to go on record." Her mom beamed at Luke and Ruth. "I heard that you and Tyler are dating."

"What?" Blabbermouth Lillian had struck again.

"Seeing one another. Hooking up. Whatever you call it now." Her mom held up her glass. "A toast to the lovely couple." She leaned in toward Ruth. "I worried it would never happen."

"I'd rather not discuss it yet. Everything's new." Ruth flushed, wondering at their relationship status. She recalled their latest kisses and what might have happened if Luke's police lights hadn't interrupted.

Mary Jo said, "Not that I mind. In fact, Joy and I have always wanted the two of you together."

How would their mothers regard the perfect match if they knew Tyler wanted to roll in the hay without commitment? Usually, the lasagna was delicious, but tonight it was gummy as a wad of bubblegum. She changed the subject. "Can you teach me how to make this?"

Mary Jo nodded. "Sure. It would be good if at least one of you could cook."

Luke asked, "Can I get you a piece of pie? It's lemon meringue."

"Thanks. I'll get it." Relieved at the distraction, Ruth took the pie from the fridge and began cutting it into wedges.

She finished her dessert as quickly as possible, but she wasn't fast enough.

Mary Jo looked at Luke. "Can you imagine how cute their kids would be? Probably strawberry blondes." She sighed. "And smart. Talented." Her mom was legendary for having a loose tongue when she had a buzz on from a glass of wine or two.

"You're being premature, honey." Luke looked at Ruth and winked. "I don't spot an engagement ring yet."

"May I help you clear?" Ruth sounded as icy as possible.

"No, thanks. It's Luke's night for the dishes." She patted her daughter's hand. "You go on. I'm sure you have an early morning."

"Thanks for dinner." It would've been great without the editorializing.

Luke walked her to the door. "Want a ride?"

"I'm fine, thanks."

"Are you sure?" Luke crossed his arms. "After what happened?"

Ruth held up her phone. "I have this, and I promise I'll get in touch right away if something's wrong."

He gave her a brief smile. "She means well."

"I know." A full moon illuminated the night sky, drowning out the stars. "Well, goodnight."

"Take care." Luke closed the door behind him, leaving her awash in moonlight and the glow of small lamps lighting the pathway. She took the long way home, enjoying the night. She craned her neck toward the heavens and her annoyance with her mother melted away. Instead, she recalled her dad, who taught her to identify constellations with a small book and a flashlight.

When Tyler visited, her father had included him, despite all the questions from the precocious little boy. For the first time, remembering her dad didn't cause a stab of pain. She recalled him running his hands through his hair when he found the interrogation by Tyler too daunting. "Boy, you're gonna grow up to be a regular Einstein," he'd predicted.

The lights were full on in some RVs, while others were faint glows where residents had retired for the night. In the distance, an owl hooted. She passed by Betty Bling's Allegro motor home, outlined in twinkling white party lights. Luckily for Lillian, her trailer was dark. Ruth would have a chat with her about blabbering to her mother and volunteering her for the talent show.

When she came around the corner, the office was lit up in the darkness of night. Debi had parked her minivan in front of her trailer. Then she spotted a pile of something white along the side of the road. It looked as if someone had dropped a pillow. She cursed. Some campers sure were litterbugs.

She made out the form more clearly as she drew closer and broke into a run. Kneeling on the gravel, she felt a faint pulse. She speed-dialed her mother with shaking hands.

"Come now. It's Gandalf. He may have been hit by a car."

Ruth ran her fingers down the goose's body, relieved there were no apparent broken bones or blood.

Poor Gandy. Hang in there.

Minutes later, Luke drove her mother's Jeep to where Ruth had directed. Mary Jo carried a large towel and a wire crate. Her mom sobbed as Ruth and Luke carefully lifted the goose into the padded carrier.

"How bad is he?" Her mother's voice was heavy with worry.

"I don't know. He's alive." She gave her mom a quick hug. "Go now. The sooner you get him to the vet, the better."

The Jeep tore off into the night. She scanned the area, but whatever happened to Gandy was probably off camera either by coincidence or plan.

Using her phone as a flashlight, she surveyed the area. Perhaps in daylight, Luke might better detect what happened. As she walked home, the night took on a more sinister appearance. What if the person who hit Gandalf was still around? Aware Luke was off premises, and she was out of camera range, an icy current of fear went through her. Leaves rustled in the dense bushes. Clouds obscured the moon, and the breeze turned cold. Night predators were on the move. Owls hunted prey, and raccoons foraged for food, sometimes robbing bird nests.

She was thankful to see the porch light still on and quickly opened the front door, pushing it shut and locking it with the deadbolt. With shaky thumbs, she texted Tyler about the goose and asked him to examine the security camera footage. He texted, asking her if he should come over, but she assured him she was fine.

As she waited to hear from her mother, Ruth glumly stared at her computer screen. Nothing bad happened at Dairyland Acres before her arrival. The trouble she attracted at Golden Years had seeped into the quiet, safe campground.

With a beep, Tyler's text told her what she already feared. Whatever had happened to Gandy was outside camera range. He promised to study the tapes from the evening to spot who might have been on the road.

To kill time, she checked her email. There was the usual junk she'd been meaning to unsubscribe from, advertising things she had no intention of purchasing. Most messages offered discounts, and she vowed never to pay retail when one day she had some disposable income.

One email, however, held her attention as she read and reread the message from a hospital in Madison.

Dear Ms. Ruth Markson,

The position for which you applied has a recent opening. If you are still interested, please contact us at your earliest convenience. Your credentials impressed us, and we would like to schedule a final interview.

CHAPTER 23

Ruth drove to town by fields of towering cornstalks and carpets of soybeans. Her heart quickened. The hospital's email offered her a potential way out. Soon, she might be in the middle of Madison, returning to an anonymous life in a large city. She recalled her favorite haunts, including her go-to sushi restaurant.

Trouble seemed to follow her return home. Someone vandalized her car, invaded her trailer, and injured her mother's pet.

Her stomach clenched at the agony her mother had been through the night before. Mary Jo had texted repeatedly from the veterinary waiting room until two in the morning. Fortunately, the vet had determined Gandalf was only stunned, but kept the gander overnight for observation.

Luke had sent separate texts, asking if Tyler had anything on camera. He guessed a vehicle had grazed the goose, and they were lucky the collision hadn't been more direct.

If I hadn't come home, none of this would have happened.

A new job might solve a host of problems. Not only would she take her vortex of danger away from home, but she'd also be ahead financially. The salary range for the position was generous, making a studio apartment affordable. She had already cost her mother additional expenses like the pricey internet connection. If Ruth left now, her mom may rent the trailer for the season, and sell the Saturn to recoup her investments.

No more Head Nurse Steele threatening to fire me. The idea sent a rush of pleasure through her.

A familiar black sports car gained on her. She deliberately slowed the Saturn. Bobby McKay honked his horn, waved, and flew past her, headed toward town.

No more Bobby McKay in my face. No stupid talent show.

She arrived at the yellow brick building and parked in the employee area. The police tape on the recycle dumpster was absent, but an acrid smoky odor permeated the air.

The Viper pulled into the lot, and Miriam emerged from the passenger side. She spoke to McKay through the open window, and he sped away. Funny. He should have arrived before her.

No more Miriam. It would be a relief not to have to endure the recreation director's inane sayings and corny attire. As Ruth entered the building, she passed by the atrium filled with dusty weeping fig plants that needed watering. Scattered magazines littered the coffee table instead of in the usual neat stacks.

A group of aides on break called friendly greetings. Yolanda separated herself from them and rushed over to her.

The aide spoke in Spanish. "I made you tamales. They are in the icebox."

"That's so sweet. Aren't they a Christmas tradition?"

Yolanda grinned widely. "I made them for you."

It touched Ruth, who knew how much work they were to assemble.

"*Gracias.* Thank you. I will share them with my friends."

"Oh, your handsome *novio.*" Yolanda rolled her eyes. "Enjoy."

Boyfriend. She thanked the aide again. Tyler. Whatever their relationship, it would change if she moved to Madison. Sure, she enjoyed a good-looking man. Intelligence always attracted her. But kindness won her heart. He treated everyone from delivery people to waitstaff with respect. She'd marveled at his easy ways with animals and kids.

Ruth stretched her neck from side to side to fight the familiar knots of tension in her shoulders as she entered Hatty's room.

"I feel terrible arguing with Nellie now, God rest her soul. Such a stupid thing to fight about. Who cares so much about an election?" Hatty squinted at her. "Are you ill, Nurse Ruth?"

"I'm fine, thanks." The right side of her head throbbed.

Ruth had finished giving Hattie her medications when a wave of nausea crested over her. She hustled down the hall and ducked into the unisex restroom where the fluorescent lights bounced off the all-white tiles and fixtures. She hurried into the accessible stall, breathing hard. Kneeling, she retched, and wiped her lips with toilet paper.

She rinsed her mouth at the sink and waited for the vice-like pain to begin. Nothing happened. It occurred to her she hadn't had a migraine since she left her ex-boyfriend and came home.

Ruth stared in the mirror at her pale face, gathering herself. The door slammed open, and Debi stepped in.

I'd rather have a pap smear than see her right now.

Debi swished by her and entered the stall. Before Ruth finished scrubbing her hands, her coworker called out.

"Are you all right, Markson? I mean Ruth."

She listened for a note of the usual sarcasm, but didn't catch one. Whatever.

"Just tickety-boo." She strode from the restroom.

No more Debi. Now that thought had a genuine appeal. Bad enough seeing her at work, but living next door was reason enough to propel Ruth back to Madison.

As Ruth made her way through the corridor, Tony Bettini walked toward her, towing his oxygen tank behind him.

"Greetings, Nurse Ruth. When will the newsletter be complete?"

"Soon, Tony. I've finished the first draft."

"No rush. I know you have many important things to do."

He hadn't been so bad lately, she reflected. Still, he would be one less burr in her side if she took the new position elsewhere.

At lunch, she spotted Howard in the dining room. He ambled toward her with the use of his cane. "You look pale."

She appreciated his concern and patted his hand. "I'm okay, just up late last night."

"I heard about your mother's goose. Any more on how it happened?" After her negative reply, he scanned the room. "I know about the election."

"Luke told you?" Goosebumps rose on her arms.

Howard nodded. "After you confided in him. I'm glad you did."

Ruth scanned the room. "Why do you think they'd rig it?"

"Tell me, does Tony ever raise issues?"

She recalled their meeting. "Only about the Italian sauce."

Howard harrumphed. "That's what I mean. I keep asking questions of anyone who'll listen to me. Anything else besides what you told Luke?"

Ruth remembered her arrival at work. "Miriam rode in today with Bobby McKay."

"He gives her a lift when she drops off the recreation van for service." Howard's forehead scrunched. "Although it seems like it needs a lot of work."

"I'll have Tyler check on the van's records."

Howard squeezed her hand. "I don't know what I'd do without the two of you."

The two of you. She and Tyler were a team. If she returned to Madison, who would help solve the mystery before more residents died? She wasn't sure if she was helping or hurting the cause. So far, they weren't any closer to determining the reason for the deaths. They weren't even certain there was any criminal activity. Still, when she considered abandoning Howard and her patients, tendrils of unease crept through her.

. . .

After her shift ended, Ruth finished printing the newsletter, *The Golden Years' Ears.* She quickly reread the copy she'd written after speaking to Nellie Wilson's daughter.

Nellie Wilson, free spirit, and accomplished danseuse, died this past week while practicing her victory dance for Howard Engel, who sadly lost the election. She was in her nineties, but rarely admitted it, thank-you-very-much. The family asks in lieu of flowers, donations in Nellie's name to Greatwill of Golden Years.

Ruth added Nellie's poem beneath her obituary, along with a funny clip art of an older couple racing in their wheelchairs. She smiled, thinking Nellie would approve of the additional humor.

Her phone announced a text from Ty, wanting to know of any update on Gandalf.

She hesitated and texted, *No news may be good news.* She didn't want to share her letter from the hospital with anyone yet, especially Tyler.

Noting the time, she headed to the storeroom next to the beauty salon. An excited murmur greeted her as she rounded the corner. Residents and aides crowded the hallway. A hand-lettered sign proclaimed: *Greatwill Clothing (and Other Stuff) Exchange.*

Lillian held a large pair of scissors and handed them to Ruth.

"I didn't expect this." Ruth gaped at the crowd who held cell phones aloft, ready to take photos.

"This was your idea." Lillian tapped her foot.

"But you made it happen." Ruth snipped the red ribbon tied across the doorway and they entered the room. "Look what you did, my friend. This is amazing!"

Phones flashed and illuminated the neat rows of clothing, organized on racks by type, size, and season. Baby strollers and car seats lined the wall. Cardboard boxes held books in Spanish and English. One contained medical textbooks donated by Ruth.

Yolanda carried in an armful of women's clothing. "Mrs. Wilson's family gave these." She held out the muumuu. "This was her favorite, no?"

Ruth nodded. "I bet it will go in a flash."

Lillian took the clothing and hung the dresses where they belonged.

Boys and girls inspected the boxes of toys. One little girl looked familiar in a white tutu and tiara. "Grandma, look what I found!" She held a baby doll with a missing arm, also dressed in tulle.

Lillian sighed. "Now Princess, what did you bring to replace it with?"

Her granddaughter turned her mouth into a pout. "The box of toys there. Mama told me I *had* to." She shook the doll by its one arm, causing it to blink.

Lillian leaned over. "We share with those who have less than us, right?"

Princess shrugged and meandered to study the children's picture books.

Lillian shook her head. "I'm trying to teach her to be good."

"Didn't she blackmail you for cussing?"

"Yep." Lillian ran her fingers through her hair, pushing it into a wavelike ridge. "I didn't say my job was easy."

More people streamed in and crowded the small aisles. Others carried boxes and set them where Lillian pointed.

Ruth spotted Stanley with clothes on his arm, scrutinizing more. A boy next to him held jeans topped with a pair of new-looking Nikes. Someone tapped her arm, and she turned.

Yolanda had her hand on a young woman's shoulder. "Ruth, I would like you to meet my daughter, Maria."

"How do you do?" Ruth shook the woman's hand, noting one of her own nursing textbooks in the other.

"I've heard so much about you." Her brown eyes shone with admiration. "I want to become a nurse like you."

"Maybe you could talk to her? If you have time?" Yolanda asked. "She gets the highest marks in school."

"I'll be happy to." Ruth recalled others who had helped her with her own scholarships.

Maria thanked her with a shy smile and handed Ruth a scrap of paper with her contact information. Mother and daughter walked away, and Ruth's heart sank. How would she mentor the young woman long distance?

Smiling people packed the crowded room, who by sharing had gained something of value. *At least I make a difference here.*

CHAPTER 24

Lillian rode shotgun on the way home from Golden Years. She stared out the window of the Toad. "Thanks for the lift. Chuck needed the truck."

"No problem." Ruth drove slowly around the square. Scaffolding shrouded the old department store. "Did you know about Tyler's building?"

"Sure. Who didn't?"

"Me, for example." Ruth pumped the brakes as a maroon sedan pulled in front of her. Whoever drove it barely cleared the wheel.

As they passed Ed Foo Young's, Lillian spoke. "Is that a reason you don't think friends with benefits is a good idea?"

"What do you mean?" She glared at Lillian.

"Watch out!" The huge gunboat had come to a complete stop for apparently no reason, and Lillian cursed and grabbed the safety handle. "I guess that's another donation to my cuss fund."

"You were saying?" The Saturn crept forward.

"Well, he stays here, but you go to Madison."

"What?" Ruth slammed on her brakes and automatically checked her rearview mirror. A pickup truck behind them screeched to a halt, nearly rear-ending her car. "Why would I do that?"

"How's Gandalf doing?" Lillian looked out the window.

"We'll know more when we get home." Ruth let off the brakes and drove to the one stop-and-go light in town. It had to be red, drawing out this discussion. The Saturn idled roughly. She should probably get a tune-up as McKay had suggested, but she hated to see him again, reminding her of the almost-offer letter.

The light turned green. "Madison?" she prompted.

Lillian harrumphed. "When you go back to school. To become a doctor."

Ruth banged on the steering wheel. "Who told you?"

"No need to get your panties in a bunch. I think Mary Jo mentioned it first."

"*My mother? When?*" She stepped on the gas, and Lillian clutched her seatbelt.

"You came up with the idea to come home. None of us could figure why you were so gung-ho to save money to pay off your loans. Plus, you always played the doctor when you were little."

"That's what Aunt Cordy told me." She drove past the Piggly Wiggly into the open countryside. "If they find out at the Home, I'm in trouble."

"Those ninnies can't guess their way out of a paper bag. I wouldn't worry about it."

"And Mom has spent a bundle on me all ready."

Lillian shrugged. "You're her world. If she had the dough, she'd have paid everything for your college. In fact, we all wanted to try funding an Internet whatchamacallit to help you, but she vetoed the idea."

"No kidding?"

"Yeah, she was afraid you might be too proud to accept it, with your Only Child-itis." Lillian rubbed her neck.

"How are you feeling?" Ruth regarded Lillian's pale complexion.

"Must've slept funny." She glanced out the window. "Looks like the corn's good. Knee high by the Fourth of July."

"Lillian, Chuck didn't need the truck, did he?" She slowly drove into the entrance to Dairyland.

"Ah, no." She motioned toward the recreation building. "The Walkie-Talkies want to meet with you."

"Why am I not surprised?" Now she had more reason than ever to leave and take the job in Madison if they offered it. Her mom was giving her money, and because Ruth was so proud, she had to do it indirectly. Besides, the interference and nosiness by her foster-grannies were getting old.

"This won't be so bad." Arm in arm, Lillian and Ruth made their way to the office. In the recreation center, piles of clothing decorated a long table.

"Hi, Pookie." Aunt Cordy nodded as she tried on a turban.

"Let me guess. We're getting ready for the Talent Show."

Betty Bling held up a feathery number, a red corset costume with sequins. "What about this?"

"Nice."

"Picture it with fishnet stockings."

"On you, Betty, it will be stunning."

Ruth lifted a few G-strings and examined a pair of high-heeled pumps decorated with marabou feathers. She idly wondered at the intended wearer.

"I shall be Cordelia the Clairvoyant." Aunt Cordy reached for Ruth's hand. "I will read your future in your palm."

Ruth pulled her hand back. "I'll wait for the show."

Lillian went under the table and handed Ruth a gift-wrapped box topped with a pink bow. "Here."

"We noticed you have been redecorating your car," Betty said. "I'm all about décor." She owned Betty's Beautiful Interiors, Eureka's dubious answer to interior design.

Ruth untied the ribbon and tore open the paper. Under the tissue, she discovered a pair of fuzzy dice.

"I knit those." Lillian beamed. "Only took me a week."

"Thank you." Ruth studied the cockeyed fuchsia and black-spotted cubes. "I'll hang them from my rearview mirror." From the large box, she removed a rosy knit circle.

Cordelia beamed. "It's an angora steering wheel cover to moderate the temperature on your hands."

"It's beautiful. Thank you, Aunty."

From the bottom of the box, she pulled two hot pink carpet floor mats with black crowns inscribed with *Princess Ruth.*

"Obviously, I didn't fabricate them myself, but I had them custom made. They'll add to your design scheme." Betty winked. "And the Prince Harry motif."

Ruth hugged Betty and was enveloped in Chanel No. 5. "Thank you. They'll go well with my zebra print seat covers."

"*Très* shabby *chic*," Betty said. "Perhaps a crystal chandelier?"

"Know your limit," Lillian warned as she rubbed her jaw. "You don't want to turn the car into a death trap."

"True." Betty frowned. "Now for your musical number, Ruth. I've researched the film, and Ann-Margret wears tight black slacks and a yellow sweater during a duet with Elvis." She held up a marigold pullover. "I assume you have black leggings and flats."

Ruth rolled her eyes. "Yes, I guess."

Betty held the top up to Ruth and pulled it tight. She frowned. "Do you have a Miracle Bra?"

As Ruth bit back a response, Lillian slowly stood and wiped her perspiring brow. "Well, time for me to get Chuck's dinner ready."

"Thank you. I appreciate all your gifts. My car will be cool."

Lillian interrupted her. "Come on, kiddo, it's time to go." She rubbed her shoulder, and then her neck. "Could use a massage."

Then, as if in slow motion, Lillian bent over, vomited, and collapsed.

Ruth leaped into motion and grabbed the AED hanging on the wall. "Call 9-1-1, now!"

Cordelia stood with her mouth agape, but Betty grabbed her cell phone.

Ruth searched her memory for Lillian's medical history of a pacemaker. She took a chance. She cleared Lillian's airways, ripped open Lillian's shirt, and applied the pads.

"Analyzing."

Ruth studied the bluish tinge of Lillian's lips.

"Analyzing complete. Stand clear."

She pressed the button marked *shock*. She detected a slight change on Lillian's face, but wasn't certain.

"Continue CPR."

Ruth returned to the rhythmic pushing, the muscles in her arms tensed. Inside her head, she sang "Staying alive" and kept the beat.

"Come on, Lillian. Stay with me."

Out of the corner of her eye, Ruth spotted her mom entering the doorway, followed by Luke. Then Debi moved into her field of vision, standing a distance away.

Two paramedics stormed into the room, and one of them pulled Ruthie away from Lillian.

"You did good," he said. The other paramedic administered to Lillian.

Ruth's arms shook with adrenaline, as Mary Jo rushed to Ruth and placed her arm around her.

The two men loaded Lillian onto a gurney and then wheeled her away.

Ruth sprinted toward the ambulance. "I'm a registered nurse."

The men exchanged quick looks, and one of them nodded. "Let's get a move on."

"Right." She hopped into the ambulance. The door clanged shut.

. . .

Hours later, Ruth sat at Lillian's bedside. She checked her friend's vitals, and her eyes grew heavy. Then Ruth sensed Lillian stir, and she sprang up.

Lillian's eyes fluttered open. "Hey, kiddo."

"Hey." Ruth felt her friend's pulse. "How're you feeling?"

"Like a Mac truck ran me over." She coughed and winced. "What the hell happened?"

"You had a myocardial infarction."

Lillian asked in a fuzzy voice, "A card? What in fart?"

"A heart attack. You have had an angioplasty procedure, and the doctor's put you on medications. You'll need further tests, but so far, so good."

"All I remember is falling down." Lillian breathed heavily through the oxygen tube in her nose.

Ruth moved her hand over Lillian's forehead. "Take Doctor Kelly's lifestyle recommendations to prevent further trouble."

"No more sweets?"

Ruth smiled. "Chocolate is good for you. In moderation."

Lillian blinked. "Where's Chuck?"

Ruth explained her husband had spent the night at the hospital but was now resting in a visitor's room. Lillian's eyes fluttered closed, and Ruth waited until Lillian spoke.

"Damn. I missed Doctor Hottie-Pants."

"You're feeling better." Dr. Greg Kelly, Tyler's dad, had half of Walworth County's Medicare set crushing on him. "You'll have to wait till tomorrow."

Lillian sighed. "His son is as good-looking. You're lucky."

Ruth had a twinge of guilt as she lied. "Yes. I am."

"He'll make a good husband."

"Yes, he will." For Ms. Right.

"I've seen the way he looks at you. He loves you." Lillian opened her eyes. "Don't hurt him."

Lillian fell asleep before Ruth replied.

Birdsong greeted Ruth as she left the hospital. The sunrise was a rosy glow in the tree-lined distance. She inhaled the aroma of freshly mown grass and clover as she jumped into her car.

A tornado of texts had swirled all night to keep her mother—and therefore the Walkie-Talkies—updated with Lillian's progress. Yawning, she rubbed her eyes. She'd also sent a text to

Golden Years, taking the day off, explaining the emergency, wondering briefly if Steele would consider it an infraction.

So what? Lillian is alive.

Rolling down the Saturn's window, she let the warm wind blow over her face. Dew-drenched spider webs decorated thriving crops. Cows nursed calves in the fields. Black-eyed Susan blossomed in the early morning sunshine.

She drove into Dairyland, smiling at the campers outdoors who were enjoying their coffee. As she rounded the bend toward her trailer, she spotted Luke on her porch with Gandalf cuddled next to him.

He grinned at her. "Good morning."

"It is a good morning, isn't it?" Ruth pet the goose, running her hand over his soft white feathers. "How's my boy?" The gander clucked softly. She took the proffered cup of steaming tea from Luke and sipped it gratefully.

"Gandalf was in shock, but we got him to the vet just in time. Lucky you found him when you did." He smiled. "Your mother is beyond grateful."

A rush of satisfaction flowed through her. "I'm glad I helped."

"Check out your bounty." He pointed to the pile of covered dishes that graced the deck.

"What's this?" Next to her, behind the tower of casseroles, she found a bouquet of filigreed Queen Anne's Lace, delicate pink peonies, and her grandma's Peace roses. The note read, "Thank you so much. We don't know what we would do without you." Chuck, Rupert and Cordelia, Betty and Bernie, and her mom and Luke had signed it.

Ruth glowed with pride. "That's so nice of you all. When I was giving CPR, it surprised me you didn't step in."

"Why would I?" Luke regarded her. "You did a remarkable job. Even Debi commented on how well you did."

Pleasure at his praise rushed through her. "Thanks."

"Lillian might well have passed if it weren't for you."

"And Mom's foresight to buy the AED." She reached over and absently pet Gandalf's head.

Luke took a sip from his coffee mug. "Your mom and I lost Betty's fiancé, John."

Ruth nodded, remembering how upset her mother had been when he'd died in Dairyland of a heart attack.

"Your training served you well."

Ruth's eyes filled with tears. "I couldn't stand to lose Lillian."

Luke stood and patted her arm. "You need a well-deserved rest."

A surge of fatigue washed over her. "You're right."

Inside the trailer, Ruth stripped off her scrubs and showered until the hot water ran out. After feeding Oreo, she shut the blinds and fell into a deep sleep. She awoke around five, hungry. She set a shepherd's pie in the oven and then checked her messages.

Texts from Tyler congratulated her for saving Lillian. Howard's message praised her. It filled Ruth with gratitude that she was there for her dear friend at the right time.

She reread the letter from the Madison hospital. Lillian labeled her as having "Only Child-itis." "Onlies" often were "First-Borns" on steroids, driven to successful careers, highly motivated, responsible, older than their years. Controlling. Perfectionists.

Did she decide for others instead of letting them choose for themselves? She'd run from Madison in the first place to break from her previous relationship. Now, was she running again?

She wasn't much of a fatalist. Instead, she believed life was a series of small choices until they became large moves. If she left now, she would be a quitter, leaving Howard and her patients to fend for themselves.

And Tyler. Was she running from him too, afraid of the consequences of an intimate relationship?

She was clearing her inbox email folder when she spotted a message with no subject. Opening it, she gasped.

It showed a cartoon bird on its back. Below it: YOUR GOOSE IS COOKED BITCH.

CHAPTER 25

Ruth rushed to the deck where she found Gandalf curled on her Crocs, illuminated by a full moon. A cool breeze scattered a few of his feathers like snow. He lifted his head and gave a small honk. She looked across the way to the office with the nearest security camera. She took a piece of lettuce and opened the front door of her trailer. Gandalf nipped at the treat, and she lured him inside. Relieved, she forwarded the threatening email to Tyler.

Her phone rang in less than a minute.

"How are you, Ruthie?" Tyler's voice was laden with concern.

"Gandalf and I are fine." She reached over and petted the goose's head.

He promised to look for the sender. "But I don't think I'll find them."

"How can that be?" A jolt of anxiety shot through her. If Tyler couldn't identity the culprit, who could?

He explained they used a free email account, and he suspected a proxy email server would keep their identity secret. "But I'm forwarding it to Luke."

Ruth didn't argue and wished him goodnight. Weariness settled on her like a fog. She grabbed a comforter off her bed and fashioned a nest on the kitchen floor. Once Gandalf settled, she curled up next to him.

. . .

After her shift ended the following day, Ruth ventured to Tony Bettini's room with her copies of *The Golden Years' Ears*, where he distributed the newsletter to all the pickup points. She rapped on the shut door.

"*Entrare.* Come on in."

Frank Sinatra crooned in the background as she pushed open the door. Clad in his usual tracksuit, Tony reclined in his La-Z-Boy, speaking to a woman with her back to Ruth.

"Oh. I didn't mean to interrupt. I can leave these here." Ruth showed him the newsletters.

"No, no. Don't rush out, Nurse Ruth. This is my daughter, Caprice."

The plus-sized brunette turned around and smiled.

Ruth was stunned as the unforgettable name hit her. Caprice! She composed herself quickly.

"How do you do? I'm Ruth Markson." She stared at the woman, remembering.

Caprice's face darkened, then paled. "Nice to meet you."

"Well, I must go," Ruth apologized, breathing hard as she turned to leave.

As the door clicked shut, she heard Tony say, "What was that all about?" to the woman who had helped ruin her family.

. . .

Ruth waited in her car for Caprice to exit the building. She carefully followed Tony's daughter, staying far enough behind all the way to The West End Tap. Ruth had avoided the tavern since returning home, but seeing Caprice brought everything back. She turned down the potholed street, determined to confront the memory, and parked her Saturn across the street.

Ruth studied the West End Tap as Caprice disappeared inside. The old volleyball net was gone, and morning glory vines wound their way along the sides of the peeling white clapboard. Flanked by a vacant storefront and a weed-infested lot, the bar rippled like a mirage in the late-afternoon glare.

As a kid, Ruth had often gone to the tavern with her parents, where her dad taught her how to play Pac-Man. But by the time she was in her teens, her mom avoided the Tap, and her father spent more and more time with his drinking buddies.

Ruth had sensed her parents' tension and tried unsuccessfully to ignore it. They never fought openly, but the distance between them grew larger every day until they appeared to be reluctant roommates rather than husband and wife.

In her senior year of high school, Bobby McKay asked her to prom. When she refused him, he'd punched her locker. A few days later, she'd found a note taped over the dent that read *Your dad likes more than just drinks at the West End Tap.* Bobby smirked more often afterward.

That same night, Ruth borrowed her grandpa's pickup truck and drove to her father's haunt. She waited with sweating palms. Her father exited the bar with a mini-skirted brunette clinging to his arm, one of the regular servers, Caprice Bettini. Ruth ducked lower into the cab and watched as they kissed. Then her dad hopped into his vintage Corvette and sped away.

Ruth's hands shook with fury. She wanted to follow him and run him off the road, demanding answers. Had he promised Caprice he'd get a divorce? But Ruth knew she needed to think this over first. Before she had a chance to confront him, he'd been diagnosed with pancreatic cancer.

Her dad stayed with his family as he wasted away. If Caprice was naïve enough to believe he would leave Mary Jo, it must have crushed her.

A hot wind blew in across Ruth's arm, rousing her from her reverie. It was all history now and besides, Caprice looked pitiful, a middle-aged woman with few prospects in life, a job in a run-down tavern.

Ruth put the Saturn in gear with shaking hands but braked as the Viper pulled into the bar's parking lot. But Bobby didn't get out. Curious, she waited. Two teenagers arrived in a red pickup truck, their rap music booming down the street. One kid remained in the vehicle with the engine running, while the other ducked into the Viper. After a few minutes, he exited and hopped into the truck. They sped off. McKay showed no sign of leaving.

If Bobby was dealing drugs, where did he get his supply?

Ruth hoped he didn't spot her as she quietly pulled out and headed toward the cemetery, weary but wiser.

. . .

The setting sun cast long shadows as Ruth turned into Our Lady Cemetery. Fourth of July decorations adorned neat graves, and their ancient tombstones leaned toward one another like old friends gossiping.

She parked by her maternal grandparents' graves. Exiting the car, she stood at the side-by-side markers. Both had vases of artificial flowers studded with small American flags. Her mother must've taken care of the decorations.

"I miss you both," she said aloud. Birds twittered in the gnarled ash branches above her, their shade dappling her arms.

She walked toward the newer section of the cemetery. There were fewer mature trees, and all the markers were flat against the ground in the modern fashion. It took a minute to get her bearings, but she easily found her father's grave. His name and dates of his birth and death were carved in the granite. Ruth did the quick calculation; he was fifty-six when he died. Too young. His grave was decorated exactly like her grandparents' plots. Her mother must've arranged care for both gravesites. Since it was impossible to keep an affair secret for long in Eureka, her mother, Mary Jo, certainly knew about Caprice. Did that mean she had forgiven her husband's transgressions?

Her mom called her late one night when Ruth was away at school. Theo, Ruth's lover, had answered her phone. Mary Jo didn't know Theo existed and pressured Ruth to meet him, but Ruth let slip Theo's marital status. The exchange degenerated into anger and Ruth, resenting Mary Jo's lecture, blurted out she'd known about her dad's affair and her mom had no right to advise her on relationships. They'd never discussed it again.

Kneeling, she touched the cold stone, tracing "Loving Father" with her finger and paused at "and Husband." Guilt rushed over Ruth for her defensive response to her mother. She needed to apologize and not ignore the exchange.

"I still miss you, Daddy." She wished she could talk to him, try to understand what he did, make some peace with it.

"I once was lost and now I'm found," she sang aloud and then allowed grief to overwhelm her.

The opportunity to resolve issues with him had passed. Now she must deal with the living and do her best to right any wrongs. Her dad had wounded her mother to the core. Luke had helped her mom heal and rebuild Dairyland and her life. He'd been nothing but good and kind to Ruth, and she vowed to stop comparing him to her father and let him into her heart, not as a replacement, but as an addition.

Ruth stared at her dad's grave. She had been running all her life to avoid confronting the uncomfortable. No way would she leave until she was ready. She took out her phone and pulled up the email she'd composed earlier.

Thank you for thinking of me, however I cannot follow up with an interview.

She hit the "send" button.

. . .

Ruth drove to Lillian's and found her at her picnic table with her Chihuahua on her lap. She looked gaunt, and her white, short-cropped hair lay flat against her head.

Lillian attempted to stand.

"Stay put," Ruth said as she walked to her friend and kissed her on the cheek. Taco attempted to include her in his doggy kisses, but she moved away in time. Her friend's hands shook as she stroked her quivering dog.

"How are you doing?" Concern flooded her as she regarded the dark circles under Lillian's eyes. She flashed to the image of her friend on the ground, her face ghastly pale.

"Doc Kelly says I'm okay." Lillian looked down at her dog. "I guess I am." She kept taking deep breaths, as if to test her ability to do so.

Ruth touched her friend's arm. "Look, it's normal to experience some anxiety after a major illness."

Lillian screwed up her face. "Anxiety? I'm waiting for the other shoe to drop."

Ruth put her arm around Lillian, skillfully avoiding the dog. "Talk to me."

Lillian complained she noticed every twinge in her chest. "What if you're not here to use the machine on me?"

"I've trained the others. We'll all be watching out for you." Ruth squeezed her shoulder. "What else?"

Lillian looked hopefully at Ruth. "Doc Kelly told me to follow a Mediterranean Diet. Does that mean a lot of pizzas?"

"Vegetarian ones are best."

Lillian made a face. "I can have fish, which I hate, except at a Friday fish fry. With French fries and creamy coleslaw."

"No. Deep fried is a no-no. How do you like vegetables?"

Lillian's face fell. "Only with lots of butter or cream of mush-room soup."

"Fruit?"

"I love taffy apples. Does that count?"

"But he told you to have a glass of wine at night?"

"Yes. A little red was okay, even good for me."

"And he didn't say you couldn't have anything you like, only in moderation, right?"

Lillian nodded. "I can even resume normal sexual activities."

Ruth half-smiled at her. "In moderation."

Lillian sniffed. "I'm not like Betty, working her way through the *Kama Sutra*. She'll be the death of poor Bernie yet."

"But he'll die with a smile on his face, won't he?" Ruth patted her friend's hand. "A wise lady once told me life isn't worth living without some fun."

"What are you saying?"

"Do what Dr. Kelly tells you, but don't forget to enjoy yourself as much as you can along the way."

Lillian set her dog on the ground, who ran circles around the picnic table. She hugged Ruth hard. "You're going to be a brilliant doctor."

"Thanks, Lillian. I hope so."

Lillian regarded her with eyes, regaining their sparkle. "How's the deal with Tyler going? Any benefits yet?"

Ruth imagined the X-rated conversations of the Walkie-Talkies regarding her love life.

"He's still looking for Ms. Right."

Lillian snorted. "Bull-pucky. The way Tyler looks at you would melt an ice cream cone from fifty yards."

"He didn't contradict me when I gave him permission to keep looking. Anyway, I'm leaving next fall for med school. He's signed on for two years at his building. Do you remember what you told me in the hospital? About Tyler?"

"No, I was pretty doped up. Speaking of the devil." Lillian reached into her purse, pulling out a prescription bottle. "I don't want these. They make me kind of goofy. And they bind me up real good."

"I'll properly dispose of them." Ruth examined the OxyContin bottle. They were worth a small fortune on the street where the drug problem continued to grow. "Kids are overdosing on these."

Lillian sniffed. "I hate the notion of someone addicted to the stuff. What did I say to you in the hospital?"

"I don't remember," Ruth lied.

Chuck called out from inside the trailer. "Dinner's on, honey."

Lillian made a face. "I'm afraid I'm doomed to eat healthy stuff the rest of my life. Rupert was in my kitchen with his organic crap for hours." She turned toward her husband. "What's on the menu, honey?"

Chuck called back in a load voice. "Tofurky. With roasted vege-table and chickpea stew."

"Torfucky." Lillian grasped Ruth's arm dramatically. "See what I mean?"

Ruth laughed. "Go enjoy a glass of wine. It'll cover up the bland taste."

"And you, my dear, should take your own advice and enjoy Tyler while you can."

"That's one approach." Ruth nodded. "But I'm afraid of who'll get hurt."

Probably both of us.

CHAPTER 26

Ruth carried Lillian's unused OxyContin to work the next day, intending to give the bottle to Nurse Steele for DEA pickup and disposal. She made it as far as the Head Nurse's door. Then, a question occurred to her. Oxy was worth a fortune on the street. How were unused drugs kept until pickup, and who was responsible in the interim?

She stuffed Lillian's prescription bottle into her computer bag. During her first break, she headed toward an alcove in the unused visitor area and booted her personal laptop. She easily signed into the system using Tyler's ghost password, allowing her to navigate without leaving a trace.

Footsteps. Peering around the spindly Ficus, she stared down the vacant hallway. The drone of television programs came from open doorways, along with muffled snores. Sunlight poured into the window behind her, which framed a large elm. Below, raised bed gardens dotted the lawns. Residents in wheelchairs tended their tomatoes, eggplants, and zucchini. Another program instituted by Howard designed to give them healthier food.

She checked the drug inventory, restricted to the Head Nurse. Studying the transaction history, she found purchase orders, receipts to inventory, and then the disbursements to the daily medicine trays. Transactions confirmed each patient received their medication, but no data regarding unused drugs.

She scrolled to the date of Nellie's demise when the soft swish of boots interrupted. She slammed the lid as Debi peered around the plant.

"Ah, there you are." Nurse Peterson scanned the area. "Nice. Fairly secluded." She pulled up one of the hard orange plastic chairs. "What have you found?"

"I don't know what you're talking about."

"Well, it's a process of elimination. Either you're watching porn during work or snooping around the computer." Debi regarded her with ever-changing eyes. Today they were murky green.

"You won't find me in the system where I don't belong."

Debi nodded. "Probably true. Your boyfriend's way too smart to let that happen."

Ruth crossed and uncrossed her legs. "I was shopping. On my break."

"Is that how you found the parrot granny cam?"

Ruth's heart sped up. How had Debi figured it out?

Debi continued, as if reading her mind. "I recognized it from the luau. Your boyfriend was wearing it on his shoulder." Ruth remained silent. "Then I watched the video of Betty's wardrobe malfunction." She paused. "The next day the parrot showed up in Nellie Wilson's room."

"It's a toy. I gave it to Nellie because she collected stuffed animals."

Debi gave a small laugh. "Right. And I have a swamp to sell you if you believe it." She leaned forward. "What did you discover?"

Ruth bit the inside of her lip and glanced up to find Yolanda briskly walking toward them.

"Nurse Ruth. I'm glad I found you," Yolanda said in Spanish. "The Big Nurse is as angry as a hornet. She is using your name."

Ruth packed up her computer. "Do you know why Steele is looking for me?"

Debi shrugged. "Don't have a clue."

Liar. She hurried down the hall and knocked on the office door. Her heart pounded, worried Debi had outed her about the granny cams and her sleuthing around the computer system.

"Where were you?" Nurse Steele's face was red.

"I was on break." Ruth wiped her palms on her scrubs, and surveyed the usually neat office. Copies of her newsletter littered the Head Nurse's desk.

"Obviously." Steele held up a crumpled *Golden Years' Ears*. "What on earth did you have in mind when you wrote this?" She stabbed at the newsletter.

Ruth squinted at the document. "Oh. Nellie's obituary." Her heart rate slowed. At least the reprimand wasn't about the parrot granny cam.

"I must approve all material before publication."

"It's cute."

Steele clenched her jaw. "Cute, is it?" She read from the paper. "Her only regret was not seeing her candidate, Howard Engel, elected so she could perform a victory dance."

Ruth's stomach twisted. "That's what her friends told me."

A vein visibly throbbed on the Head Nurse's temple. "Do you realize what you've done? Howard Engel is demanding a recount of the election results."

Ruth bit her bottom lip. Good for him. They weren't able to recount missing ballots. "I wasn't aware of that."

"The original documents are long gone. The next step might be a run-off election." Her hand shook as she pointed at Ruth. "You've stirred up everything since you arrived."

Ruth suppressed a smile. "I didn't mean to cause a problem."

"Whatever you meant doesn't matter. I was afraid to hire you with your family connection. I shouldn't have listened to Doctor

Kelly. I want to remind you the probation period doesn't end for three more weeks." She slammed her fist on the desk. "One tiny infraction and you're terminated. Do you understand?"

"Yes, ma'am."

. . .

After her shift ended, Ruth knocked on Howard's apartment door. When he opened the door, she blurted, "Debi suspects we've been snooping, and Steele's pissed about another election."

"Come on in, honey." He gave her a brief hug. "Lemonade?"

She nodded, and he returned with the ice-cold glasses.

"Now tell me about it." He regarded her with warm brown eyes.

She sipped the sweet-tart drink with a shaking hand. "I'm afraid Debi's figured out our granny cam plan." She recounted most of their conversation. "And she suspects Tyler and I were in the computer system."

"Did you confirm or deny the accusations?"

"Neither. She caught me off guard."

"Perhaps she was fishing." Howard grimaced.

"I figured Debi had told Steele, and I was getting fired for snooping." She recounted the conversation with her supervisor. "Why did you ask for a recount?"

Howard shrugged. "Wasn't me. A bunch of my friends insisted. They took a straw poll and can't understand how Tony won."

"They fixed the election. I suspect Miriam and Steele are in cahoots to keep you from becoming reelected." She fidgeted on the leather sofa.

"Are they desperate enough to start the fire in the dumpster to get rid of the evidence?"

"We know someone set it deliberately." Luke had told her about the fire chief's findings. Her phone rang with a text notification. "Tyler's found the records for maintenance of the recreation van. It shows a normal amount of servicing."

Howard harrumphed. "It's in the shop more than it's out."

"Why is Miriam always taking the recreation van to McKay's garage?"

Soft jazz infused the air as Ruth took in the apartment. He'd updated the family collage with her picture from her mom and Luke's wedding.

With a shrug, he nodded toward the collage. "Do you like the one I chose?"

"It's sweet." She studied the photos. "You still have a few empty frames."

He nodded. "Room for when the family grows. I had to remove a few pictures when Luke's wife left him and took his girls with her to Chicago. Couldn't stand to look at her."

Ruth winced. She'd heard the story of his exercise-crazed ex who had left him for her personal trainer. "She's the one who lost out."

"Luke's happy now. Of course, it would've all been different if he took Mary Jo to the prom. Instead, somehow, they got their wires crossed, and he ended up going with Miss Buns of Steel."

Ruth hadn't known her mom and Luke went that far back. She wondered what else she didn't know about her family's past. "Wow. One date and it all might have been different."

"Lots of times, our paths diverge with the smallest of decisions." Howard sipped his lemonade.

Ruth checked her watch and finished the rest of her drink. "Have to run. I go to kickboxing class tonight."

Howard placed a gnarled hand on hers. "Be careful. I fear we're stirring up a hornet's nest."

"That's what Yolanda called Steele, mad as a hornet."

"I once ran over a ground nest of yellow jackets in the tractor. Got stung twenty-two times. Good thing I'm not allergic to them or I would've kicked the bucket." Howard scowled. "And once they're angry, they'll follow you anywhere to kill you, even if they die in the attempt."

The employee parking area was empty when Ruth left Howard's apartment. The sun had lost its intense heat, and shadows had lengthened. She pulled up short. Her car was off kilter, and she soon discovered why.

Dammit. The rear left tire was flat, the second time in a few weeks. After she'd placed the spare on the car, she decided she'd need to have the damaged one fixed and not risk traveling without a backup tire. She sent a quick text to Tyler, asking him to review the parking lot security footage for the last hour.

At McKay's garage, Ruth spotted the Golden Years recreation van parked beside the building beneath his cheesy pun sign. She honored a hunch. Until Tyler examined the security videos, there was no way she'd go to McKay's with the evidence. She drove home, intending to take the tire to a shop in Lake Geneva the next day.

When she arrived home, she stared at a message from Tyler. The news wasn't good. She studied the grainy video clip he'd attached. Someone had been near her car, the figure's face shielded with a hoodie.

.   .   .

The next morning, Ruth jogged with Luke along the winding asphalt road at Dairyland Acres.

As they rounded a bend in the road, Luke turned to Ruth. "How was your kickboxing class last night?"

"Good. The teacher says I'm a natural."

"I bet." Luke's smile dimples showed. "Do they go over self-defense, too?"

She nodded and took a swig from her water bottle. "I need to finish early this morning."

"No problem." He checked his fitness watch. "How come?"

"I have to drop off a tire in Lake Geneva before work. I can't leave it with McKay." She then told him how she'd found the Toad with a flat.

"Nail?"

She shook her head. "Nothing obvious."

"We'll examine the security tapes."

She hesitated. "Tyler already did. There was someone near my car while I visited Howard."

"Could you identify the person?"

"No. Whoever it was wore a hoodie."

"Perhaps our expert can get a general description."

He didn't chastise her or Tyler and then she described McKay with the two teenage boys at the West End Tap.

Luke stopped short. "We suspect he's a small-time dealer, probably pot. He only works with friends who won't say a thing." Luke resumed running. "I don't have the resources to launch a sting operation. We hope he does something stupid, and we can catch him in the act."

They ended the run at her trailer, next to the Toad.

"May I see the tire?"

She nodded her assent and opened the trunk for him.

Luke inspected it, rotating it methodically. "I can save you a trip to Lake Geneva. Let's go to the house. I have an air compressor in the garage."

As she drove up the road, she asked, "They only let the air out?"

He nodded. "I'll take the parrot granny cam, too."

"Sure. It's right on the rear seat."

Luke turned around. "Don't see it."

A shiver shot through her. "Petey was there."

"When did you notice it last?"

"I haven't paid attention," Ruth said.

"Do you keep your car locked?"

She shook her head, noting his severe expression. "I will from now on."

"I'll patrol the lot myself for the time being. In the meantime, be careful."

Ruth thought of Steele's ire, McKay's hostility, Debi's disdain, and Miriam's fake niceties. "Sure, Luke."

Too late. The hornet nest had been stirred, and they wouldn't stop until someone had been stung too many times to count.

CHAPTER 27

A Fourth of July tangerine sun rose through a gray mist. Ruth tried to recall the adage about sunrises and sunsets. Was it "Red sky in morning, sailors take warning?" And did orange count as red?

She was determined to take a holiday from the worry of Golden Years and enjoy a day off. She walked across the road to the office, clipped the Stars and Stripes on the flagpole, and hoisted it to the top where it lay limp. Her mom had assigned her the job this morning, and she warmed at the recollection of raising the flag with her grandfather as a child.

The campground came to life, signaled by a whiff of pancakes on the grill, two sleepy children wrapped in beach towels trudging toward the bathhouse, and a couple in folding chairs outside their tent sipping coffee. A man strode by, walking a Pomeranian. When he waved at her, she waved back.

Kathy, the Workamper, arrived to open the office, and nodded a greeting to Ruth.

"Supposed to storm tonight." Kathy busied herself counting the cash in the register's drawer.

"Typical Wisconsin Fourth, isn't it? We always just hope the rain will hold off until the fireworks are over," Ruth said. "I have to judge the contest before I head over to the parade in town."

"Your mom gave you the tough job."

Ruth shrugged. "I don't mind. The kids are cute."

The sun had burned off the fog, and the temperature was rising accordingly. Ruth adjusted her sun visor with the Dairyland logo of a cartoon Holstein and RV camper. A small crowd milled around the building. Tricycles with red, white, and blue crepe paper threaded through their spokes sat behind two wheelers with silver streamers on handlebars.

Parents stood next to Red Flyer wagons filled with toddlers. A petite blonde girl on a tricycle was dressed as the Statue of Liberty, complete with a foam crown. A scrawny red-headed boy wore an Uncle Sam top hat, leading a white terrier with a matching miniature hat strapped to its head. It would be a tough to choose a winner.

The parade took off with the ringing of bike bells. Guests had set up lawn chairs along the route and waved and tossed candy at the procession. The group slowed every time a child bent to pick up the goodies and, as a result, the parade stretched out.

Ruth followed up the rear and found the participants waiting where they'd started. The terrier had twisted its leash around a wagon wheel and one of the littlest toddlers was crying, her mom trying to calm her with a pacifier.

From the porch she waved her hands, requesting silence. "Thank you for taking part in our Independence Day parade and contest. You all look patriotic." She awarded the third-place ribbon to a boy with a bike covered with crepe paper and stars. Second place went to the Statue of Liberty.

"And this is for you." Ruth knelt by Uncle Sam and his miniature canine version. The terrier licked her hand as she gave the boy the blue ribbon.

"What do you say to the nice lady?" his mom prompted.

He adjusted his askew goatee. "Thank you, ma'am."

"You're welcome. I like your freckles."

"I don't." The boy looked down and frowned. "The kids make fun of them."

A swell of pity washed over her as Ruth recalled the teasing Tyler had endured in school. "They're a sign of intelligence."

He looked up at her, hopefully. "No kidding?"

"You bet. The smartest person I know has red hair and freckles." She recalled her mother's comments about hoped-for grandchildren with Tyler.

As the kids dispersed, she checked the time. She'd have to hustle to Tyler's loft if she wanted to catch the town parade with him.

. . .

Downtown, the citizens of Eureka lined the square beneath a Federal-blue sky. Warm wind blew from the southwest, ruffling American flags along the town's parade route. Tyler and Ruth nursed carryout Chai teas from Lucy's Café and rested their elbows on the windowsills of Tyler's empty apartment, furnished only with a sorry-looking futon, which Ruth surmised was a leftover from Tyler's college days. Painter's tape outlined future walls and fireplace. Through the open window, the aroma of grilled meat wafted in from the annual Beer and Brat Fest.

Tyler gestured toward the barbeque. "They're donating the proceeds to the Main Street Program."

Ruth recalled the legend of how the town came to be in 1820, when an early settler found a spring in the center of the future square and shouted "Eureka!"

"We need some water balloons up here." She nodded at the crowd below. "There are our moms."

Mary Jo sat with Joy Kelly in their traditional folding chairs, sipping from Styrofoam cups, their heads bent and deep in conversation. They might be planning the next parade or developing more ideas for the Main Street program. Or they could've been plotting to get their children together permanently.

Tyler grinned. "We could easily make a direct hit, figuring the trajectory."

"We'd better not." She leaned closer to him, resting her arm against his. "Though it is tempting."

Tyler gestured toward a far corner of the square. "Look who's here."

Ruth squinted in the direction he'd pointed. "Debi. Dressed like a nun, relatively." Ruth scanned the crowd. "I wonder if those are her kids. She doesn't have custody of them. I wonder why." A young girl and boy walked up to Debi, holding cotton candy. McKay stood in the square, surrounded by his cronies. "And she's not with Bobby."

He craned his neck. "Interesting."

As was the custom, the American Legion led the way, some marching, others riding in a shiny Model T borrowed from the local car dealership.

Amid the veterans, Ruthie spotted a familiar face. "There's Howard!"

Their moms below stood and cheered. Luke's father grinned, saluting them as he strode past. Ruth put two fingers in her mouth and whistled loudly.

Tyler stuffed a finger in each ear. "Who needs eardrums?"

Howard looked up and waved.

Various-sized girls in brown or green matching outfits carried handmade troop signs. Ruth recalled one parade when she was about eight years old, straggling along, her sash backwards and her shirt untucked. Her dad, though, had acted as though she was the star of the entire event.

Their counterparts, the Boy Scouts, followed behind, holding banners, or grabbing at their shirt collars. Ruth nudged Tyler. "I remember it petrified you to let the American flag touch the ground."

"Scout Leader Browne told me I'd be expatriated if I did."

"I doubt he used those exact words." Ruth looked at his handsome profile.

He turned to her and held her gaze. "Maybe he threatened to call the flag police?"

The Fire Department trucks' sirens screamed, sending a chill through Ruth, followed by paramedics. Young kids along the route waved their pennants and clapped their approval.

The Dairy Celebration float appeared from around the square's corner, towed by a farmer's tractor. Festooned in tissue paper, it featured a life-sized statue of a Holstein, gazing contentedly at the crowd. Arranged around it, five high school girls clad in billowing prom dresses surrounded the Milk Day Queen, waving in proper royal fashion.

"Your mom was a queen, wasn't she?" Her mother's best friend was the center of social life in Eureka in high school and maintained her position even now.

"Yeah, but don't remind her. Looking at a cow for hours and waving like a zombie left her with permanent psychological scars."

"She seems to have overcome them." Ruth regarded his youthful mother animatedly greeting passersby.

Sirens whooped, and Luke rode in a black and white squad car driven by one of his officers.

"I think he sees us." She waved from the window.

"There's a surprise ending."

"Yeah?" Hard to believe since the Eureka Fourth of July Parade format hadn't changed since her childhood.

Tyler pointed toward the street corner. "Yep. There they are!"

Five tall phallic figures emerged, with heads like Easter Island statues wearing hats. As they neared, Ruthie made out the costumes of the sneaker-clad runners. The crowd along the route cheered and waved American flags as the enormous sausages sprinted by.

She shook her head in wonderment. "How did we ever get the Brewers' Racing Sausages in our tiny parade?"

"Our mayor is distantly related to a former racing bratwurst."

"I can believe it." They looked at one another for a moment and then burst into laughter. "Thanks. I needed that." Ruth wiped a tear from her eye.

When the finale passed, the crowd dispersed as quickly as they had assembled, presumably rushing off to their cookouts and picnics.

He nudged her. "The sausages are giving autographs."

"I wonder if they sign in mustard."

"Certainly not ketchup. That's not Sconnie." He grinned and his smile dimple showed. The aroma of brats and corn he'd picked up for them at the roast below wafted through the room. "Are you hungry?"

"I bet you are." She lightly punched his arm.

"Guilty as charged." He reached into a cooler and handed her a New Glarus Spotted Cow Ale and then doled out their lunches from brown paper bags. He spread extra napkins, and they took seats on the futon.

Ruthie munched on a row of roasted corn and licked butter off her lips. Tyler's gaze lingered on her face. Then he tore it away to regard his own lunch.

"Good, isn't it?" He chewed vigorously on an ear of corn.

"Never had a better one. And yours?"

Ruth noticed Tyler looking at her long, tanned legs in her running shorts as he took a bite of his brat. "Hmmm."

The tension thrummed between them as they sat on the futon.

"You have a dab of mustard. Right here." She reached over and rubbed a thumb on the corner of his mouth.

"Thanks." His gaze held hers.

"Is that where the fireplace is going?" *It's as hot in here as if there's a roaring fire.* She wondered if he too could feel the waves of heat playing dodge ball with them.

"Yeah. It's a gas, wood combo, you know, sometimes it's hard to get firewood up three stories."

"Romantic." She wiped her lips with a napkin and set her paper plate aside. "It's nice, Ty."

"I'm so glad you approve." He reached over and held her hand. His thumb trailed along her pulse point.

She laced her fingers through his and set their hands next to her bare thigh.

He swallowed hard. "Looks like you've been running. And kickboxing."

She released her hair from its ponytail. "Uh-huh. I like the connection to my body."

"I love your hair like that." His green eyes stared into hers.

"Thanks." Ruth took in the high ceilings, the exposed brick walls. "This will be a perfect bachelor pad."

"Or an apartment for a couple."

"Oh. You mean you and Ms. Right might live here?"

He sat back. "What?"

She ran a hand down his muscled arm. "Ms. Right. Describe this person."

"Well, she's smart, funny, and beautiful."

"And are you still looking?" Ruth raised her eyebrows.

"I think I've found her."

"And where might that be? Eureka?"

"Just outside of town." A flush crept up Tyler's neck.

"On a farm?" she teased.

He winced. "In an RV park?"

"Oh, my god. It's Debi!" She opened her eyes wide in feigned surprise.

After a shocked moment, he laughed at her joke. "You know she's you."

"Why did you lie to me? I almost didn't take dating you seriously."

"I didn't want to screw up our friendship."

"From now on, let's have an agreement. Absolute honesty. Can you do that?" She looked anxiously at his handsome face. "I mean it. I've had enough lies to last a lifetime."

He held her hand and traced it across his heart. "I promise."

"You're a lousy liar anyway, just so you know."

"I haven't had much practice."

"Good. Keep it that way." She ran a hand through his thick auburn hair. "Now, there's one more thing to iron out."

"What's that?"

She took a deep breath. "I am leaving for school in a year. I need you to promise me, no matter what happens, you will support me in my goal." She hesitated. "If we become closer, I need to know you won't stop me, or even try to influence me otherwise."

He grabbed her hand again, traced his heart, then kissed each finger. "I do."

"Can I be Ms. Right-Now?"

"Ruthie, you always have been and always will be right for me." Tyler leaned closer and framed her face with his firm hands. He looked into her eyes and kissed her. He smelled so good, a combination of soap and clean clothes.

She returned his kisses and smoothed her hands under his T-shirt across his flat, toned stomach. When she moved lower under his belt, he moaned. Standing, she lifted off her tank top and heard his sharp intake of breath. Then she slid out of her shorts. In her pink lacy bra and matching cheeky panties, she twirled for his inspection.

"Do you like my new lingerie?"

"You look delicious." His green eyes darkened.

She swallowed hard. If his appetite for sex was anything like his was for food, they were in for quite an evening.

"You like the color?"

"The pink is nice, but my favorite color is your alabaster skin."

She obliged and slipped out of her remaining clothes and stood before him naked, her long, golden hair cascading around her shoulders.

He shook his head. "You are heart-stoppingly beautiful."

She grinned. "Do you have an AED in the building?"

"Not yet. I should add one to my shopping list."

"Or we might try mouth-to-mouth instead." She knelt next to him and set about removing his clothes, marveling at his cut body. She traced his firm chin, ran her hand down his arm. "Do you remember what I like?"

He reached into the back pocket of his shorts and removed a condom from his wallet, then pulled her on top of him, nuzzling her collarbone. "I have an eidetic memory."

She shuddered as he skillfully kissed her ear. "That you do." Desire flooded through her limbs, slow and thrilling.

He kissed her, his tongue pushing gently into her mouth, which she opened wider. His hands ran over every inch of her as if memorizing her body. She moaned, and a warm fluttering started in her belly. She ached to be closer to him with the full length of her body.

"I need you. Now."

"We have all night." He kissed her firm, small breasts, her nipples already tingling from his skillful caresses. "I want to taste you."

Her skin grew damp, and she gasped as his mouth moved down her torso, lazily kissed her belly and nibbled his way to her thighs. She moaned and cupped her hands behind his head, pulling him closer, letting herself forget everything but the pleasurable sensations running through her.

She closed her eyes. Never had she been so cherished. Heat rose in her, and she traced his strong shoulders with her fingertips. Her back arched, her toes curled, her belly tightened. The tension was almost unbearable and then, one last aria of ecstasy pulsed through her, grew note after note until she cried out in one long chord.

Pulling him up, her eyes fluttered open and met his look. Something shifted inside her. She surrendered, no longer protecting herself, and she drew him even closer. As she relaxed her guard, the boundaries between them melted. She had no reason to withhold a part of her. He was her best friend who understood her past, her present, her very core.

And she knew him as well. She trusted him. He'd always been there for her, and he always would be. As if he sensed her faith, their kissing became more passionate. She trembled under his hands and mouth. He groaned as she slipped the condom on him, and her hips arched as he lifted them.

With urgency, he entered her. Their bodies merged, and she drew him deeper into her, hooking her long legs around his back. He wrapped her golden hair in his fists, pure concentration on his face. She moved against him, matching his rhythm skin to skin, soul to soul. Arching, she held her breath until a rhapsody of pleasure hummed through her and she sang out his name.

Outside, fireworks burst, casting their light on them in shades of red, white, and blue. The explosions continued, and after a long while, Tyler shuddered in release, murmuring endearments. Finally, they came apart, her limbs still trembling with shockwaves of bliss. Spent and enveloped in each other's arms, they held each other until they slept.

CHAPTER 28

Ruth awakened, spooned behind Tyler. Thin sunlight filtered through the high multi-paned windows, washing the exposed red brick wall next to them. Somehow, during the night, she'd ended up wearing his Comic Con T-shirt. She ran her hand down his side to his boxers, marveling at his lean line, the feel of his individual ribs.

He stirred and rolled over to face her.

"Good morning." He pulled her close.

Her body responded immediately, ready for more. They slept little during the night. They'd cuddled, snoozed lightly, and then one of them would wake up, arouse the other, and make love again.

Then awareness hit her, and she sat up. "What have we done?"

He ran his hand along her hair to her shoulder. "I could tell you, blow by blow, pardon the pun."

"Ha ha." She found her headband on the floor and trapped her golden hair in it. "I'm not kidding. What about a year from now?"

"Ruthie, I will not let you ruin the memory of the best night of my entire life worrying about the future."

"I'm serious."

Tyler stretched and yawned. "I'm serious too." He slapped the futon. "This has to go. My back is killing me."

"What did we do last night?" she asked.

"What I've wanted to do since you sang at your mother's and Luke's wedding. You were always my friend, but when I heard your voice, I lost it."

"What'll happen now?" She grabbed her phone. "Look at this." She thrust it toward him.

"I see a cheap phone." He frowned. "We need to get you a new one with more functionality."

She blew air out of her mouth. "That's not what I'm talking about."

He sat up. "Okay, Ruthie, I'll bite. What's the problem?"

"No text from my mom, wondering where I am."

Tyler yawned. "That's an easy one. She knew you were up here with me watching the parade."

"Exactly." Ruth stabbed a finger toward his chest. "My mother didn't have to wonder where I was. All she needed to do was call your mom, who'd tell her you hadn't come home either."

"So?" He grabbed his tablet and swiped. "Let's see how soon I can get a king-sized mattress and box spring delivered before my back gives out. Although, I won't be able to get a certificate of occupancy until September sometime."

"You don't get it, do you? We can't live together."

"Why not?"

"Two words—our mothers."

"Just ignore them." He returned to his tablet.

"Easy for you to say. There are the Walkie-Talkies, the store-keepers, everyone in town." She stood and walked toward the window overlooking the town square. Below, Lions were picking up trash and dismantling the grill. About half of the shops still had *For Lease* signs in the windows.

"It's this town."

Tyler showed her the screen on his tablet. "What do you think about these mattresses with sleep numbers? Each person can dial in their own softness or firmness."

She motioned toward the window. "Eureka's a commitment vortex. It will suck you in. Do you know anyone who left here? I mean, other than those who've died?"

He stopped typing. "Didn't Bill Bell go to Chicago?"

Ruth snorted. "He ended up with a life sentence in Joliet prison."

"When people leave, they usually come back here to raise a family. If they're going to have one." He patted the futon. "I planned to get rid of this, but now, I might have it enshrined."

"Hilarious." She stood over him. "You know, my ex-boyfriend, Theo, wasn't always right, but he had a point."

"I have a point, too. I'll hit him hard if he ever shows his face around here."

"Truly?" The image of Tyler decking Theo sent a pleasant thrill through her.

He nodded. "I didn't get a chance to punch his lights out when I came to pick you up from Madison." He typed for a few seconds. "Anyway, what about that douche?"

"He theorized there was a master manipulator at work. My mother." She frowned. "Why did you want to hit him when you helped me move? Did you know about him then?"

He looked her straight in the eye. "Yes."

"From our mothers?" When he didn't respond, she gritted her teeth. "Yet, you let me tell you about him."

Tyler shrugged. "I wanted to know your side of things, not what our moms believed."

Hot anger coursed through her. "Turn around. I need to get dressed."

He set his tablet down and paled.

"You're serious?" He turned his back to her, facing the brick wall.

"See you around." Ruth grabbed her purse and headed toward the door.

"Ruthie."

One word. Her name. It went to her ears, then to her heart and stopped her with such force she was breathless. She turned to face him.

Tyler walked toward her, his boxers low on his slim hips.

Her body thrummed as he neared. He gently put his hands on her shoulders and her knees weakened. She closed her eyes so she wouldn't stare at his chest.

He lifted her chin and tenderly kissed her. "Look at me."

She did and regarded his handsome face shining at her with such affection, she wanted to swoon.

"Listen. I'm not making light of last night. I meant it when I said it was the best time of my life. Wasn't it good for you, too?"

Good isn't the word. Everything he did, every move they made together, was heaven. He was so loving, so cherishing, it made her head spin. She cupped his face, touching his morning stubble.

"Why did you choose now to pick a fight?" He ran a hand down her jawline. "Did I get too close for comfort?"

She looked down at the scarred maple floor and the truth rang a bell inside her. She looked back into his moss green eyes, which looked at her with alacrity.

"I hate you sometimes, Tyler Kelly."

A shadow of a smile crossed his face. "At least it's one side of the same coin." He pulled her close, and she yielded to his embrace. She listened to his beating heart, so in synch with her own. "We can take it down a notch. Let's go for a bite to eat tomorrow night, catch a movie, whatever. No pressure. Just have fun like we always have."

"Sure." But she understood it wouldn't be the same as it used to be. Not when she didn't want to spend a minute without him, preferably naked in his arms. The warning from the internet quiz she'd taken regarding friends with benefits haunted her.

Dammit, I'm in love with this man.

.   .   .

Tyler dressed and insisted on escorting to her Saturn, which was parked in the alley behind his building. Ruth squinted at the crystals glistening in the sunlight on the asphalt next to her car. As they neared, she found they weren't jewels. Broken glass from her driver's side window littered the ground.

"Shit." She started forward, her heart pounding. She intently scanned the interior. Green safety glass littered the zebra seat covers and Princess floor mat. At least nothing appeared to be missing. Then she looked at Tyler, who stood behind the car, staring at the trunk.

He met her midway and wrapped an arm around her as they walked to the back of the Toad. "I am so sorry."

Spray painted large red letters spelled out, "WHoRe."

His brow furrowed, Tyler grabbed his phone. "Is it okay with you to notify the police this time?"

Ruth nodded. "Call Luke."

. . .

An officer dusted for fingerprints as Ruth looked on. Backs of shops lined the alleyway, their various shades of brick crisscrossed with fire escapes and studded with garbage cans. A black cat licked its paw and studied the police commotion.

Luke, uniformed and intense, asked, "No surveillance, Tyler?"

"No, Chief. I was going to have a system installed this week."

"What about the other shops? Any cameras there?"

Tyler checked his tablet. "Sorry. None I can find."

Luke sighed. "I'll go have a chat with the shopkeepers." He moved closer to Ruth. "Did you hear anything last night?"

She colored. "Fireworks. Then the thunderstorm. That's all. It might've been vandalized any time."

"The whole town was here yesterday, with the parade and events."

"Debi was in the square, but she had her kids with her. Bobby McKay and his posse were hanging around too."

Luke crossed his arms. "Would you mind texting your mom with your whereabouts if you deviate from your usual routine?"

Tyler put his arm around Ruth. "Like coming here? Working late?"

"Anything." A muscle in his firm jaw twitched. "I couldn't forgive myself if something happened to you."

His concern warmed her. "Okay."

"I'll take you to get a rental car, and we'll impound the Saturn." He patted her shoulder. "They will repair her in no time, just like new."

"I owe you the deductible, at least."

Luke hesitated. "We'll work out a split sometime." He walked toward a detective.

Ruth squeezed Tyler's arm. "I'd better go with Luke."

"Before you do, take this." Tyler handed her his phone. "It has the latest apps on. Use this as a backup."

"Don't you think that's overkill?" She read the resolve on his face and hugged him. "All right."

CHAPTER 29

Red velvet curtains framed the recreation hall doorway with sign-age welcoming everyone to Golden Years' Casino Night. A disco ball rotated on the ceiling, casting a festive glow. At the entrance, Miriam took donations and exchanged them for gambling chips. On the wall, a sign read *Win one of our many prizes! McKay's Garage for a free tune-up, Ed Foo Youngs dinner for four, Lucy's lattes for a month, and Hair on the Square, free perm or color.*

Red, white, and black balloons covered the ceiling. Paper hearts, diamonds, clubs, and spades decorated the walls. Lillian stood in the corner, spinning a roulette wheel, raking in chips by the second.

The crowd spilled into the hallway where Aunt Cordy advertised, *Cordelia the Clairvoyant, your future is in your hands. Only five chips.*

Ruth wore black slacks and the yellow form-fitting sweater that Betty insisted on. Tyler stood next to her, looking especially handsome in his dress clothes.

Ty had kept his word, and they hung out with little more than a friendly kiss on the cheek. Ruth was in a quandary. Her head told her she would feel much worse leaving him in a year if they continued as lovers, but her body yearned to hold him whenever he was near. She had to decide. The present state of detente was torture.

Surrounded by his cronies, Tony Bettini wore a gray suit with a dark shirt and white tie. *Could he look more retro gangster Las Vegas?* Frank Sinatra crooned over the speakers, followed by Dean Martin.

Debi swished by, dressed in an off-the-shoulder black cocktail dress. On her feet were a pair of ebony stilettos with red soles, emphasizing her shapely legs. She took her place with Tony, who stood and kissed her hand.

"She looks great," Ruth said to Tyler.

"Not as good as you." He flipped her ponytail over her shoulder.

"Yellow's not my color." She fiddled with the large black bow holding her hair.

"Any color is your color." His green eyes crinkled. "I can't wait for your performance." He gave her a quick hug and left to chat with a group of his friends.

Rehearsals for "Viva Las Vegas" last week had been tense. Bobby McKay had wanted to end their duet with a kiss, but Ruth had insisted the song had to be true to the film. She'd pointed out the lyrics were about denying she was in love.

He'd reluctantly agreed. It always helped to cool his ardor when Tyler showed up to watch the rehearsals. The animosity between the two men was palpable.

With a look at the stage, she mentally rehearsed her number with McKay. If she remained spry, she might out-maneuver seedy Elvis every time he closed in on her. Just.

Nurse Steele arrived next, surrounded by a group Ruth surmised was her family. In her chic sharkskin pantsuit, and her tight curls smoothed into a fashionable hairdo, she greeted people as she glided through the crowd like a celebrity. As Ruth drew closer, the corners of her mouth turned upwards into a half-smile.

"Break a leg, Nurse Markson."

Although a standard show sendoff, Ruth wondered if Steele meant it literally.

Betty entered the building, striding by in a full-length cape. Her fiancé, Bernie, walked behind her, carrying two large feather fans in one hand and holding Pucci's leash in the other. The poodle yanked repeatedly on the lead as he sniffed people's legs. Finally, Bernie slowed enough for Pucci to grab his quarry, Eureka's mayor, and the dog humped the incumbent's limb.

Betty wagged her finger. "Pucci, no coochie."

Bernie hauled the dog off the irritated mayor's leg and raised his brows in a what-can-you-do look. Betty forged onward, heading toward the storeroom designated as the green room, but not before giving Ruth and Lillian significant looks.

The plan was in place, and Ruth acknowledged the butterflies in her stomach were because of her scheduled detective work later in the evening rather than her stage performance. Why she had agreed to the harebrained idea befuddled her. *Maybe it's hormones.* She hadn't been the same since her first kiss with Tyler.

Miriam flicked the overhead lights. She climbed onstage and grabbed a mike.

"Viva Las Vegas!" The lights glistened off her sequined Queen of Hearts tunic. "Please support our generous donors, including our local Piggly Wiggly bakery, who supplied the red velvet cupcakes. All proceeds will go toward our new recreation van. Thank you for your support!"

After a scattering of applause, the familiar melody of Elvis' film played over the loudspeakers.

"And now, the one, the only Elvis!"

Bobby McKay sprinted in, sporting tight black slacks and a pink sport coat. With a sneer, he leaped onto the stage and swung his hips to the rhythm, strumming his guitar. Screams erupted from female members of the audience.

Ruth glanced at the AED on the wall—she might need it. Someone tossed something white onto the stage. *Panties?*

Ruth caught Howard's eye, who gave her a thumbs up.

Tyler walked over and put his arm around her. "Ready?"

She rolled her eyes and nodded. Elvis hopped off the stage and worked his way through the audience, weaving and bobbing to the blaring rock and roll.

"That's my boy!" Mrs. McKay beamed. Bobby kissed women, shook men's hands. *He sure knows how to work the crowd into a frenzy.*

Ruth readied herself. When the spotlight shone on her, she pouted.

Elvis stopped, and silence filled the room. He strummed his guitar and crooned, "The lady loves me. She doesn't know it yet."

Ruth responded singing the lady loathed him, and he didn't know it yet, then strode across the stage protesting she wasn't in love, but Elvis insisted she was. He suggested they'd have dinner, and she sang back she'd rather eat with Frankenstein. Elvis sneered and maintained he was right. At least the song had a ring of authenticity.

When the duet ended, after calling him "all wet," she turned to the audience, grinning. In the film, Ann-Margret shoved Elvis into a swimming pool. Unfortunately, she only imagined doing so to McKay. After a burst of applause, Ruth bowed and caught Tyler's eye. He gave her a thumbs up and rose to his feet, whistling. She sprinted through the crowd, accepting congratulations.

Miriam grabbed the mike. "And now, Ms. Betty Fontaine, star of Eureka's Senior Talent Show."

Betty strode in with her red velvet cape swirling behind her. Elvis strummed and belted out "Hound Dog." She stripped off her cloak, revealing a sequined sweater, satin short-shorts, and fishnet stockings. Betty tapped and spun around in circles. Tony Bettini wolf whistled from the front row. The audience clapped in time to the beat. Betty dipped, wiggled her hips, and smiled seductively at Elvis.

Bernie set Pucci onstage and handed Betty a hula-hoop. The dog hopped through the circle on command, leaped into the air, and danced on his two back feet.

After thunderous applause, Betty returned the dog to Bernie, and ripped open her sweater, revealing a scarlet bustier. The crowd tapped their feet and heads bobbed. Someone called out, "Shake it, baby!" Ruth recognized Howard's voice in the flurry of encouraging shouts. This was Ruth's clue. Betty was going strong. Bobby was scheduled to sing three more songs in the set, followed by intermission. Ruth checked her fitness watch. She had exactly eleven and a half minutes. She snuck out the door, followed by Lillian. In the corridor, Aunty Cordy nodded, and provided them with two walkie-talkies from underneath her expansive caftan.

"Remember your warning phrase?" Ruth turned to Cordy.

"I see trouble in your future." Aunt Cordy waved her hands over a crystal ball.

Ruth and Lillian hurried to Tony Bettini's room. Lillian stood at the corner of the hallway, ready to alert Ruth.

"You remember how to use this, right? Hold the button here." Ruth's heart raced.

"Over and out." Lillian grinned.

Ruth slipped into the room. She didn't even know what she was looking for. The padlock on his closet was usual for residents who wanted to keep their belongings safe. She glanced under the bed and spotted boxes. As she examined one, she stifled a laugh. He was stockpiling Italian gourmet marinara sauce and biscotti. Shaking her head, she was going to leave when the door slowly opened.

She dove under the bed, her heart beating staccato. All she saw were Tony's shoes coming toward her. If he'd called it a night, she was toast. What the heck had happened to Lillian? A commotion in the hall rang out, followed by nails clicking on linoleum, the snap of heels, voices calling out in the hallway.

Tony's shoes froze in the doorway. The door opened wider, and a furry ball ran straight toward Ruth. Pucci's wet nose met hers.

She hoped he wouldn't nip her. Instead, he licked her, causing her to smother a gag.

"There you are, my darling," Betty crooned. She reached for her poodle, and her wide-eyed expression motioned Ruth to the door. "I am so sorry. Mr. Bettini, is it?"

"Call me Tony, dear." He cleared his throat. "I enjoyed your act tonight. You are extremely talented."

Ruth peered from beneath the bed. Betty had Tony backed against the closet, waving her feathered fan. She held it up, blocking Bettini's view and mouthed, "Go."

Ruth scurried across the floor, and Pucci yipped. She slid into the hallway where Lillian stood holding the walkie-talkie.

"Why didn't you warn me?"

"I was looking one way, and he came in the other. By the time I spotted him, I had to call Betty. It worked, didn't it?" They hurried down the dimly lit hallway.

"Yes. It also aged me ten years." Ruth sighed.

"Did you find anything?"

"Only that he hoards Rao's marinara sauce."

"That stuff's not cheap. Any Alfredo?"

Ignoring her friend, they halted by Steele's office.

"This could get me fired." Ruth's heart pounded.

"More likely, you'll find something to end this trouble."

"I hope so." Ruth waved at Aunt Cordy, who held up her walkie-talkie and nodded. She glared at Lillian. "And you look both ways, all right?"

Lillian rolled her eyes. "Hurry. You're running out of time."

With the sound of Bobby singing "Love Me Tender," punctuated by an occasional scream, Ruth entered the dark office. She fervently hoped Steele was an Elvis fan. Narrowing in on the desk, she recalled Dr. Thompson had locked it. She rummaged for the key holder under the drawer with slippery palms, but she finally located the magnet.

She flipped it open and retrieved a tiny key. Unlocking the drawer, she used her phone's flashlight. Amid the pens, pencils, and rubber bands was a pile of papers.

She gasped. There must've been thirty or more prescriptions for everything from pain drugs to codeine, all signed by Dr. Thompson. The corner of the drawer contained a large bottle of cough medicine. She skimmed the label. Codeine.

Nellie had told her Steele had cough medicine on her breath. Was she an addict? If so, what did she do to sustain her habit?

McKay's last refrain sounded, and she hurriedly locked the drawer. Her walkie-talkie beeped.

"I *really* see trouble in your future," Aunt Cordy's reedy voice warned.

Crap. Ruth flew to the door and peered into the hall. Steele stormed in her direction. Lillian stood against the wall, her mouth agape. Aunt Cordy attempted to persuade the Head Nurse to have her palm read, but Steele was having none of it.

"I don't believe in that rubbish." She shook off Cordelia's imploring hands.

This is it. I'm done.

Then all the lights in the building went out.

. . .

Ruth eased out the door into the ensuing chaos. The emergency lighting kicked in and the exit signs glowed red. She wiped her shaking hands on her pants as she pushed her way through the crowded hallway.

With a variety of beeps and squeals, the overhead lights came on. At the corner, she spotted Tyler leaning against the wall, wearing a lopsided grin. He slid his phone into his sport coat.

"Just a power blip, Ladies and Gentlemen." Miriam clapped her hands. "Come back to your seats, please!"

"Did you?" Ruth cocked her head. When he only smiled, she blew out her breath. "You saved my butt."

"And a nice one it is." His burning look sent a thrill through her.

Still shaky with adrenaline, she took his arm and led him to seats in the back row.

"What did you find?" His voice was low.

"Shh. I'll tell you later."

"When?"

She grabbed his hand. "Did you order the sleep number bed?"

"Ah, no." He frowned. "I wasn't sure if you wanted me to."

"Get a king-sized one. In the meantime, would you like to come over for a nightcap tonight?" She paused. "And breakfast in the morning?"

"PowerBars and tea?"

"Breakfast of champions."

"My pleasure." He kissed her. "Anytime."

CHAPTER 30

If this was Tyler's idea of taking their relationship down a notch, Ruth wondered what would happen if they amped it up.

The room looked like a tornado had torn through it, with clothes and pillows everywhere. They'd had a pleasant dinner after the Las Vegas show and strolled along Lake Geneva in the moonlight. A tsunami of desire had washed over her, combined with the realization she couldn't stand to be away from him.

She'd been so focused on the future, and worried about the past, she'd missed the present as it unfolded. If they were together, if only for a year, so be it, she'd reasoned. Their lovemaking had been more torrid, more urgent than their time in the loft.

She'd been weak and shaking after his passionate devotion to every part of her body and had enjoyed treating him to the same heart-pounding ecstasy. Afterward, they lay in each other's arms, talking, laughing, and exchanging small kisses until desire built up in them again.

Her mother's rooster yodeled his morning call. Ruth rolled over and studied Tyler in the shade-darkened room. He had a perfect body, broad shoulders, and a lean stomach. And a great butt. She stretched catlike.

Tyler's eyes fluttered open. "Ruthie." He traced his finger along her jaw, stopping at the cleft of her chin.

"Good morning." She kissed him on his lips. "Are you hungry, my prince?"

"Sure, I can oblige you." He crawled down the bed.

She grabbed his shoulder. "No, I meant for food. My mom gave me some eggs. Let's try to make a proper breakfast."

"You sure?" He reached over and ran a hand down her thigh. "I think there was a series of bets made last night in the heat of things."

Her heart immediately sped up, and she grew moist as a thrill of desire shot down her lower belly.

"I guess I can wait. For food."

"Mmm." He pulled her on top of him after grabbing a condom from the nightstand. "As I recall, you like it on top."

"Any way you want me."

■　■　■

Later, they rested in each other's arms. Oreo curled at the foot of the bed.

"What do you do in the winter?" Ruth murmured.

"I cross-country ski a bit." He played with a strand of her hair.

"I meant what do you do when you can't ride in your car with the top down?"

"Oh. My claustrophobia." He looked at the ceiling. "I leave the windows cracked open in my bedroom. Drives my mom crazy. And I drive a big-ass SUV for the snow."

"How did you get locked in a closet?" It wasn't like his parents to be careless.

"I was around three or four. I snuck into the pantry for a snack. When the contractors left, they piled a bunch of stuff against the door. They trapped me in there for hours."

She regarded the tiny bedroom. "You must hate the trailer."

"I did at first. But I'm better when you're around."

"That's good. Because I want to be around you a lot more." She kissed him. "I'm glad I didn't take the job."

"What job?" His arm tensed against hers.

"I-I had an offer for an interview at a hospital. In Madison."

"Oh. And why didn't you tell me about it?" He sat up.

She flushed red. "I guess I wanted to decide without any influence."

"And what made you stay?"

"I can't let more people die if I can help it."

"How noble of you." He sat up and reached for his boxers.

She put her hand on his arm. "And I can't leave you now." She laughed nervously. "I mean, we have a year, right?"

"Ten months, one week, and three days, but who's counting?" His smile was sad.

She wrapped her arms around him.

Me.

.   .   .

After Tyler left, Ruth answered the door.

"Hey. Want to join me?" Lillian motioned toward the stoop.

"Sure." Ruth plopped down next to her friend.

Lillian fanned herself. "It's hotter than a firecracker lit on both ends." When Ruth didn't respond, she asked, "What's up?"

Ruth shrugged. What was there to say? She was in love and the clock was ticking.

Lillian eyed her up and down. She placed her hands in mock prayer. "Oh, for those first few days, of the blush of love."

Ruth sighed. "Okay, what do you want to say?"

"I figured you might want to talk."

Irritation rose in her. "Everyone knew about Theo, didn't they? I mean, even before I came back."

Lillian shrugged. "Common knowledge, yes."

"Because my mother told everyone. You knew Tyler was crushing on me, too?"

"You have to admit he was pretty obvious, honey."

Ruth didn't argue the point. As she gathered herself, she stared at the enormous burr oak across the way. "Do you know the tree was here when my great grandpa homesteaded this land?"

"And that has to do with what?" Lillian's nose wrinkled.

"It's this place that's so rooted in the past. When people are born here, they may go away for a time, but eventually, they end up in this town until they die."

Lillian guffawed. "So? You make it sound like it's a condemned sentence."

Ruth swatted a fly away. "It's just all so conventional."

Lillian looked deeply into Ruth's eyes. "We believe in commitment, if that's what you mean."

"You mean marriage. It's a sham." There, she'd said it, finally admitting her worst fear.

"Tell that to me and Chuck after sixty years." Lillian snorted. "And Cordelia, now your mother."

Ruth frowned, recalling her dad's infidelity. "Yeah. And my father."

"So, that's it." Lillian looked toward the tree. "Honey, life continues to go on despite the past. People will or will not marry. Those like Joe Schultz will wonder where their life went until it's too late." She put a ring-laden hand on Ruthie's arm. "But you have to have some faith in love. Mostly, things work out."

"And what if they don't?"

"Tennyson wrote about better to have loved and lost." Lillian reached over and hugged her. She pointed toward the green and white hostas surrounding the trailer. "I see you've fixed up those plants."

"Yeah. Aunt Cordy and I get together once a week and get the slugs drunk." Purple blooms on delicate stems sprouted from formerly decimated leaves.

"It would impress Joe Schultz. Cordy was always on him to use an organic solution rather than pesticides." She patted Ruth's arm. "You should take a good nap. Everything looks better after a rest."

Ruthie stood. "I guess you're right. I'm working a late shift tonight. The holiday schedule is all balled up." She smiled down at her friend. "I like your hair. It looks like one of Luke's pies."

Lillian looked up at her. "And I love you."

. . .

Her shift was over. Ruth wandered down the darkened, quiet hallways of Golden Years, lined with new posters demanding a runoff election between Howard and Tony. She knew Steele had the janitors taking them down as soon as they sprouted up. From open doorways, televisions cast blue glows onto the polished linoleum floor, their muted sounds lulling patients to sleep. She yawned. Her shift was over.

As she passed one room, it startled her to see Howard next to a bed. A quick glance at the patient's nameplate—Mike Cherry—identified him as one of Debi's patients. She remembered Howard pointing him out to her, a forty-something man who had suffered a severe brain injury in a bar fight. Enough to keep him in care for the rest of his life.

She tapped on the door.

"Hi, honey. What's up?" Howard looked up at her.

Walking in, she studied Mike's sleeping face. His black hair stood in sweaty spikes, and she noticed the dent in his skull where he'd been injured years ago.

They'd set the muted television to the Food Channel, where chefs were battling it out to become the king of cupcakes.

"You tell me."

"No need to be quiet. He's snoozing pretty sound now." Fatigue had lined Howard's face. "I'm here on suicide watch."

"Did you tell Steele? Debi?"

"What good would that do? They'd pump him up with more pills."

"How did you find out?"

He grimaced. "Mike told me at dinner he didn't want to live anymore."

"Why tonight?"

"Nellie died two weeks ago."

Ruth sat in the other plastic guest chair. "You mean they were close?" She remembered the journal Yolanda had recovered with its entry of "M" visiting, a gentleman caller.

"They were lovers." Howard looked at her as if to check her reaction.

Nellie, how vibrant she had been. Ruth looked at Mike's wheelchair, and the sticker on its side, the sign that stated he was single.

"How was he going to do it?"

Howard produced a handkerchief filled with pills. "I convinced him to give me his stash, after promising not to leave him alone tonight."

Ruth remembered how Nellie had told her some residents pretended to swallow medication and then hoarded it.

"May I have those? I need to dispose of them properly."

Howard handed them over. "I believe they're pain pills. Would they be enough to do it?"

"Absolutely." Her heart sank as she watched Mike turning over, muttering.

Ruth sent a text to her mom, telling her where she was, and then told Howard, "We'll take turns sleeping. If Mike wakes up, I'll be here."

"Thanks, honey." Howard looked frail in the television's light as he stared at the screen where the Food Channel had degenerated into infomercials.

He pointed at the television. "Who buys this stuff?"

"I don't know, Howard. Lonely people in the dead of night, I guess."

.   .   .

Ruth checked the time on her computer. Four o'clock on the dot. She yawned and stretched. Both men snored lightly. The only other sounds were the occasional footsteps in the hallway. It must be hard waiting for an aide to help you get to the bathroom before you lost it.

"What's going on, Nurse Ruth?"

She spun in her chair to see Debi standing in the doorway. "What are you doing here?"

Debi stepped into the room. "I might ask you the same thing. Your shift ended hours ago."

"Mike was depressed, and Howard was keeping him company. I sat here with them." Ruth raised her brows, trying to look matter of fact.

"That's kind of both of you." Debi walked to Mike and frowned, examining his chart. "His antidepressants should have helped."

Mike smacked his lips, and Howard snored louder. Debi nodded toward the doorway. She and Ruth walked into the darkened hallway.

Debi crossed her arms and tapped her foot. "I woke up and couldn't get back to sleep. I found you were in the system looking at Mike's records."

Ruth had signed on with her usual password, not using Tyler's all-powerful access.

"So?"

"I was worried about my patient." She stared at Ruth hard. Tonight, her eyes were gray.

Ruth wondered how Debi had administrative access. Then again, Mike was in Debi's care. "All right, we'll go. Both of us could use a rest. You shouldn't leave Mike alone."

"I'll monitor him, don't worry. He's a good guy." Debi shook her head. "Too young to spend his life in an institution."

They returned to the room, and quietly awakened Howard, who struggled to consciousness.

Ruth kept her voice low. "Debi will sit with Mike now and give us both a break."

Howard looked doubtful, then checked his watch. "Well, it's only for an hour or so."

"And he's my patient." Debi smiled at them. "He'll be in expert hands."

Howard moved more stiffly than usual, relying heavily on his cane. "Not used to sleeping in a chair."

"I'll walk you to your section." Debi volunteered. "Ruth probably wants to get home and get some shuteye as soon as I get back."

"Don't need any help," Howard muttered. Then he stumbled a bit, and Debi caught his elbow as they crept toward the independent living apartments.

After a check on Mike, Ruth ducked into his bathroom and splashed water on her cheeks to wake herself up enough to drive.

Beep Beep Beep.

The rhythmic ear-ringing alarm blasts rang out. Ruth rushed from the bathroom, adrenaline-fueled to shake Mike awake. He looked confused as she said, "Fire!"

She helped him sit, lowered him in into his wheelchair, and clipped the safety belt shut. She pushed him into the hallway chaos where aides scurried in and out of rooms, loading patients into wheelchairs, as others quickly rolled them a safe distance from the building.

The emergency lights cast an eerie red glow, and the fire alarms strobed white flashes on the walls. She pushed the chair outside and put Mike in his designated area where clipboard-carrying senior aides were already accounting for patients and staff.

"Everything's all right, Mike." She patted his arm.

He nodded. "Tha-nks, Nurse Ruth."

Fire engines wailed their arrival, followed by police and paramedics.

Then she spotted the source of the alarm. Vivid orange flames burst from the independent living section. She took off at a full run, heart pumping.

As she stumbled to a stop, emergency vehicles painted the building in blood red flashes. Firefighters operated hoses, spraying water in gigantic arcs. Luke and other uniformed officers formed a semi-circle around the center of the black acrid smoke.

She surveyed the clusters of residents and fought down panic. No Howard. Gert screamed and wept, surrounded by friends.

Wide-eyed, Ruth ran to Luke. "Howard!"

"We'll find him." Luke's face was hard, red lights strobing across it.

"I'm going in after him." She lurched forward.

"No!" He gripped her arm.

Firefighters wearing headgear and fire suits resembled an invading military force as they moved toward the building. Something exploded, sparks flew, and they retreated.

Ruth scanned the group on the sidewalk. "He was with Debi about ten minutes ago."

"She wasn't on the duty list." Luke cursed and sprinted toward the fire chief, who shouted at his people to move forward.

Another bang rattled the scene. Gert screamed. Embers erupted from a beam as it crashed. Then, emerging from the blaze, two figures crawled forward, one pulling the other. The firefighters rushed into the billowing smoke and snatched them to safety just as the inferno burst into a sinister parody of a fireworks finale.

CHAPTER 31

Monitors steadily beeped as Ruth studied Debi's chart: Superficial first-degree burns on arms. Treatment for smoke inhalation with oxygen, no intubation is necessary. The patient stirred, eyes fluttering open, and Ruth rose from the chair.

"How's Howard?" Debi asked in a hoarse voice, then coughed. Ragged strands of singed hair framed her pale face. She inhaled deeply through the oxygen tubing in her nose.

"Treated for smoke inhalation, then released." Ruth monitored her pulse. "Are you in any pain?"

Debi closed her eyes briefly. "Can't feel a thing. What did they give me?"

Ruth checked the chart. "Lidocaine. With a prescription for Vicodin when you go home."

"And these?" She raised her bandaged forearms. "What's the prognosis?"

"You're lucky. Superficial, hopefully minimal scarring." She pointed toward the pitcher of ice water. "Are you thirsty?"

"That would be great."

Ruth poured it into a cup and held the straw to Debi's lips.

"Thanks." Debi sucked greedily at the water. "For a guy with a cane, Howard sure can move. I turned away, and he took off." Debi coughed. "What the hell was he running in there for, anyway?"

Ruth recalled picking up the framed piece the paramedics had thrown to the side. "His collage of family photos." She'd shown it to Luke, who only shook his head.

Debi rolled her eyes. "Old people and their pictures. Unbelievable."

Ruth shrugged. "It's the recording of his life."

"True," Debi said. "Where's Howard going to live now?"

"My stepdad asked him to move in with him and my mom, but he wants to stay with Gert."

"Stubborn, isn't he?"

"Howard was a farmer. Enough said." Ruth gave Debi another sip. "Is there someone I should call?"

"No. No one. My ex won't care."

A ripple of pity washed over Ruth. She made her voice sound light. "What about Bobby McKay?"

Debi winced. "He dumped me after I didn't put out."

A shock of surprise ran through Ruth. "You two weren't an item?"

"He enjoyed having an ex-beauty queen on his arm as eye candy." She coughed. "And he paid for dinner. I made sure I ordered steak or lobster. No hamburger joints for me."

"He flashes the cash and drives a car that flaunts it."

"He wants to overcome the fact he can't get the grease from under his fingernails. He's constantly scrubbing them." Debi took another sip of water. "Have they determined how the fire started?"

"It's under investigation." Ruth set the cup down. "Coupled with the burning dumpster, they're considering both suspicious."

Debi breathed in deeply, filling her lungs with oxygen. "I knew things were bad."

"You did?" Ruth arched her brow. "In what way?"

Debi's eyes were red rimmed, but the irises were a cool gray as they held Ruth's gaze.

"You've got to be kidding. Howard's complaints have hardly been a secret."

"And so?" A frisson of fear ran through her. Had Howard been the target for arson?

"Something's wrong at Golden Years. I've been trying to find out, but—" She stopped and coughed. Ruth held a tissue to her mouth as she spit up dark mucus. "I thought Bobby might know something, but he's as tight as a drum. Far too smart to say anything."

Ruth's pulse quickened. "You suspect he's involved?"

"Believe me, I wouldn't go out with the creep unless I did."

"You looked pretty tight when I saw you around." Ruth remembered the way the two of them looked at one another.

"At first, well, he was cute in a rugged way. I was lonely. Plus, he used to phone me and sing Elvis ballads. He was so romantic."

"Yeah." Ruth recoiled at the image of McKay wooing someone.

Debi sighed. "He sure is one to hold a grudge. He's still pissed at you for something in the past."

"He didn't tell you?" Ruth asked. "I beat the crap out of him in grade school." She related the story. "Later, I wouldn't go to prom with him."

"I can understand why you wouldn't. He sometimes said the crudest things. I couldn't imagine those dirty hands on me, so I told him to back off." Debi held Ruth's stare. "You should be careful. He really doesn't like you or your boyfriend."

The image of UGG boots near her Saturn on the security video flashed through her mind.

"Do you think he keyed my car?"

"No." Debi looked down at her bandages. "I did."

"Why?" Confusion flooded Ruth.

"You were nosing around, installing granny cameras, looking at the computer system where you didn't belong." Debi shrugged. "I was trying to scare you off for your own good."

"How did you get around the computer system so easily? Most of us don't have admin capabilities."

Debi pursed her lips. "I dated our technical guy in Janesville."

"He told you everything?"

"How could he resist?" Debi looked coyly at Ruth.

Ruth ignored the question. "Did you flatten my tires? Or spray paint my car?"

Debi shook her head. "I don't know anything about graffiti. Or your wheels."

"And someone was in my trailer. I think Gandalf chased him or her out." Ruth looked for a reaction.

Debi shrugged. "There were lots of strangers in the campground. I noticed a couple of teenagers hanging around the office before I left town."

Ruth's mind raced. If Debi wasn't involved, that left Head Nurse Steele, the only other person with regular access to the meds. She considered Mike's hoarded drugs, the street value of Lillian's pain pills, her suspicion McKay was a drug pusher.

She checked her watch. "I should go. Steele will have a fit with both of us out today."

Debi gave a weak smile. "True. She might have to get out from behind her desk and work with patients."

Ruth grinned. "They're discharging you this afternoon. Can I give you a ride home after work?"

. . .

Golden Years' gloomy atmosphere surrounded Ruth like smog. Residents wheeled themselves along the hallways, forming small groups where they gossiped like middle school students. Whenever she passed, they would acknowledge her respectfully and inquire about Howard's health. The male residents asked for updates on Debi's condition and when she responded that the nurse would soon return, they cheered at the news.

Yolanda approached her at midday. "How is your grandfather?"

When Ruth answered he was okay, tears welled up in her eyes.

Yolanda put her arm around Ruth and led her to the unisex bathroom. Ruth threw her arms around the aide. Throughout the embrace, Yolanda muttered terms of endearment in Spanish, a beautiful daughter, an angel.

"Howard might have died."

"But he didn't." Yolanda hugged Ruth tighter.

"You're right." Ruth wiped her eyes. "I'll see him soon."

"The last I heard, he is with his beautiful woman." Yolanda regarded her with soulful eyes. "Get some rest soon. You have been through a lot."

"*Gracias,* thanks, Yoli."

At the end of her shift, Ruth strolled to Steele's office, who had paged her several times. She tapped on the door and, not expecting an answer, came in. "You rang?"

The Head Nurse stood. With a ruddy complexion and shaking hands, she pointed toward the side chair across from her. "Sit. Down. Now."

Ruthie lowered into the chair and crossed her legs. "Great. I'm pretty beat."

"You're tired? You're the one who spent the night here. You're the one who rode to the hospital. And came in late, with only a text to me."

"Right." Ruth studied her nails. "I might have broken one of these last night in the ruckus."

Steele shook with fury, with her face a study in shades of purple. "That's it. For your attitude, I am terminating your employment. You've refused to comply with my instructions to phone if you are late for work. You've also taken it upon yourself to work unauthorized hours." Nurse Steele looked triumphant, and then her frown turned quizzical.

Ruth polished her nails on her scrubs. "You wouldn't have an emery board, would you?"

"Did… you… hear… what I said?" Steele thumped down on her chair. "Are you deaf?"

"No. I heard you. I refuse to acknowledge it."

"When you stop getting a paycheck, you will." The older woman wore a smug smile.

"Oh, I don't think that will happen. First, even though I'm on probation, you must establish a rational cause." She held up her phone. "It's in the bylaws. I found it last night, doing some research."

"That's, that's—"

"That's the way it is. I notified you as soon as I knew I would be late for work, via text, since early in the morning you aren't in yet. Secondarily, I have access to a member of the Board. And for once, I *will* use my personal influence."

"Oh, Miss-High-and-Mighty, as if you hadn't already pulled strings to get this job." Steele sniffed.

"I didn't. But never mind." Ruth stood and looked down at Steele. "I will find out what's going on here. If I have to call for impromptu audits, I'll do anything to save as many lives as I can."

Steele turned from bright purple to a sickly yellow.

Ruth leaned over the gray steel desk. "And if anything suddenly happens to another resident here, I will sic the dogs of hell on you, proof or no proof."

"Get out. Now!"

Ruth walked from the room, sneaking a quick glance back at Steele, who'd gone ghastly pale staring at her desk, looking exactly like a woman on death row.

.   .   .

Ruth waited at the hospital entrance as a young volunteer wheeled Debi out of the lobby.

Debi plopped down on the rental car's front seat. "What's new?"

"Steele ripped me a new one today for coming in late to work and only texting her. She also didn't like the fact I spent the night at Golden Years."

Debi awkwardly patted her arm. "I'm sorry. I'll be back shortly to help you fight the Dragon Lady."

"I could use the support. I called her bluff when she wanted to fire me." She summarized their conversation and her commitment to find any wrongdoing.

"Ballsy of you." Debi gave her an appreciative look.

Ruth shrugged. "It's worth it to find out what's happening. She looked guilty."

"Good for you." Debi gestured toward homes as they drove through Eureka. "Do you know the best neighborhood in town for middle school kids?"

"Sure, I grew up here. We can drive by some areas if you like." Ruth was so far away from buying anything, she'd be lucky to afford a shed in someone's backyard once she paid back her student loans.

Ruth gave Debi a tour of Historic Eureka, pointing out the best areas.

"This one, for example, is within walking distance of school. And it has potential." She parked at a rundown Victorian with a large, sagging porch, and a handmade *For Sale By Owner* sign. "Of course, it's a family home."

"Perfect." Debi beamed a beauty-contest-worthy smile. "I'm trying to get a house for my kids to join me. They're with my ex and his bitch of a wife who's poisoned them against me. If I get pro-moted to Head Nurse once Steele retires, I'll be able to afford one."

"Good for you." So that's why Debi didn't have custody of the two tweens Ruth spotted on the Fourth of July.

Ruth pointed out the Kellys' Painted Lady, festooned in hues of mauve, sea green, and deep purple. Metallic gold highlighted the intricate detailing along the windows and the wraparound porch.

Debi craned her neck. "Beautiful, but way out of my price range. I'd need to find a sugar daddy to finance it."

Ruth briefly wondered at a life spent bartering beauty for what a woman wanted. "Not necessarily. The Kellys did lots of work. You can remodel a fixer upper one step at a time."

Debi scanned the blocks of neat homes and well-tended yards. "Is this the neighborhood you would live in?"

Ruth recalled a Victorian house with the sagging porch. It could be as pretty as this Painted Lady and was on a large corner lot as well.

"When I have kids, yes." Where had that idea come from?

In Dairyland Acres, when Debi's trailer came into view, they found its deck railing decorated in metallic helium balloons glisten-ing in the lowering light.

"What the—?" Debi's mouth was agape.

They exited the car and walked toward Debi's trailer. Casse-roles, desserts, hand-decorated cards, and flowers filled the deck.

Frowning, Debi grabbed an embossed thank-you card. "Who is this from?"

Ruth grinned. "Everyone here." She picked up the lemon me-ringue pie she recognized as baked by Luke. "You're in for a treat."

Debi said, "I don't get it. I thought they didn't like me."

"You saved Howard's life." Ruth accumulated the presents. "Come on. Let me warm up something for your dinner. I'm an ex-pert at this."

CHAPTER 32

The next Monday morning, Ruth answered Lillian's page to come to the reception desk. When she walked to the lobby, it surprised her to see Luke in uniform, standing by the front door.

"Hey, Ruth." He grinned. "Do you have a minute?"

"Sure." She wondered what he had to say. If he hadn't been smiling, she would've been worried.

He pointed toward the front door. "Care to switch?"

Parked in front of the building, the Saturn's green paint shone in the sunlight.

"Oh, it looks great." The front door swished as she walked outside with Luke. She ran her hand down the side panel with its smooth finish. They must've fixed the keyed area, and when she made it to the back of the sedan, the trunk showed no signs of graffiti.

"We put on four new tires and gave you a new spare. Good as new, huh?"

"Better." Ruth regarded the interior décor, filled with presents from the Walkie-Talkies.

Luke glanced toward the assisted living area, still surrounded by yellow tape. "The Fire Marshall officially called this arson. I've also spoken to the Board here about hiring nighttime security and installing better surveillance." His face hardened. "Meanwhile, keep your car parked where it's in view of a camera."

"I will, Luke." She patted the car's hood.

"Good. I'll do some off-duty patrolling myself. My officers will keep tabs here, too."

"Don't worry." She gave him a brave smile.

He gently placed his hands on her shoulders. "I'd worry even if it wasn't my job."

. . .

Toward the end of the day shift, the Head Nurse called Ruth to her office, where Debi and Miriam had already taken their seats. Ruth took the chair next to Debi.

"I've called this meeting to discuss the additional security measures here." Her mouth twisted into a grimace. "The Board of Directors has taken actions to provide for the safety of all residents and staff." She looked straight at Ruth, who strove to maintain a neutral face. "New procedures will be in place, including nighttime security guards." Steele stood and looked out the window. "Also, they will install more cameras with a higher resolution."

Debi cast a side-glance at Ruth behind Steele's back. They both raised their eyebrows and made small shrugs. Miriam frowned at them quizzically, then tapped her Mont Blanc pen on her writing pad.

Steele spun around. "Especially in the medication dispensing area." She placed her hands on her gray desk and leaned forward, addressing the three women. "We don't have an extra dime in the budget for pay raises, or other improvements, but the Board has found the money for *this*."

People are dying. Steele is worried about pay increases, and someone might have intentionally set the fire that almost killed Howard and Debi. She took out her pad and paper and wrote *some priorities, huh?* She moved the note closer to Debi.

Debi stole a look at the pad and gave a slight nod.

The Head Nurse grabbed a stack of stapled papers, handing them to each of the women. "Please sign and return to me." Ruth looked down at the new safety procedures, noting they agreed to be on camera when performing their duties.

Steele sighed. "Last, I need to inform you we will hold another election for Resident Council President." Her look at Ruth was venomous enough to burn skin. "None of us will be involved in the counting of ballots. The Board will appoint independent observers." Steele's face reddened. "Just one more way to waste our time and money."

The room remained silent, save for the tapping of Miriam's fountain pen on her tablet.

"Miriam, can I ask you to stop that irritating noise?" Steele rubbed both temples.

"Sor—ry." The recreation director's voice was as gooey-sweet as a sundae at one of her Ice Cream Socials. Today she wore a T-shirt with a cartoon cow in a frame entitled *The Moo-na Lisa*.

Debi tapped her foot. "Is there anything else?"

Steele waved her hand at them. "Isn't that enough?"

As they shuffled out the door, Ruth asked Debi, "She's a barrel of laughs, isn't she?"

"A real hoot."

Ruth's phone chimed with a text. "Howard would like to see us after our shift at his new place."

"Sure." Debi smiled, her eyes a deep blue today. "As long as he stays out of trouble this time."

.   .   .

Ruth and Debi walked through the parking lot toward the Independent Living section of Golden Years. Ruth winced at the decimated end of the building where Howard's apartment had been. A front-loader lifted singed debris, sending an acrid stench into the air. Construction workers in hardhats kicked at the scorched ground. They had cordoned off piles of charred brick with yellow police tape.

"Are you all right?" Ruth noted how Debi's face had paled.

"Yeah. I just haven't looked at this since the fire." She rubbed the bandages on her arms.

They entered a side door and walked toward Gert's apartment. The far end of the hallway was boarded up and a light stench of burned material lingered in the air.

Howard flung open the door after a single knock and welcomed them into the cozy apartment. He grabbed Ruth in a bear hug. After a second of hesitation, he gruffly embraced Debi, who patted his shoulders.

"Gert's at her bingo game, but sends her regards." He nodded at Debi. "And her thanks. As do I." His gnarled hand shook on his cane. "Have a seat. Lemonade?"

They sat on the sofa festooned with needlepoint pillows, and Howard returned with their drinks. The aroma of citrus and pastry filled the room.

"Gert makes a great lemon meringue pie with Meyer lemons." He leaned toward them. "Don't tell her, but Luke's is still the best I've ever tasted."

Debi studied Howard's family photo collage. "Been making any rescue efforts lately?"

He grinned wryly. "Not my best decision." He looked pointedly at her bandages. "How are you doing?"

"I'm fine. Not even taking my pain meds." Her flawless complexion shone in the evening light.

"Ruth tells me you think something's going on here, too."

"I do." Debi explained she'd dated McKay to find what role he might play, and how she'd been in the computer system searching for answers. She grinned her beauty-contest smile. "Our tech guy told me how to do everything, of course."

"But nothing, huh?" Howard asked. When she shook her head, he continued, "Well, if you find out anything, I'm sure you'll let us know.

Debi shrugged. "We should probably leave it to the authorities to investigate."

"At least for the arson," Ruth said.

"That would be smart. My son's quite a capable man." Howard stood, leaning heavily on his cane. "Well, I'm sure you young ladies have something better to do than sit around with an old man all evening. I just wanted to thank you, Debi."

"You're welcome, Howard." They started out the door, and Debi turned. "Good luck with the election."

As they walked toward their cars, Ruth asked, "I thought you were a supporter of Tony."

Debi shrugged. "May the best man win. I see you have your car back."

"Good as new."

"I'm sorry about the keying. Say, let me make it up to you. I have tons of casseroles left. Would you like to have dinner sometime?"

"Tyler's working tonight, so I have an open calendar."

"Great. Come over when you're ready."

. . .

An hour later, as Debi fussed with the old stove, Ruth studied the trailer identical to hers with its matching plaid couch, harvest gold dinette, and shag orange carpet. The only thing missing was the odor of Bengay.

Outside, Gandalf honked.

"What's with him?" Ruth looked out the window as the goose paced back and forth on Debi's porch.

Debi joined her. "He looks agitated. You should calm him down."

Ruth knocked on the glass. "Cool it, Gandy." He ignored her and continued his pacing.

Moving to the sofa, Ruth took in more of Debi's trailer. A shelf held a picture of two kids, a cute little girl in a pink dance leotard, and a boy in his soccer uniform.

"Your kids, I take it?"

"Yep. The lights of my life. Is iced tea okay? I don't drink."

"That's fine."

Debi joined her on the couch. They chatted about Eureka's best neighborhoods for families as they sipped their drinks. When Ruth felt a sneeze coming on, she reached inside her purse for a tissue and found Mike's handkerchief containing his stash.

"Oh. I've been meaning to give these to Steele. But—"

"You haven't trusted her?"

"No. Other than us, who else handles the meds? And we know people are overdosing on Oxy and fentanyl in town." She reached into her bag. "Like this?" She showed Debi Lillian's unused bottle. She spread out Mike's handkerchief and began counting the pills. Then she pointed to the meds. "Some are definitely a different shade, but they're all supposed to be OxyContin."

Debi raised a brow. "You're right."

Excitement shot through her as she realized what she held. "There's a chance someone's been substituting placebo or black-market pills for the real thing."

Debi went to check on the lasagna and returned with their refreshed teas. "Won't be long now. How are we going to proceed?"

"I'll turn this over to Luke when I leave here. I'm sure they can test them. After that, there're probably be an immediate audit."

"Brilliant. But who set the fires?"

"McKay and company? He's probably the pusher."

"Wow. It's lucky we were both there when it happened."

"I guess." Ruth's stomach cramped. "I need to use the restroom. Don't worry, I know where it is." She hurried to the bathroom, afraid she might have picked up a bug. A message notification dinged, and she dug the phone out of her pocket.

She found a text from Howard. *Holsteins don't change their spots.*

The hair on the back of her neck stood up. She needed a plan. Make up an emergency, beg off from dinner, and get up to the house as soon as possible with her evidence. Trying to appear nonchalant, she stepped from the bathroom, glancing toward the bedroom. In a corner, something bright and multicolored attracted her. She sidled closer and squinted. Someone had slit a stuffed animal open— Petey.

A flood of nausea swept over her and then a heaviness. She spun around to see Debi blocking the hallway.

"I need to go. Not feeling well."

"I know, Markson."

Ruth sank to the shag carpet as the hallway spun around her. The last thing she saw before she lost consciousness was an UGG boot swinging at her face.

CHAPTER 33

Ruth struggled to awareness on a cold cement floor, inhaling the acrid aroma of grease and cigarette smoke. Voices in the garage murmured in the background. She opened her eyes to a slit. The pinup girl on the wall calendar smirked at her. Her head throbbed, and she gingerly touched her cheekbone. Nothing seemed broken, probably because the boot softened the blow. She reconstructed what had happened, but it was a blank after she saw Petey's carcass and the last kick to her face. Somehow, Debi had moved her here.

She fought down the panic that made her limbs feel like lead. Sweat trickled down her armpits. Taking deep breaths, she called on her training at the Y for calm despite the terror gripping her. She glanced toward the one window. In the pitch black, only a faint glow shone underneath the door leading to the garage.

Call for help. She reached for her phone. Not there. Probably the first thing they took away. Rolling cautiously onto her side, she checked her back pocket and found the phone Tyler had given her for backup. They must've assumed her phone was the only one, and didn't bother to search further. Hope flooded through her. *My wonderful geek.*

Debi and McKay argued in the garage bay. Ruth located the outside door. Could she make it out?

McKay's voice loomed closer, and with shaking hands, she hit the emergency app Tyler had shown her. *Please work.*

The metal door opened just as she jammed the phone in her pocket. She feigned unconsciousness as McKay strode toward her.

He shoved her hip with a work boot. "Wake up."

Ruth moaned and stirred a bit, hoping to buy time. "Wait. Wait."

She opened her eyes a bit to see McKay standing over her, a smug look on his face.

"I said, get up." He grabbed a handful of her hair and yanked.

Pain shot through her scalp. She attempted to sit.

"I feel sick." She feigned retching and bent close to the floor, spitting into a crack on the concrete, leaving some DNA. *In case, in case.*

She looked wildly around, searching for potential defensive objects. The rolling office chair could be wedged between them. There might be a letter opener, and failing to use it on him, cut herself leaving some blood on the garage floor. If… if… she fought to keep the fright of death from her mind. Focus on the present, she reminded herself as she gritted her teeth.

"We have plans for you, bitch. A drive in your beater of a car to Madison, where they won't find you for a long time. Then a nice permanent sleep." He unzipped his pants. "But first, I'll show you who's boss. I've been wanting this for a long, long time."

Debi strode in, her face a grimace.

Pure terror gripped Ruth. "Please! It doesn't have to be like this."

Debi looked with gunmetal-gray eyes at her, then addressed McKay. "Don't leave any DNA on her. Be quick about it. We haven't much time before the plane leaves." She walked into the garage, muttering, "Men. Such fools. You can lead them anywhere by the cock."

He grumbled and reached into his back pocket, presumably for his wallet and a condom. Ruth strained to hear any signs from the police. Nothing. She took as many deep breaths as possible, getting oxygen into her core as her kickboxing teacher had taught her. She forced herself to focus as she prepared for her one chance.

"Will you fucking get up?" He moved to grab her hair again.

"No, don't." She stood, bent over, and wobbled closer to him. "Just a second."

With a silent prayer, she gathered her strength and with all of her being, kicked out her leg, striking McKay squarely on his right kneecap. He squealed and leaned to the side. She aimed her next kick into his solar plexus and the breath *whooshed* out of him. It sent him sprawling backward, where he crashed into his desk. She aimed a last kick into his open fly and his eyelids fluttered shut.

She rushed to the outside door and yanked at it. Locked.

From behind her, a voice snarled, "We figured you might try something." Debi glanced at the now unconscious McKay. "Always thinking with his dick." She rolled her eyes. She held a full syringe. "I understand overdosing is a good way to go."

"Murder? Debi, right now it's drug charges. McKay with attempted rape." When Debi remained silent, Ruth looked out the window at her Saturn. "If you want it to look like an accidental overdose, you'll have to get the syringe in me."

"When Bobby wakes up, he'll help me hold you." McKay stirred. "Or we may go to Plan B. Once you're addicted, there's a market for natural blondes, even if you are old."

Trafficking. "You won't get away with it. They'll find me wherever you take me."

Debi cackled. "You won't want to be found. An addict used by countless men."

How to take her down? Whenever Ruth moved closer, Debi inched away.

"Not falling for it, Markson. I don't think with my cock."

"What about your children, Debi?" Try for humanity. Use her name. Link to her family.

Debi snorted. "They're gone. I lost their hearts years ago." A flicker of an emotion crossed her face. Sadness or guilt? Then her expression hardened. "This is all your fault. If you would've just gone along, ignored Howard, and done your job, you wouldn't be here."

A siren screamed in the distance. "It's the police, Debi. Give up before it's too late."

"Nice try. I have your phone. No one will notice your car here."

Ruthie pulled Tyler's phone out of her back pocket.

"Drop it!" Debi moved closer. She lunged, giving Ruth an opening. She kicked viciously at Debi, who danced away with every attempt. "I'm too quick for you, Markson." Debi grinned maniacally. McKay groaned and muttered.

Ruth spoke into the phone. "Dial emergency number now!"

"Give me that." Debi's eyes shone yellow as she turned to stare at the red lights flashing through the window.

Ruth seized her opportunity and charged forward, kicking the syringe from Debi's hand. When she lunged for it, Ruth grabbed her neck and jabbed two fingers into her trachea. Stomping her heavy work shoes on Debi's instep, Ruth crashed her forehead into Debi's nose, the crunch of cartilage unleashing a fountain of blood as she sunk to her knees.

Luke's voice boomed, "Police! Open up!"

Ruth shakily straightened and regarded Debi whimpering on the floor. Ruth delivered a final, ferocious kick to her ribs.

"This one's for Nellie, bitch."

The police rushed in, weapons drawn, with Tyler behind them. He grabbed Ruth and held her close. "Are you okay?"

Ruth nodded into his shoulder. "I am, now that you're here."

They watched as the police handcuffed Bobby and Debi and read their rights by Luke. Led by two uniformed officers, Bobby, still groggy, limped out the door. Debi stared at the floor as she winced in pain with every step.

Tyler glared at his nemesis. Then he kissed Ruth's head, saying, "You beat him up again, didn't you? That sonofabitch. If you hadn't, I would've."

Luke approached them, laying his hand on Ruth's shoulder. "You can give me your statement when you're up to it. Meanwhile, let's get you to the ER. That bruise on your check doesn't look great. Come on, I'll drive you myself."

Tyler kissed her temple. "Don't worry. I'll follow right behind you, sweetheart."

As Luke walked her to his squad car, she asked. "Mom?"

He smiled. "Don't worry, honey. She and the Walkie-Talkies are already on their way to meet us at the hospital. I couldn't keep them away."

.   .   .

Ruth pressed the cold compress to her face as Tyler drove home from the hospital along the cornstalk-lined highway.

"That's some shiner you have, Slugger." Tyler patted her arm.

"You should see the other guy." Her cheek and forehead throbbed, but she'd refused anything but ibuprofen for the pain. "I guess that should be plural."

"It's your destiny to keep beating the crap out of Bobby McKay." He grinned at her. "Just never get mad at me, okay?"

A chortle rose in her, causing her to wince. "Don't make me laugh. Your 9-1-1 app saved me."

"Well, I meant to tell you. There was a slight snag." Tyler shrugged. "It's beta software. The emergency operator didn't ex-actly know what to do with the text."

"You're joking. Then how did the police find me?"

"I got worried when you didn't answer your phone. I checked the office surveillance cameras and there was a sizeable gap. Apparently, Debi scrubbed them like I did."

"She was that good." Ruth had underestimated her coworker.

"Lillian noticed Gandalf making a fuss, and your car was missing. Your mom was going crazy with worry since you hadn't contacted her. When I said you weren't with me, Luke called an emergency." He squeezed her hand. "I was on my way to your place when I received the text from my app with your GPS location here."

"For once, I'm glad everyone kept tabs on me."

Luke had told them the District Attorney would determine the charges against Debi and McKay. He'd brought Steele in for questioning, and the Head Nurse had broken immediately, wanting to make a plea bargain.

"All four of them were in on it." Steele had swapped out fake or illegal pills for real medications. Miriam delivered the drugs in the recreation van for Bobby to sell. Debi had come up with the lucrative plan and manipulated the computer system to cover up any discrepancies.

He nodded. "Yesterday, I finally figured out the system was slow because of duplicating transactions. They had one complete set of false records in case of an audit. I called you to tell you, and that's when I realized you were missing."

A wave of sadness swept over her. "So, people died because of drug interactions, or lack of the right medication."

Tyler nodded. "My dad says it's possible. Steele said it was Russian roulette, which patients got what. Bettini was certain there was something wrong, but promised to keep quiet if they gave his friends the proper drugs."

She clenched her fists. "Tony was blackmailing them. Will they charge him?"

"Likely not. He'd probably deny it, and there's no proof. But here's the latest. Steele admitted Miriam has flown the coop, along with all the recreation money. She had a gambling jones, big time. No wonder they didn't want you working there." Tyler frowned. "If my dad hadn't recommended you, this all wouldn't have happened."

"He was trying to do me a favor. They didn't want me around listening to Howard." She sighed. "What threw me was Debi running into the fire."

"Luke thinks she set it herself to convince us of her heroism and throw us off track."

"But she didn't fool Howard." He hadn't articulated exactly why he didn't believe Debi. He'd just used the same judgment as when he chose crops to sow, and it worked for him for over sixty years.

They made their turn in the town of Lake Geneva, where the water glistened in the lowering sunshine. Sailboats and launches rocked their moorings behind the Riviera Docks.

Tyler slowed the car to a crawl as tourists strolled across the street in crosswalks. People crowded restaurants with outside seating, taking photos with their phones.

"I haven't been here in years during the summer." She eyed the vacationers flooding the town.

He braked hard as a car with Illinois plates backed out of a diagonal parking space. "You're not alone. Locals avoid the crowds in town during the season."

She eyed the tourists who crammed the sidewalks while licking their dripping ice cream cones.

"You don't want this for Eureka, do you?"

"Nope, but it's not likely, anyway. We don't have a lake lined with nineteenth-century mansions."

By the time they drove to the west end of town, it seemed they'd run a gauntlet. "What do you envision for our Eureka?"

His face animated. "A square with enough commerce to bring tourists. Stores for people to shop for one-of-a-kind handcrafted gifts, art, or antiques. Better restaurants, like a brew pub, even food trucks."

"Wow. That's quite a change. How do Lucy and Eddy regard more competition?"

"If the town does well, so will they. I've already been working on the website and social media."

Tyler slowed as they approached the center of Eureka. Men in orange vests stood on the corners of the square, as the central cow statue seemed to watch benignly.

He slammed the steering wheel, cursing. "The surveyors are here. There've been rumors there's renewed interest in straightening out the route and eliminating the square."

"Can't you stop them?"

His mouth set in a gloomy line. "The Village Board can fight it. We'd have a lot more leverage if we qualify for the Main Street Program."

"How long before that happens?"

"I'm not sure. But we're running out of time."

.   .   .

At the campground, mylar balloons and crepe paper decorated her trailer's deck. In contrast, yellow police tape outlined the singlewide next door. As they neared the pyramid of dishes and flowers, Tyler grinned. "I don't think you'll need to learn to cook just yet."

Ruth's throat tightened at the sign *We Love You. Our Hero!* Next to it, Gandalf nested on her Crocs and softly honked at her.

Tyler walked her across the deck, picking up packages along the way. "Dad says I should watch you for symptoms of concussion. Okay if I spend the night?"

She reached for his hand and pulled him close. "The adage that nurses and doctors make poor patients is wrong. We appreciate good care and will show our appreciation." She grinned. "Over and over."

. . .

The next morning, Tyler took off early to supervise the installation of new windows at his building, leaving Ruth with strict instructions to rest and recuperate. She sipped her tea, watching the campground awaken and then fed Oreo a carrot.

She was giving Gandalf a lettuce leaf when Mary Jo knocked on the door. "You-hoo, anybody home?"

"Come on in."

"Aw, honey." Mary Jo set her packages down and hugged her daughter. "How are you doing?" She caressed the side of Ruth's face.

"Sore, but okay." Ruth moved toward the Keurig machine she'd recently purchased. "Coffee?"

"That would be nice." Mary Jo set a large rectangular, brown-wrapped package against the wall and placed a basket on the dinette. "I brought you some of Luke's rolls. They're divine." As she removed a gingham napkin, the odor of cinnamon set Ruth's mouth watering. "Doctor Greg told me they're bringing in a temporary staff at Golden Years. I understand the Board wants to offer you the job of Head Nurse."

"No. They need someone who'll be there for the residents and provide some continuity." She hesitated. "I'll be gone in a year."

"I figured as much." Her mom's face glowed. "You'll make a brilliant doctor."

Finally, the truth between them. "Thanks, Mom." She hugged her mother. "I'll give the Board my recommendations." She mentally listed them: a new computer system, a total review of residents' meds, surprise audits, and the replacement of Dr. Thompson. Even if he wasn't guilty in the drug scheme, he was at least irresponsibly over-prescribing medications. He was also likely aware of Steele's codeine addiction.

"I'm sure they'll appreciate your suggestions."

Ruth pointed to the large package. "Okay, Mom. I can't stand the suspense. What's that?"

"It's an early Christmas present."

"I'll say." Ruth unwrapped the parcel, tearing off the brown paper, sending the odor of linseed oil into the air.

The painting displayed the burr oak silhouetted against a rising sun. A little girl sat on a tire swing on one of its old limbs. A beatific smile glowed on her face beneath a halo of golden curls.

"Oh Mom, it's beautiful." She squinted closer at the painting. Two thin arms reached behind the tree, seeming to propel her. "Is that who I think it is?"

"Tyler. He was in the picture I worked from."

"What ever happened to the one of me in your house? Where I'm looking fat and cranky?"

"It sold." Mary Jo took a bite of her cinnamon bun. "Aren't these great?"

"Yes, they are. But sold to whom? Who would buy it?" The look on her mom's face gave her the answer. "No. He didn't."

Mary Jo shrugged. "Tyler loves the artwork and plans to put it in his loft."

"Oh well. There's no accounting for taste in subject matter." Ruth looked around the cramped trailer. "You should hang onto my painting for me until I get a place."

"Sure, honey." Mary Jo half-smiled and took a bite of her roll.

Ruth regarded the tree outside. "Why didn't you sell Dairyland Acres when you had the chance?"

Mary Jo took a long sip of coffee. "I was ready to. Then, I called you the night before the meeting, and found out about the professor."

Ruth winced. "I'm sorry for what I said about Caprice. I was wrong to bring it up. My apology."

"It stung," Mary Jo said. "But it highlighted something for me. I was trying to escape my failure with Dairyland and run from my past." She locked her gaze with Ruth's. "I didn't set the best example for you. I loved your dad when we first married. Over the last years, we had nothing in common, but we stayed together. I worried you were settling for someone like I did. Eventually, I vowed to let myself love again, so I met with Caprice."

Shock flooded Ruth. "How could you do that?"

"Forgiveness is a choice. Once I let my anger go, it made room for the good feelings in life, like love."

"I'm glad you're happy now. I couldn't ask for a better stepdad."

"Thanks, honey. I only want the same for you, no matter what you do with your life." Her mom reached inside her purse. "There's one more thing." She took out a legal-sized envelope and handed it to Ruth.

The return address was a law office in Chicago.

"Go ahead. Open it." Her mom's face shimmered with excitement.

The letter was from the estate of Joseph E. Schultz, naming Mary Jo Engel, sole heir. The amount was considerable. "Oh, good for you, Mom!"

"Mr. Schultz had no relations and changed his will a while ago. It took years to settle. He would open bank accounts all over Chicagoland, back when you got a toaster or transistor radio to do so. Interest adds up. Look at what's attached."

Ruth had never held a check with so many zeroes. "Fantastic. Your retirement! I'm so excited for you."

"Look at the back."

Underneath her mother's signature, the check was endorsed to Ruth Ann Markson.

"What? You can't mean this."

Her mother beamed. "Oh, but I do. It's for your education." She glanced over at the photograph. "Mr. Schultz would want it for you, too."

Ruth's hands shook, holding the piece of paper that would not only pay off her student loans but cover most of her medical school tuition.

"I-I don't know what to say. I can't thank you enough." She blinked through tears of joy.

"There's no need, honey. It's your inheritance. Just early."

"I've checked. I can start as early as this September. Oh my god, oh my god." Ruth jumped up and ran over to her mother and hugged her. "I need to call them, find a place to live..." She trailed off. "Does Tyler know?"

Mary Jo nodded. "Joy told him this morning."

This was everything she'd desired. Still, her heart sank.

CHAPTER 34

The following weekend, Ruth sat on her trailer's porch encircled by labeled boxes, with Oreo's cage at her feet. Gandalf snoozed on her Crocs that she'd donated to the next tenant.

Her stomach lurched when the Budget moving van arrived on time. Tyler emerged and strode to her. He grabbed her hands, pulled her into a hug, and kissed her lightly on the lips. "This it?" He looked at the piles surrounding her. When she nodded, he said, "You carried this all by your lonesome?"

"I'm strong enough. You call me Slugger for a reason."

He hooted. "Oh, yeah. McKay's still singing a falsetto 'Jail House Rock.'"

She laughed, remembering the satisfying kick to his groin. "My destiny."

After they filled the truck with her possessions, as they drove away, she took a long last look in the rearview mirror at Dairyland. She'd had a tearful farewell party the night before in the recreation hall. She begged the Walkie-Talkies and her mom not to come for a last goodbye. This was hard enough.

Tyler glanced at her. "How are you?"

"I'll make it." She reached into the cage at her feet and stroked Oreo's soft fur.

They drove past apple orchards laden with fruit and farms golden with crops waiting to be harvested until two hours later they arrived in the Capital.

The corners of his mouth lifted. "Cheer up. Nothing beats being a Sconnie."

"Yeah. My dream." She'd experienced a mixture of excitement, anxiety, and sadness since her inheritance.

He pulled into the loading zone of her six-flat brick apartment building. Cooking aromas of bacon, cabbage, and curry filled the hallway as they carried the boxes filled with her belongings.

"Well, that's it." Tyler gave her the smallest of grins. "I'd better be going. I need to return the van." He embraced her tightly, drawing her close to him. She relished the aroma of his fresh laundry, his aftershave.

He kissed her softly at first, then passionately. She returned his kiss, as if to imprint herself on him. They reluctantly pulled apart.

"You study hard." He ran his hand over her face, still bruised from her fight with Debi. "And try to stay out of trouble, Slugger."

"I will. To both." She fought back tears.

He smoothed her hair. "I'll miss you."

"Miss you too."

With a wave, he headed down the stairs. It took all her will-power not to beg him to stay.

. . .

Ruth immersed herself in her classes, finding them interesting and challenging. Her classmates deferred to her, especially in discussions of medical ethics after one of them had read of her Golden Years' exploits. She seemed older, even if they were the same chronological age. Somehow, her experience in the "real world" had altered her and given her an aura of sophistication the others lacked. She occasionally joined them after class and sipped iced tea at the bars they frequented. Two of the men asked her out for dinner. She declined, citing study time.

In truth, there was no one for her but Tyler.

Days bled into weeks. She studied diligently, ever certain her vocation was the right one. She narrowed down her choices, moving toward General Practitioner, with a specialty in geriatrics. Some of her fellow students were aghast at her decision, warning her that choosing to become a specialist or surgeon was more lucrative and higher in status.

She honored her gut feelings, remembering her patients, in particular Nellie Wilson. She studied reports of the lack of doctors in rural areas where the situation looked bleak for small towns like Eureka.

If she only wanted money and glory, what was the point?

Ruth hung on to her contact with Eureka like a lifeline. She heard from her mother daily, mostly stories about the town and Dairyland. Gandalf appeared to miss her, forlornly refusing to leave the porch.

Luke texted her repeatedly about the status of the case against Debi, McKay, and Steele. Justice was slow, as he explained the constant legal delays. They'd been unable to find Miriam, who remained at large with a warrant for her arrest.

Her stepfather was, however, more upbeat about his plans to avert the opiate disaster. With the small-time pushers like McKay out of the picture, large drug cartels might move into Eureka. He reasoned that if the addicts were helped, the demand would lessen, and the supply would dry up.

Luke found programs in other towns where the addicts only had to arrive at the police station, declare their need for help, and with no questions asked, officers would deliver them to a drug treatment center. The individual's insurance often covered the cost of the treatment, but if not, Eureka had secured a fund for the uninsured. So far, the incidence of overdoses had decreased. He also asked for Ruth's input for his plans, to which she responded enthusiastically.

Doctor Kelly, Tyler's father, had taken over as Golden Years' doctor. He often wrote to her for ideas to improve the facility. "But," he'd written, "my workload has increased proportionally. Would you consider a partnership in my practice? I will eventually retire."

It was a tough choice because of Tyler. She'd heard from him daily, but they had limited their conversations to jokes and funny stories. She hoped he was keeping to his promise to support her by playing it light.

Howard occasionally texted Ruth about "breaking in the new administration." He stated the people seemed all right, they just needed to get the lay of the land. He was relieved and grateful to her since his friends were no longer at risk and he looked forward to Thanksgiving when the family would be together.

Ruth vowed to practice living in the now, neither the past nor the future. "Where are you?" she would ask herself.

"Here."

"What time is it?"

"Now."

I can do this.

. . .

She took the stairs two at a time. The apartment was empty except for her pet.

"Mama's home, Oreo." She reached into the cage and gave her guinea pig a carrot. "Who's a good girl?" The loneliness always hit her hardest this time of day.

She flipped on a light, illuminating the gloomy room. Her heart sank. Matching reading lamps flanked a sagging sofa. A pile of textbooks covered the coffee table. Her jogging shoes sat next to the front door. She automatically picked up a dirty teacup and placed it in the stained kitchen sink.

She settled with her computer, studying until her eyes crossed. It wasn't so bad during the day when she was busy with classes. At night, she crawled into bed longing for Tyler, often unable to sleep. She picked at her dinner, no matter what the takeout meal. Her clothes hung on her. All her life she'd watched her weight, now it peeled off her.

Then she allowed herself to text Lillian and confessed her loneliness.

I am heartsick.
He misses you too
Doesn't seem like he does
There was a long pause.
Maybe he is trying to support your decision.
Maybe. Fingers crossed.

.   .   .

Running errands, Ruth had taken refuge when a deluge sent her scurrying into a brightly lit drugstore. With a start, she recognized the plump woman in a sweatshirt. Winding her wet ponytail into a knot, Ruth stepped an aisle back, pretending to muse over cosmetics.

She hasn't noticed me.

Miriam reached for a bottle of Clairol *Just for Gray*. She had dyed her mousy hair red, but Ruth recognized her trademark corny saying on the shirt *I'm a Pabst Blue Ribbon drinker, not a fighter*. The older woman paid for the hair coloring, and Ruth followed her out of the store.

Ruth debated what to do next. Somehow, she needed to alert the police without alerting the fugitive.

Miriam picked up the pace as a crowd of students engulfed her, and Ruth made a run for it before she lost her quarry. She pushed forward, nudging people aside.

"Excuse me," she panted.

"What's your hurry?" a heavily tattooed guy asked.

Ruth didn't answer intent on the escapee and shoved past anyone in her way. The resulting ruckus garnered Miriam's attention. She turned around wide-eyed with recognition and ran.

Miriam was no match. Ruth easily caught up with her and threw her arms around the portly woman.

"Get your hands off me. Help! Help! I'm being accosted."

Ruth kicked Miriam's legs out from under her, and the older woman landed heavily on the sidewalk. Astride her, Ruth pinned her arms to her sides.

Miriam screamed and turned the air blue with a string of curses.

"Now that's not nice talk." Ruth tsked.

More students gathered and were apparently recording the proceedings on their phones.

"Get off her."

"This is fascism at its worst." A woman with a heavily pierced face shrieked. "Make sure you get this on video."

Ruth rolled her eyes. "Someone please dial 9-1-1. The police will explain everything."

Miriam struggled like a slippery pig in a pen, with tears running down her reddened face.

"Relax, Miriam. Remember, a frown is just a smile turned upside down."

.   .   .

The Walkie-Talkies mailed Ruth a copy of the *Eureka Gazette* with a note.

"You're the cover girl!" Betty penned.

"A heroine," Lillian added.

"I read this in your palm," Aunt Cordy asserted.

The newspaper amused her. A bystander's photo of her straddling Miriam with the caption, "Local woman arrests suspect," portrayed the fugitive's face smashed against the sidewalk, wearing an ugly snarl. The rest of the story recapped Ruth's involvement exposing the drug ring at Golden Years. Luke and Howard had praised her.

The sugar maple outside her apartment was transforming from flaming orange to crimson. Ty had moved into his building and sent pictures. She thought longingly of his loft. He'd taken her advice for finishes, and it looked wonderful.

She glanced around her lonely apartment. It served its purpose. She ate, studied, and slept here. The walls were bare except for the painting her mother had given her. Who cared?

A text beeped, and Ruth read the message from Lillian.

Are you doing anything for Homecoming this weekend?

Ruth snorted. Classmates had invited her out, but a football game or partying was the last thing on her mind.

Nope. Home studying. Looking forward to Thanksgiving, though.

For the first time in years, she'd be going home to Eureka for a holiday. Her mom had planned a large dinner in the Dairyland recreation building with all her friends and family. That included the Kellys.

Can't wait to see you then.

U 2. Ruth followed the message with a heart emoji.

She looked forward to seeing Tyler again but dreaded having to leave him afterward.

Ruth looked at the clock and studied on her computer. Instead of supper, she made do with a PowerBar. Eventually, she stretched and checked the time. Two hours had flown by. With a yawn, she fed Oreo and headed toward the bedroom.

Someone knocked. She sighed. It was probably a delivery driver with the wrong apartment. Flinging open the door, she was ready to clarify that she hadn't ordered pizza when her breath caught.

Tyler stood on the landing with a lopsided grin. He waved the *Gazette* at her. "What did I tell you, Slugger?"

She threw her arms around him and burst into tears of joy.

"Hey, hey." He stroked her hair and kissed her temple. He pulled back a bit. "Are you unhappy to see me?"

She swiped her cheeks. "You know better."

"May I come in?"

"Oh sure. Sure." She stepped backward, embarrassed by the disarray. Most of her books were still in boxes. "I'm still getting settled."

He nodded toward her tiny kitchen. "You learn how to cook yet?"

"Nope. You?"

"Naw." He looked her up and down. "I love your outfit." Her bright red sweatshirt read *SCONNIE* in bold white lettering.

"I am what I am."

"You look amazing, Slugger."

He looked as good as ever. She eyed the duffle bag he carried. "Are you staying?"

"If it's okay with you."

More than okay. "Sure." She walked to the window. "Where did you park? They're fussy around here." She frowned. "I don't see your car."

He stood next to her. "Down there."

Immediately below her apartment was a black SUV towing a small moving trailer.

Her heart pounded. "That's your big-ass winter vehicle, right?"

He nodded. "I brought a few essentials. A flat screen television, another for the bedroom, a sound system, my desktop, my laptop, a new laptop for you if you want it." He kissed her lightly. "Clothes, Luke's baked goods, and casseroles from the Walkie-Talkies."

Her eyes widened. "How long are you planning on staying?"

"As long as you'll let me." He kissed her, tasting of mint and smelling of his aftershave and leather jacket.

Her knees weakened. "What about your building? It's your life savings."

"Ruthie, I would lose everything and live on an ice flow with you."

"How about a cave?" She grinned.

"That would be a stretch with my claustrophobia." He kissed her again. "I've worked through the problem with the contract. I approached the bank and explained the circumstances. At the urging of the Historical Committee, I can live part time in the building."

"Our moms convinced the bank?"

He nodded. "The caveat is I… we… must return to Eureka for holidays and breaks. If, and I quote, your studies are not affected. Coincidentally, my mom is the Administer of the Main Street Program as of this morning."

"She'll be great! Nothing like a popular ex-Milk Day queen to help." Ruth paused. "You said 'coincidentally.' Your mom knew you were worried and wouldn't leave town, even part time if no one stepped up."

"True. And she's been looking for something more to do."

"Did she keep my inheritance quiet?"

"She only told me."

"Someone kept a secret in our town? It's a miracle."

"It's been a miraculous day." He rubbed the small of her back. "If Lillian hadn't told me you were free this weekend, I wouldn't be here."

Ruth grinned. "I let her know how much I missed you." A rush of affection for her meddlesome friend coursed through her. She hugged him hard. "I've missed you so much."

His kisses left her panting and breathless Desire coursed through her loins.

"I love you, Ruth."

"I know you do. I love you too."

He caressed her shoulders. "I *love* you like I can't stand to be away from you and think of you day and night. I wanted to honor your wishes, or I would've turned around the day I dropped you off here. You were right about our mothers not wanting us to live together without a plan for the future. I don't want that either."

He reached into his pocket and took out a small jewelry box. Then he sank down on one knee. "Will you, Ruth Ann Markson, make me the happiest man on earth and marry me?"

"Yes." Ruth pulled him to her. "My silly, wonderful, brilliant man."

He slipped a ring on her shaking finger. "It was my grand-mother's. If you want a different one, we can go shopping."

"No, it's perfect." The sapphire and diamond ring sparkled on her hand. "It looks like Princess Di's. How long ago did your mom give this to you?"

"Right after we kissed, when I told her I might have a chance for something permanent with you." He ran his finger along her cheek. "Should we tell them?"

"They're probably already planning the ceremony."

He pulled back a bit. "I'll call and ask Luke and your mom for your hand in marriage right now."

"You're so old-fashioned." She kissed him. "But I love that about you." The image of Luke walking her down the aisle pleased her. Gandalf could be the ring bearer. On further consideration, probably not.

"Would you think about eventually moving back to Eureka? I'm considering a run for Village Trustee. There's still a lot to do in town."

She nodded. "I might join your father's practice."

"That would be great. Two Doctor Kellys in town." He paused. "If you want to change your name."

"I would. Debi called me Markson so often I hated the sound of it."

Their phones beeped, announcing text messages. Ruth thumbed a few words.

"What did you tell them?" Tyler hugged her.

"I told my mom I said, 'yes' and messaged Lillian I'd get back to her later."

"Much later." He easily scooped Ruth into his arms and carried her across the bedroom threshold.

"Much, much later," she agreed, kissing him with all her heart and soul.

ACKNOWLEDGEMENTS

I want to send an enormous thank you to the team at Black Rose Writing for their faith in this story and for helping bring it into readers' hands. A huge thank you goes out to my writing buddies, Beverly Jackson, editor extraordinaire, Margo Carey, Glenn Erick Miller, Robert Erickson, Rosie Weidner, Jayden and Sana Flynn. Your sage advice and generous critiques have made me a better writer.

To my beta readers, a big thanks for spotting anything I missed and for your other suggestions. I truly appreciate the time you took, Laura Gillice, Micki Stern, Valerie Nuti, and Kerri Lukasavitz. Thank you for your friendship and your encouragement.

Cheers to my instructors, Christine DeSmet, and Angela Knight. You have been instrumental in my writing journey.

The seeds of this story were sown years ago when my mother was elected President of the Resident Council of DuPage Convalescent Center. Her campaign slogan "All the Way with Juliet A." won the election for her, representing over four hundred residents.

There were, however, no unexplained deaths at the Center, and all the nefarious activities at the mythical Golden Years Retirement Village are completely products of my imagination. Other places mentioned in the book exist, but Eureka, Wisconsin and Dairyland RV Park are only composites of my experience camping and living in Southeastern Wisconsin.

Thank you to all my readers who have many books to choose from. I'm grateful you came along on this adventure with me.

And most of, thanks to my husband, Paul. We've been on a wonderful life journey together that I never would have taken without you.

Michelle Caffrey www.MichelleCaffrey.com

ABOUT THE AUTHOR

Michelle is the best-selling author of *Bring Jade Home: The True Story of a Dog Lost in Yellowstone* and the award-winning picture book *Jade—Lost in Yellowstone*. She is a former full-time RVer and Workcamper. Once, when checking in at a rundown campground, she and her husband were accosted by the owner's pet goose that was "only posturing," inspiring her *Dairyland RV* series of novels. No longer nomadic, she currently lives with her husband Paul, in Lake Geneva, Wisconsin, where she safely avoids confrontational poultry.

NOTE FROM MICHELLE CAFFREY

Word-of-mouth is crucial for any author to succeed. If you enjoyed *Desire in Dairyland*, please leave a review online—anywhere you are able. Even if it's just a sentence or two. It would make all the difference and would be very much appreciated.

Thanks!
Michelle Caffrey

We hope you enjoyed reading this title from:

www.blackrosewriting.com

Subscribe to our mailing list – *The Rosevine* – and receive **FREE** books, daily deals, and stay current with news about upcoming releases and our hottest authors.
Scan the QR code below to sign up.

Already a subscriber? Please accept a sincere thank you for being a fan of Black Rose Writing authors.

View other Black Rose Writing titles at www.blackrosewriting.com/books and use promo code **PRINT** to receive a **20% discount** when purchasing.